THE MAN ON THE RUBBER BALLOON

or

OPTIMISM

THE MAN ON THE RUBBER BALLOON

or

OPTIMISM

PAUL KELLY

NORTH
OAK

First published in Great Britain in 2022 by
North Oak

NORTH
OAK

A CIP catalogue record of his book
is available from the British Library.

ISBN
978 1 7398376 00

Typeset by Hewer Text UK Ltd, Edinburgh

Copyright notices

The End
Words and Music by John Densmore, Robby Krieger,
Ray Manzarek and Jim Morrison
Copyright ©1967 Doors Music Company, LLC
Copyright Renewed
All Rights Administered by Wixen Music Publishing, Inc.
All Rights Reserved. Used by Permission of Hal Leonard Europe Ltd.

Mickey Mouse March
Words and Music by Jimmie Dodd
©1955 Walt Disney Music Company
Copyright Renewed
All Rights Reserved. Used by Permission of Hal Leonard Europe Ltd.

In memory of Thomas McDonnell
(1891 – 1986)

I tell you, do not worry about your life, what you will eat or drink; or about your body, what you will wear. Is not life more important than food, and the body more important than clothes? Look at the birds of the air; they do not sow or reap or store away in barns, and yet your heavenly Father feeds them. Are you not much more valuable than they?

Can any one of you by worrying add a single hour to your life?

Matthew VI:XXV

PROLOGUE

The boat sliced through the Rio Beni, leaving a mess of blood and bodies behind. The noise of its propeller was fast, percussive and aggressive, like the burst of the Uzi that started it. Except *it* was now over.

Sitting up front, Max pulled a green plastic sheet over his shoulders, leant back and tapped the blade of a Bowie knife on his thigh; its hilt was covered in blood and snake scales, some of which fell off and dropped into a small pool of water by his feet. Just ahead, the river swirled and bounced over a submerged branch and then washed under the boat, making a man groan loudly. Turning around, Max checked on the DEA agent crumpled over some barrels of sulphuric acid lying sideways across the boat – he was barely conscious with broken ankles twisted awkwardly and a face contorted in pain. The boat bounced once more and his ankles jumped, but this time the man made no sound, having slipped into unconsciousness. Max turned back, shook some water from the sheet and tapped his feet in the pool that was fast becoming a puddle.

Further back at the pozo pit, the remnants of the battle lay scattered, dead and dying with insects crawling deep into open wounds and feeding on the flesh. By dusk, caiman would drag the bodies into the river for a merciful release, but not before the forest had taken its share of the Colombian narcos. A new war between the cartels was now inevitable, not least as Pablo Escobar was taking back control of his business; that was assuming he still had a business once the DEA had extracted revenge for their tortured agents.

Max leant back again, pulled his feet out of the water and rested them on the front of the boat – it was only then that he let out a long, slow sigh and tried to take in what had happened. Closing his eyes, he allowed himself a small smile, and thought back to the start of his journey on a spring morning in London, full of uncertainty, nervousness and maybe even fear.

PART ONE

*Sometimes not getting what you want
is a wonderful stroke of luck.*

14th Dalai Lama

CHAPTER ONE

The idea only really came to him the day he hit rock bottom. But for now he was feeling pretty good.

It was Friday, after all, which meant lunchtime beers at the Seven Stars, followed by a few more beers at the Rat & Parrot, or some other Covent Garden pub that evening. London was in a severe recession, but he was not going to let that affect him. He was twenty-six, working in the best city in the world in a role he had worked damned hard to get. It's no wonder he had a smile on his face strolling into Lincoln's Inn Fields.

It was a crisp spring morning and the daffodils and cherry blossom sparkled in the sun. Today looked like it could well be the first session of the year outside the Stars, which would be a welcome change from the cramped bar and its wall of smoke that had half choked them all winter. He only had a couple of things to sort out before his meeting with Roe and Tony, but they should not take long. The morning was going to fly by.

Crossing into the park, Max rehearsed his negotiation strategy for the meeting in his head one final time. He was going to push firmly for a ten-per-cent salary increase, making sure to highlight all the deals he had helped close that year. Fine, he was willing to accept six per cent, in line with inflation, but definitely no less. He was qualified now, so that seemed perfectly fair.

Not all the graduates had a meeting scheduled, so rumours had been circulating all week about their purpose. With the sheer numbers involved, staggering them seemed like a sensible thing to do. The general view was that the new contracts were being issued and so the hot topic became just how generous the starting salary would be for a newly qualified chartered surveyor.

So, where should he spend next month's extra salary? He could do with a new suit, but then again he also needed some new vinyl. *Maybe head over to Fat Cat Records and City Sounds first and worry about a suit later?* It was an easy decision, and with the prospect of a visit to City Sounds the following week, he pushed on the revolving door, spun into reception and winced at the firm's dated 1970s logo that conjured up images of flared trousers, bad suits and even worse hairstyles whenever he passed it.

After a couple of relatively productive hours at his desk, he grabbed his coat and headed back down to reception. He would want it when standing outside the Stars, pint in hand, and he might as well go straight there after the meeting. In all fairness, he did not like Roe Tarburt or Tony Rowan, and he certainly was not looking forward to sitting across a table from them. At least it should be short. Roe would drone through the HR issues and Tony would discuss performance before getting down to the heart of it all: remuneration.

The receptionist told him Roe was waiting and to go straight down to the boardroom.

The boardroom. Sounds a bit formal, he thought on his way downstairs.

Pausing at the bottom of the steps, he adjusted his tie and realised that his hand was shaking a bit. He took a deep breath, knocked on the door and walked in.

Oh shit, you're joking!

A middle-aged man faced him in a checked Prince of Wales double-breasted suit, crisp white shirt and blue polka dot tie. As he crossed one leg over the other, some pale, freckled skin appeared between his blue Argyle-patterned socks and turned-up trouser leg. He was fiddling with his moustache and making notes on a list of names with a Montblanc fountain pen. A small white teapot, a jug of milk and a cup and saucer were to his left, a plate of half-finished biscuits to his right.

But it was not Tony Rowan, who he had been expecting, but Terry, as in Terry Nighy, the senior partner of the firm!

His status, combined with a severe demeanour, meant that he was seriously intimidating to all graduates who were unlucky enough to cross his path.

Roe was sitting next to him and stared across the table.

'Er, I thought I was seeing Tony?' he thought to himself, but the words slipped out.

'What was that?' snapped Roe.

Terry was staring at a piece of paper, and without looking up, he gestured at a chair opposite. Max sat down and waited. It was still warm from the previous graduate, now nowhere to be seen.

'Okay . . . Max . . . ah yes, Max Hansell,' he said, looking up with a glimmer of recognition. He then leant forward, put the paper down and began.

'You're no doubt wondering why you've been asked to attend a meeting with Roe and myself? I suspect there's been some discussion amongst the graduates as to the purpose of these meetings? I've been hearing good things about your work in the industrial agency team. I know Tony considers you a valued member of staff, and I have heard the same thing from the other partners you've worked with over the past two years. I'd like to thank you personally on behalf of the firm for all of your diligence, hard work and effort during what have been challenging market conditions.'

He let his words linger for a response. But to Max it sounded like he was reading from a script, and he was not sure what to say. He simply replied, 'Thank you.'

'Now, what are your plans for the future?' Terry asked.

Max thought it a slightly odd question. Surely Terry should be telling *him* what his future looked like and not the other way round?

His eyes drifted to the ceiling as he tried to come up with something to say. And as he searched for something – anything – his eyes locked onto the gaze of the founder captured in oil above Terry, who seemed just as eager to hear what he was going to say.

'Plans for the future . . .?' he asked himself out loud, but when he spoke, his voice came out thinly.

He cleared his throat, grabbed a glass and poured himself some water. Of course, in doing so he spilled a little and was forced to swipe at the table with his sleeve. Gulping down half the glass, he pushed some hair away from his forehead and tried again.

'I just wanted to say . . .' His voice quivered. 'It's been such a privilege to work for the firm. Not to say that it hasn't been a challenge. It's really been a challenge, not least with the recession and everything.'

Shit, it's supposed to be Tony sitting there! The thought swirled around his head and stopped him concentrating on what he was about to say, not that he knew what he was about to say.

'But I think the move to industrial agency was a step in the right direction and I'm learning a lot from Tony, who has such a . . . unique style. I've been there for five . . . no, I think it's six months, isn't it, Roe?' he asked with a weak smile. She nodded. It was painful, but he pressed on.

'And I'm looking forward to getting my own clients now I'm qualified.' He could hear his voice wobbling and hoped that the conversation could now move on to his new contract.

Reaching down, he scratched his ankle, a nervous reflex.

A silence descended, enough for the rattling air conditioning grilles at the back of the room to sound even louder than they actually were. The founder in the portrait did not seem impressed by what Max had said, and neither did Terry, who was now frowning. The silence continued, and Max began to worry that he was in for a bollocking from the senior partner for something he had said. Or for something he had not said. What *had* he said, anyway? He needed to pay more attention. *No, I just need to be more positive!*

'Erm . . .' he said, pressing his palms against his trouser legs. 'I hope to get promoted to an associate once I've established myself in Tony's team . . . hopefully when the market's a bit stronger.'

Terry put down his fountain pen and leant forward further.

'What?'

'An associate.' Max's voice fluttered. 'That's my plan for the future, I guess.'

8

Terry's stare unnerved him. He now knew that he was going to get a bollocking after all. Looking away, the light from a fluorescent strip flickered over an expensive ashtray, catching his attention as he sat there, braced for Terry's outburst. But Terry was silent, and when Max turned back there was a quizzical look on his face. He appeared more puzzled than cross, and he simply went back to his list of names, starting at the top and slowly running his finger to the very bottom and back again. Finally he looked up, shook his head slightly and turned to Roe, gesturing at the paper with his hand, as if asking her to point out what he was missing.

She nodded and frowned at him, irritated by the inference that there might be a mistake in her work.

Terry turned back to Max with a slight frown.

'Max,' he said quietly and with a hint of compassion, 'I've a list of people who've been offered new contracts and your name isn't on it. I'm sure the list is correct, but would you mind checking this please, Roe?'

Max froze as the thunderbolt released by Terry shot across the table and struck him hard in the chest.

Roe did not have to take the list from Terry. 'Yes, it's correct. Max has not been offered a new contract.' She seemed to have memorised that one.

Max's heart was thumping. Shock waves pumped out of his chest and down to his shaking, sweaty palms. This wasn't happening.

'But Tony offered me a contract in industrial agency!' was all he managed to say.

It felt like he was having an out-of-body experience, on a completely different level to a bollocking.

This has got to be someone else in the basement?

The noise of the vibrating air conditioning grilles and the light flickering off the cut-crystal ashtray became sort of distant. For some reason Max's attention was drawn to some tissues in front of him that were completely out of place in a room far more used to the scent of cigars and brandy. He realised that they had been put there expressly for this meeting. *Fucking cheek.* Did they really think he was going to break down when they told him he wasn't being offered a new contract? The patronising gesture made him cross and helped him to recover some of his composure.

'If you speak to Tony he'll confirm he's offered me a contract. I don't know why I'm not on your list, but he's definitely offered me a contract . . . definitely,' he repeated, firmly.

Roe stared at Max disdainfully.

Terry, a master diplomat, took control of the situation. 'Max, I'm sorry if there's been some sort of misunderstanding, but I'm afraid the firm won't be offering you a new contract now you're qualified. The market conditions are such that we need to manage costs very closely. We had hoped to be through the recession by now, but I'm afraid it seems things are unlikely to improve again this year. Unfortunately, we won't be offering as many new contracts this year as we would have liked.'

So, the matter was settled as far as the firm was concerned. Max felt cheated.

'Okay, so if you aren't going to stand by your offer, are you going to give me redundancy and pay for help in finding another job?' he asked.

It was Roe who replied. It seemed as though her patience had long since worn thin and she had been itching to say something.

'Max, your contract is not being terminated early, so you aren't entitled to any payment.' There wasn't a trace of compassion in her voice. 'Your terms are quite clear: the contract runs until you are qualified and we can then terminate it with four weeks' notice. You'll receive a letter next week confirming what Terry has just told you. It'll formalise the notice to terminate and fix the date for your departure.'

'So, sounds like I'd have been better off if I'd have failed my exams?' Max replied, increasingly irritated by her confrontational approach. He had guessed that it had been Roe's idea to put the tissues on the table.

'Max,' barked Terry, 'I understand your disappointment. There's clearly been some error on the firm's part, and I will look into it, but the fact remains we're not going to be offering you a new contract. Please take the remainder of the afternoon off. I hope we can work with you over the next few weeks and see if we can find an opportunity to employ your talents before you leave us. I hope the letter Roe sends will make everything perfectly clear, but is there anything else you would like to raise?'

The box of tissues still loomed large, and Max felt absolutely and utterly cheated. He had to stop himself from telling Terry and Roe to piss right off.

'Yes, I'd like a copy of my contract as well, please,' was all he ended up saying.

'Of course. We'll send it out,' said Terry, gesturing to Roe, who did not look best pleased to have been given extra work to do.

Max got up and walked out of the meeting, leaving the door open behind him. The embarrassment, disbelief and anger made his face burn. He wasn't disappointed as such, nor did he feel worried about his prospects, but he was in shock and guessed that these things would follow in due course. Right now, what he needed to do was navigate the stairs up to reception and hope that he did not bump into anyone.

He quickened his step when he reached reception and averted his gaze from Simon, another graduate, who was sitting staring at the firm's gaudy logo that belonged to another era, just like the firm.

Max helped the revolving door along with some extra force and emerged onto Chancery Lane. It was midday. Walking a few yards away from the office, he stopped, breathed hard and tried to take in exactly what had just happened. He knew in that moment that he was not good enough for the firm. He would surely have been offered a new contract had the firm valued him. All that work, all those hours, pushing himself to his limit, had simply not been enough.

Last month he had been invited to an in-house lunch with three partners and five other graduates. Only now did he realise that it had not been a lunch at all, rather an informal interview, a covert means of striking through the last of those to be offered a new contract. Earlier that day he had been given some sharp, and what he felt was unfair, criticism by Tony. It had been something about the wording of a sales brochure for a milkman's depot, irrelevant now, but it had put him in a foul mood. So much so that Max could not bring himself to suck up to the partners like the five other graduates were doing. He just could not feign interest in their asinine chatter about the Five Nations rugby at Twickenham, and who would win Wimbledon that year. It was all just so boring.

The really unfair thing about it was that he was better than most of the other graduates in his year, most of whom were presumably being rewarded with contracts.

Fucking cheek.

Striding down Carey Street, he crossed over to avoid the surveyors getting pissed outside the Stars.

Up into Lincoln's Inn Fields. Right now, he didn't give a shit that it was the largest and most attractive public square in London.

Bunch of wankers.

Crossed into the middle of the park, past flimsy domed tents sheltering the homeless and hiding the sparkling daffodils and cherry blossom.

Paused briefly in the centre. Women warming up for a game of netball.

Totally crap.

Just before leaving the park, he booted the heads off some daffodils. He dared anyone to challenge him but, looking around, no one seemed to have noticed, which was disappointing.

Storming out of the square, he ramped up the volume on his Sony Walkman and music pulsed through the orange foam-padded headphones clamped to his head. It was another recording from Kiss FM. He never missed Colin Dale and Colin Faver's weekly 'Pumping House Music' and kept a stack of blank tapes by his Midi system so he would not miss recording a session.

Side A of the tape included a couple of white-label releases Colin Dale had picked up whilst playing at the Astoria and Sub Club, but Max was too cross to focus on the tracks. The music pushed him on with purpose, out onto Kingsway, past the newspaper stands and up to the tube.

It was then that the music squealed to a sudden halt.

You're fucking joking.

Max yanked the Walkman out of his pocket and flipped it open, only to find a tangle of tape springing out. He tried to salvage it, to wind it back in with his finger, but it was no use. Shoving the mass of tape back into his coat pocket, he disappeared down Holborn tube station and suffered the journey home with nothing to listen to but the whine of platform guards announcing that the closing doors in front of him were, indeed, closing.

CHAPTER TWO

Max slouched in his seat as the train raced through a series of points, throwing the standing passengers against each other and making them grab the nearest thing to hand. A few minutes later it came to a shuddering stop, and the sound of doors flying open reverberated down the carriage, followed by a handful of commuters rushing past the window.

Max was in no hurry to get to work. He was one of the last to leave the carriage and sauntered up to a bottleneck that had formed at the end of platform. Some other passengers then arrived out of nowhere, pushed up against him, and the hard edge of a briefcase rammed into his knee. He was too crammed in to be able to identify the culprit, which was lucky as he was not in the mood for lame excuses.

Pressed against the grubby coat of a complete stranger was exactly how he had expected the week to start – *miserably*.

The weekend had also been awful. On Saturday he had woken up convinced that his redundancy had just been a bad dream. But the relief did not last, and he spent the entire weekend unable to focus on anything other than the overwhelming feeling of failure.

The crowd of people finally started to move again and spilled onto the concourse, but Max stopped once more when he reached a large group gathered around a London Transport guard. She was directing people away from the concourse and out of the station. Behind her, the entrance to Paddington tube station was cordoned off. *Dammit!* There was a tube strike and he had not realised. He had caught the train early on Friday afternoon, before the *Evening*

Standard reached the newsstands, and he knew nothing about it. The underground was shut and everyone would have to walk to work, or find alternative transport. The walk to Chancery Lane would take well over an hour. Max decided to try his luck with a bus.

Outside, thousands of commuters stood confused and indecisive on Praed Street, with the odd person trying to push past the melee. Spotting a Routemaster coming around the corner, Max watched a wave of people surge towards it, forcing it to stop before its scheduled pickup. The driver leant forward on his steering wheel and looked down with contempt at the anxious faces pushing towards its entrance, whilst the conductor tried his best to stop the bus becoming overloaded, but failed. Further down Praed Street another bus was marooned in a sea of people, some of whom were remonstrating with an obstinate conductor who refused to continue with them standing on the rear platform.

The choice was clear: Max would either have to walk in the opposite direction and find a less crowded bus or walk down to Oxford Street and catch one that had just dropped people off. He chose the latter and left with the sound of Kiss FM in his ears, relieved at not having seen anyone crushed under the wheels of a bus. Strolling down Spring Street, he turned into Sussex Gardens and then found himself, almost without warning, at the top of Talbot Square, where his Great-Uncle Tom used to live.

He slowed as he walked past, and his eyes wandered up to his great-uncle's old flat, up there on the top floor of an incongruous 1950s block squeezed between Victorian townhouses. Max's grandfather, Ned McDonnell, had died when he was very young and his great-uncle had become a sort of surrogate grandfather to him. He was famous in the family for his short temper. Even into his late eighties it was easy to enrage the old man with an innocent remark, such as the one Max made when his great-uncle fondly recalled watching the funeral cortège of Michael Collins on 'a rare Dublin sunny morning' in August 1922.

Of course, Max, being fifteen at the time, had never heard of the leader of the Irish independence movement and he made the mistake of asking who he was. His great-uncle berated him for his lack of 'a proper education', but in his rage he gesticulated just a little too much and spilled the tea he was holding over his trousers. Leaving the flat a little later, Max remembered thinking how his great-uncle looked like he had wet himself. He had made sure to turn away before laughing so as not to antagonise him any further.

Carrying on down Sussex Gardens, Max picked out a gold Nissan Micra that was stuck in traffic about thirty metres ahead and used it as a marker for the speed of his journey. He reached it in no time, sandwiched between a crappy old Ford Escort and a rusty Vauxhall Cavalier. Walking was by far the quickest option until the traffic reached Marble Arch and dispersed along Oxford Street and down Park Lane. He was pleased he had not waited any longer for a bus. In fact, with the sun out and the trees in blossom, the walk with thousands of other people dashing to work was bearable.

The music playing on his Walkman was a distraction and allowed him to block out the thought of just how bad it was going to be walking down the 'corridor of shame' to his desk. Side A of his TDK SA 90 super precision anti-resonance cassette tape finished just as he was approaching Cambridge Square. Swiftly ejecting the tape, he swapped over to side B and carried on his journey.

'Yo, how's it going, gang?' crackled the tape. 'There's only one legal pressing of this in the world. This is a soon-to-be released track by Sonic Confusion on IQ Records from Germany.' The rhythmic, 120 bpm track started up, and from there on out it would be back-to-back music for the next ten minutes without interruption.

Max loved listening to Colin Dale, who had a tendency to stumble over his words and avoided talking as much as possible during his transmission. He was the antithesis of the Radio One DJs who were all identically polished and professional and played the same bland music, like the latest smash hit from Shakespears Sister, Wet Wet Wet or Right Said Fred, over and over again.

Colin Dale was out there, playing music that pushed the boundaries and elevated the soul. The other night his show was broadcast live from Canary Wharf with lasers streaming light across the dock to the beat of a track called 'Communion'. Max smiled when he thought just how much his great-uncle would have disliked the music, and wondered what he would have thought of the new Canary Wharf development. It would surely have appeared like something out of a science fiction movie to someone growing up at the start of the century?

Turning onto Kendal Street, with its mix of four-storey Georgian terraces and more modern apartment blocks, he headed towards Edgware Road. On the corner of Kendal Street and Edgware Road, the forecourt of Lellers car valet business was already full of Daimlers, Aston Martins and Mercedes, with a swarm of men in green rubber boots washing, polishing, vacuuming and waxing the vehicles. Inside, their owners or their chauffeurs sat drinking powdered coffee at sixty-five pence per cup, dispensed from a large Westomatic vending machine in one corner.

'I've put my teeth back in now,' said Colin, apologising for his last, ill-delivered announcement. 'So this is something I picked up last night at the SW1 Club.' And the wonderful music continued at the same 120 bpm pace, sweeping Max down Edgware Road along with the mass of people also heading south.

The owner of the Marble Arch Food and Wine shop had long ago finished setting out his selection of bananas, apples, oranges, grapes, pomegranates and watermelons on the pavement. Men sat smoking shisha pipes outside Asham's barber shop and old women shuffled out of Al Farabi's pharmacy with their prescriptions. The tube strike had little or no impact on the daily routine of Edgware Road, other than the hordes of office workers dashing down its length and temporarily upsetting the measured pace of life that always seemed to exist there, regardless of whatever was going on elsewhere in the city.

'A firm favourite when that was played down at Turnmills on Saturday night ... that was Rising High Collective and "Fever Called Love" released on ... um ... R&S Records from Belgium. Caspar Pound is one of London's hottest producers right now, so ... er ... check him out. And this is back on the acid tip.' The familiar sound of the Roland TB-303 machine came through Max's orange foam headphones as he turned down Oxford Street towards the C&A department store, where he was sure he would get a bus.

'That's two in a row . . . first off we had Love Inc. on Force Inc. Records from Germany, and in the background is Bizarre Inc. and "Playing with Knives", which has been absolutely massive.' Max noted the track name and scribbled it in his diary to check if City Sounds on Drake Street still had it in stock.

He had managed to board the second of two buses that had stopped, the first being too full. Luckily, it was a number 15 and would take him all the way to Fleet Street, where he would have just a short walk up to the office on Chancery Lane. It would have been quicker to walk along Oxford Street, but Max was in no hurry to arrive at work. In fact, he was perfectly happy to sit on the bus with his Walkman and watch the city glide by.

'Kiss, one hundred per cent back to back in the mix,' washed over the music playing through his Walkman as Colin added a pre-recorded jingle and the bus passed the John Lewis department store. 'The high-tech future dance sound on Kiss FM . . . that's something coming out soon on React from GTO called "Elevation",' Colin told Max whilst the bus continued down Regent Street, past travel agencies, cigar shops and tweed-suit tailors.

When Piccadilly Circus approached, the conductor announced the stop and a large man wearing ill-fitting jeans, a mustard-coloured roll-neck top and a dark blue sports jacket got up and waited at the back. The traffic in front of them slowed down for a red light, and then, just as he jumped off, the lights turned amber, then green, and the bus lumbered on towards Piccadilly Circus. But the man was now sprinting back to the bus and he just managed to reach it, grab its dirty, yellow-taped post and haul himself back inside, panting and out of breath.

'This isn't the Tower of London!' he shouted, gasping and waving his arms at the conductor, who just stared and shook his head.

Max picked up the unmistakable accent of an American tourist and guessed that he had, for some mysterious reason, thought that the Tower of London was situated in Piccadilly Circus, maybe nestled somewhere between the Trocadero and the puny statue of Eros? How he could confuse Piccadilly Circus, with its fountain covered in pigeon droppings, with the magnificent and vast Tower of London in the City was a mystery. But a very good one. Max chuckled to himself and began to appreciate his unexpected early-morning double-decker sight-seeing tour.

It reminded him of when, a few years earlier, he had been travelling on a double-decker up Northumberland Avenue to Trafalgar Square and a couple of American tourists were sitting on the seats in front of him. At the time, a large office on the southeast corner of the square was being rebuilt to exactly the same specification as the beautiful Grade I listed building it was replacing. Two monolithic sheer concrete cores stood on the site – functional but brutal stumps that would be attached to a steel frame before the cladding was bolted on. At this stage the site looked like a bomb shelter fitted with concrete ventilation shafts, standing in stark contrast to magnificent Empire-era buildings on either side.

'Jeez, how'd they get permission to build that?' the middle-aged American sat in front of Max had said, pointing at the site.

'Yeah, that's one ugly building!' her plump partner had agreed. Both had shaken their heads sadly and concluded that it was a military installation connected with the ongoing conflict with the IRA, as they were of course so close to Parliament. They were blissfully unaware that the New York accent cuts through all superfluous noise and that they had given their fellow passengers on the top deck 'a right good laugh', as they say in London.

The Strand was gridlocked, and after forty-five minutes side B of the TDK SA 90 super precision anti-resonance cassette had finished, so Max decided to swap it out for a new tape, hop off the back of the bus and walk through Covent Garden.

The streets were still full of people, most likely from Charing Cross station, but there was not the same sense of panic to get on a bus as there had been at Paddington. Once off the Strand and up into Covent Garden, it began to feel like an ordinary morning in central London, with restaurants receiving their daily provisions, postmen delivering mail and staff preparing the pubs for their lunchtime trade.

In the piazza the regular morning jester was still there jingling the bells on his red-and-yellow three-pointed hat, and tweaking his matching red nose at the end of his five-ball juggle. He had failed to grab the attention of anyone, and Max, who had seen the same act many times, thought he really needed to up his game. Walking straight past, he wondered if the jester had a normal job to go to later on. *Maybe the costume was just a disguise that allowed him to assume a different persona for the hour or so he was performing?* Max reflected that perhaps this was what he had been doing for the past two years in his black chalk-striped suit, except he did it for eight-hour stretches, five days a week. Maybe he would have to start thinking a bit more laterally about what he was going to do now that he had been stamped as useless? It was clear that he too needed to up his game.

The feeling of despondency was creeping in again, and he knew that he was going to have to make some decisions about his future very quickly. His salary would be cut off in a month's time and he was not getting any redundancy to help cover expenses whilst out of work. This really grated as he had worked so hard for the firm. He was also really quite irritated that the contract had not arrived in the post as Roe had promised. She had always had it in for him.

With his mood darkening, the streets between Covent Garden and Kingsway slipped by. The blossom and daffodils of Lincoln's Inn Fields went unnoticed and the reception of the firm's office in Chancery Lane soon appeared with its ugly logo. He made a mental note to give it a kick later when nobody was looking.

CHAPTER THREE

'**H**eather, get Ian on the phone,' Terry barked from his office.

Terry had spent the weekend going over the firm's draft quarterly figures and he was in a foul mood. The large Bishopsgate House fee that had been anticipated in Q1 was still outstanding and expenditure was barely below the previous quarter, despite the hardline measures they had taken. In fact, some costs had actually risen, such as the firm's phone bill. When Terry had checked the BT bill, he saw that there was a spike in January, largely caused by a one-off international call of £164.83 made between 11:03 pm and 11:58 pm on a Friday evening. Heather was looking into this for Terry, as whoever made the call was going to reimburse the firm, unless there was a very credible explanation.

Ian Dodds was the head of agency in London, and it fell on him to deliver the Bishopsgate House fee. It was a large letting, and inevitably complicated, but the fee had now been pushed back by two quarters and Terry had promised the firm's bank manager that it would definitely be booked by the end of this quarter.

'I've got Ian on the line, Terry. I'll put him through to you now.'

'Terry, it's Ian,' confirmed Ian. As Terry had just asked Heather to call him, it was an entirely fatuous thing to say.

'Morning, Ian. I can only assume that your weekend was better than mine, as I spent it wondering what the bloody hell I'm going to say to the bank manager this week.' The partners were all aware of Terry's fortnightly meeting with the bank manager. The firm was bridging its negative cashflow through an overdraft facility, which to date had been renewed every two weeks following these meetings.

'Terry, might one assume that you're referring to the Bishopsgate House fee missing from the draft quarterlies?' Ian casually replied. Terry knew that Ian was probably taking the call lounging in his chair with both feet up on his desk, and he bristled.

'We've been promising the fee since the middle of last year. The bank regards it as an important security against the facility. The longer it remains unbilled, the poorer the security is regarded and the greater the risk that the overdraft becomes "on demand" and we cease to exist.' He paused for a brief moment to let that sink in. 'Why are we still in this situation and what the hell are you doing about it?'

'Yaah, well, Terry, as you'll know from your days working in the City, these things are always more complicated than one wishes them to be. The tenant's solicitor has a few minor points to agree, then I think we're in the home run for engrossments to be produced, and a signing arranged. I'm assured there's nothing contentious outstanding, just a case of the solicitors wanting to get everything spot on beforehand.'

Ian was a relatively junior partner and had not properly experienced the mid-1970s property crash, unlike Terry, who knew that something more important than the 'attractive marble-clad reception' and 'latest lifting strategy' at Bishopsgate House could very easily derail the deal. He did not share Ian's confidence, and he had more equity in the business to lose than him.

'That won't wash with the bank. We'll need Throgmorton to pay a meaningful retainer in advance of the lease completing. We have had over two years of expense on the deal and they are going to have to acknowledge that we've identified and secured a tenant for their office. The closing is not something we can deliver. Pick up the phone to Peter and get him to agree to this before Wednesday as I want to present it to the bank.'

There was a short pause, and an audible sigh from Ian. 'Of course, Terry, if that's what you wish, but it does smack a little of desperation.'

Terry leant forward and made a peculiar ring-shaped gesture at the phone involving his left thumb and forefinger. 'Just get it done, Ian, quick as you can. While I'm on the phone,' he added, 'you'll recall the partner meeting we had in November? Each department presented headcounts for the year ahead and recruitment was frozen until further notice. I had the unpleasant task of telling a young man on Friday that the job he had been promised in industrial agency wasn't actually promised. Roe's double-checked, and he wasn't in the headcount presented at the meeting. So either he's lying or Tony's been a cretin. I need you to look into it. Speak to Roe.'

Terry was sure he heard the word 'wanker!' as Ian slammed his phone down. He made a mental note to take it up with him at the next partners meeting.

'Heather, get in here, I need to dictate a memo,' shouted Terry. Even though he had an intercom that could get through to her in two seconds, barking orders from his office was his preferred method.

Heather had been Terry's secretary for a couple of years now and was used to him. She was a large, blousy woman who lived in a three-bedroom detached house on one of the new estates in Northampton. A blue Ford Mondeo sat in her drive, and a wooden cartwheel was fixed to the wall beneath her lounge window. At weekends, she enjoyed taking her two dogs for a walk with her partner and drinking red wine whilst Chris de Burgh or Bruce Springsteen played in the background. She had her own office through which anyone meeting Terry had to pass, thereby allowing her to control all access to him. Her position as secretary to the senior partner meant she was the most important and influential secretary in the firm, and the other partners and their secretaries had to treat her with great respect.

Picking up her shorthand pad and pencil, she joined Terry in his office and took a seat opposite him. He did not even look at her. Instead, his eyes were shut tight.

'This is to go out this morning to all staff in London,' he began. 'As you all know, the firm needs to economise as the recession is continuing on longer than we all hoped. I know the firm's efforts are supported by the majority of staff, and this is appreciated both by me and by my fellow partners. Sadly, it has recently come to my attention that there are some employees with a total disregard for the sacrifices being made by their colleagues . . .' Here Terry paused. When he opened his eyes, Heather could see just how cross he was.

'Read that back to me, Heather,' he said, and shut his eyes again as he listened to his secretary repeat what he had just said, but without any of the gravitas he felt he had brought to it. 'Okay, that's fine,' he said, cutting her off before she had got to the end. He got up and started to circle the room as he conjured up the rest of it.

'Last week someone had six rolls of personal photos developed on the firm's account. It was only by accident that this was discovered. Moreover, the photos would actually appear to be his or her friend's photos, as we have been unable to identify any employees in the prints. But if you or any of your friends were enjoying yourself at a pretty nice-looking ski resort without a care in the world during the months of January or February, I would think long and hard about your behaviour.'

Terry paused again. He was really cross now. 'Scrap that last part.' He had failed to discover the culprit despite HR and the receptionists studying each and every face that laughed at them from the assorted photographs.

'With effect from today, no rolls of film may be processed through the firm's ProntoPrint account unless accompanied by an order form signed by a partner. In the meantime, any information on the identity of the person who has carried out this outrage . . .' Terry shook his head. 'No, change that to "act",' he said, before continuing, 'would be gratefully received.'

Once Heather had read back the memo and Terry nodded his approval, she returned to her office, where she typed it up on her electric typewriter and printed it on green paper, the colour reserved exclusively for memos. White was only for originals, pink for copies. Terry signed the memo with his Montblanc, and one of the junior secretaries photocopied it for distribution amongst the other secretaries on each of the office floors.

Phil, one of the graduates, was the culprit Terry so wanted to identify. He had put his mate's ski photos in for same-day processing, conveniently omitting his initials on the package that was collected by ProntoPrint every morning, for he knew that they would sit on reception for at least a couple of days if unidentified. The processing was delayed, which meant that he could not collect them that afternoon. He was then laid low by a virus for the rest of the week, the photos eventually found their way to the post room, and Alan then helped bring the nature of the photos to the partners' attention.

Phil was also not being offered a new contract. He was gone long before Terry discovered that he was the culprit.

Shortly after Heather returned to her desk, he thundered through his half-open door, 'Heather, get me Richard!'

Richard Baldright was the head of professional services. He was from Essex, and very well regarded by his peers on account of his senior position in the institution that governed the manner in which the firm conducted its business. He also enjoyed bird-watching and listening to Dolly Parton records. The graduates referred to him as 'Tricky Dickie', not that he was particularly slippery but he was most definitely smug, and it brought the man from Essex down a peg or two, at least in their eyes.

Terry snatched up the receiver as soon as the phone rang.

'Richard, I'm calling about the draft quarterlies. I'm going to need you to bring forward as many fees as you can into this quarter.' Terry had no need of small talk; neither did Richard.

'I'll check with my partners, but I suspect the only possible area will be insolvency practice, where fee structures are more fluid than in asset vals and rent reviews,' Richard replied.

Terry guessed that Richard was about to thrust his hand into his trouser pocket and fiddle with his balls. This was a reflex for which he was well known throughout the firm, and was triggered whenever he was asked a question to which there was a detailed, complicated and, in his mind at least, very intelligent answer.

'I'll speak to Mark,' Richard continued. 'He can front-end fees at the valuation and advisory stage and charge less for the management and disposal work that follows. You'll probably recall, Terry, from your College of Estate Management days, that applying a present value or discounting approach to projected receipts often means that whilst the overall fee may be slightly smaller, the real or present value of the total fee may actually be *larger* by front-end weighting. I remember an interesting case . . .'

Here Terry cut him off. He knew from his reply that Richard was definitely playing with his balls. Terry tried to expunge the image from his head.

'What's that, Heather?' he asked loudly. 'Line two, you say?' When Heather quickly appeared in the doorway, Terry shooed her away. 'Got to go, Richard. Speak to Mark. Let me know the outcome.' He put the phone down before Richard even had time to sign off.

And so the morning continued, with Terry speaking to all the partners in an effort to keep the show going. He felt an increasingly heavy sense of responsibility weighing him down. He knew that it was up to him to divert the firm from disaster, to prevent it slipping into an insolvency process. Not only would he lose his equity, but he also saw himself as the captain of a creaking ship that had been launched over one hundred years ago, and he was beginning to doubt that it would survive.

Heather came into his office, which was tastefully furnished and only slightly larger than other partner offices. It had a good corner position on the second floor, overlooking Chancery Lane and Carey Street. Terry was rightfully proud of where he found himself, despite the challenges the firm faced. She brought in a cup of Earl Grey tea with a slice of lemon, which helped calm him. She needed him to be calm, for her own sake.

'Terry, I've looked into that telephone charge, and I think I've got about as far as I can with BT,' she said, as Terry sipped on the Earl Grey and leant back in his chair. 'They can't trace the call to a specific extension on this occasion, so we're not going to be able to identify the culprit.'

'No,' he said firmly. 'That is not good enough, Heather. Get back to BT, tell them to trace the call and let me know when you have an answer.' Terry was tired of things not being done when he asked. It felt like everyone around him had become allergic to his very simple requests. Heather looked a little lost, as though she thought nothing could be done. But then he knew Heather. She almost liked taking no for an answer. He had been trying to teach her to be more forceful, to push for what she wanted. Or, in this case, what he wanted.

'Do we know where the call was made to? It looks like an Australian dial code. Have you looked up a list of the regional codes? Either way, we've got no business in Australia, which means no one here has any business calling Australia. The person who made that call's going to pay for it, in more ways than one.' The main way being, of course, actually paying for it.

Heather paused, as if struggling with something.

'Actually, the call wasn't made from one of the desk phones. It was made from the lift,' she eventually replied.

'What?' Terry spluttered, stunned more than angry.

'It seems someone phoned Australia from the lift. It has its own phone line for use in an emergency, which I'm told is a health and safety requirement. Current lifts have a radio alarm and intercom system, you see, with no need for a handset, but the lift in Chancery Lane's an older model—'

'I know how a fucking lift works, Heather,' Terry exploded, cutting her off as the penny finally dropped. 'And I don't need a lesson in safety regulations. Some bastard's sneaked back into the office after last orders and called his or her mate from the lift, knowing full well that it can't be traced and that I'd be paying for it.'

He jumped from his chair and grabbed the edge of his desk. It looked like he was about to flip it over. Instead, he just squeezed it.

'Get out!' he roared.

He slammed the door behind Heather, who watched him through the glass panel as he fought with the mahogany desk. Both fists delivered a crashing blow onto its leather-covered writing panel, followed by an open-hand slap on one corner and a kick with the heel of his black leather-soled brogues which only slightly moved it. Some Earl Grey dribbled down into a drawer as Terry's arms shot upwards, and he shook both fists at the powder-coated suspended ceiling tiles and recessed fluorescent strip lights above.

CHAPTER FOUR

Roe had been busy all morning in her office on the fifth floor. Pleased with her work, she took a short break, went across to the window and leant her elbows on its polished wood sill. Down below, the street was busy with people arriving for work, making deliveries and unlocking shops, but amongst it all a bloody tourist was taking photos of the phone box on Carey Street. She huffed to herself . . . *The cheek of it. They should keep out of business locations during the week.*

Earlier that morning she had caught the first train out of Basildon to avoid the disruption of the tube strike. Walking through Liverpool Street station, she always felt a sense of pride as the firm had been instrumental in the development of the huge Broadgate complex that now enveloped the old station. The offices were still largely empty and the owners bankrupt, but she knew that the firm had earned good fees on the instruction. Indeed, Donald Clarke, one of the City partners, had recently taken early retirement on his share of the proceeds.

That weekend she had met up with Helen in Antonio's, a wine bar on Basildon High Street. Helen was a self-made woman who had risen from secretary to head of Human Resources in a mid-sized professional firm, just like Roe. Neither of them had received any formal training but they had decades of experience dealing with people and staff, having risen from pool secretary to working directly for an associate and then to partner secretary. Unlike Roe, Helen had not reached senior partner secretary, but in her eyes she was better qualified on account of the personnel management evening classes she had attended at Basildon Community Centre. They met up every couple of months over some peanuts and a bottle of Beaujolais, and shared notes on running a Human Resources department. Roe's department consisted of herself and an efficient junior secretary. Helen shared her department with Janet, an elderly lady who worked on Mondays and Wednesdays, and Jason, who was a pleasant but simple-minded young man.

Whilst Roe was telling Helen about the Friday meetings and the eight graduates that she was 'letting go', she had a moment of panic when asked if her contracts had a no-liability clause. Of course they did, she replied, but then spent the rest of the weekend trying to find some suitable wording to insert into her contracts. As the Central Library was shut on a Sunday, she was forced to go to her brother's in Colchester and consult his extensive collection of Encyclopaedia Britannica. This was vexing, as she did not get along with Jeremy, and his wife made one of her underhanded remarks about Roe still being single.

There were still around a dozen contracts to amend, laid out in a neat pile on her desk. Sitting down once more, she slotted the top one into the spooling mechanism of her new typewriter. She was still coming to grips with the grey screen and release key that sent text to print once it had been checked. The so-called word processor was fine for entirely new text, but it was difficult to use for amending existing documents. It was not clear how much space was provided between lines, and the tab function was also tricky. Roe could not see why the firm had invested money in these word processor typewriters. It seemed a gimmick to avoid buying Tipp-Ex. The cost of a new typewriter was the equivalent of a decade's worth of Tipp-Ex. Roe knew this as she had told the partners in one of their meetings. But they ignored her and bought them all anyway.

Roe's typewriter jumped into life and punched out 'I hereby agree that I will not make a claim for unfair dismissal under this contract' at the bottom of the first document, which she then deftly unspooled. She had thirty-two contracts in all to amend, and even though twenty-four of them would be replaced shortly by new contracts, she felt it was only proper that they were all identical. She felt a little awkward adding the clause but was proud of her initiative. For now, it could go unnoticed by the partners, but she would make sure they all knew about it once the business was turning a profit and bonuses were being paid again.

She did not see any reason why the firm should take liability for a graduate in whom they had invested time, money and unending patience. Moreover, she did not agree with the policy of employing them in the first place. In her eyes the measure of a person was not a piece of paper stamped by a university but real-world experience and actual success. Once this was gained, they had the right to hold their head up high, but not a moment before then.

Max Hansell was a good example of the kind of graduate she disliked. He was self-confident, aloof and prone to arrogant remarks. In fact, most of the graduates from the University of Reading were exactly the same. Maybe it came with wearing a gown for a day and having their photo taken with a pretend degree certificate? She much preferred those from Oxford Polytechnic, such as Emma, who had also graduated in a gown but happened to be very pretty.

It was only Max and one other graduate who had requested a copy of their employment contracts. She would have them in the post along with their notice letters that day, but only once the wording had been added, of course. Good riddance to them. As Donald in the City had recently remarked, it was a case of 'the tail wagging the dog' with the graduates. Letting some of them go would put them back in their place. Roe had little empathy for a young person who hid their lack of confidence behind a fragile veneer of self-assurance.

CHAPTER FIVE

Ian walked into Tony Rowan's office without knocking. The first thing that struck any visitor was the tastefully framed third-class-degree certificate from the University of London on his wall. Its red-and-cream insignia certified that Anthony had graduated with a third-class honours degree in geography in 1971. It was prominently displayed for a reason, and that was to allow him to tell people that most of his time at university was spent in the bar, not the lecture theatre. He was immensely proud of his performance in that bar.

Ian was not a visitor but Tony's boss. He could walk into his office unannounced, whenever he chose, which he did so this morning.

'Morning, Tony,' he said, helping himself to a seat, sitting down and crossing his legs. He looked in disgust at the mess of papers and job files in front of him and watched some smoke spiral up from the butt of a recently extinguished cigarette. On the desk, a packet of Benson & Hedges was half covered by an *Evening Standard* that now began to ring.

'Mind if I get this first?' Tony asked, reaching for the phone beneath the paper.

Ian nodded and waited. Of course he minded, and he would make it perfectly clear that Tony needed to be snappy about it. Terry's call earlier that morning had irritated him. He knew nothing about Tony making a job offer but he should have. It was his department. He needed to find out exactly what had happened before calling the old bag, otherwise known as Roe in Human

Resources. This meant he had to cancel his regular Monday meeting with the Outer London regional office team to make time to give Tony a grilling. Ian was going to get the facts straight, and Terry Nighy would have an answer by lunchtime.

Ian was irritated that he had to miss his Monday meeting. The regional office team were the stars of the agency department. They worked longer hours than everyone else and were by far his most profitable team. He enjoyed chairing their meetings, which were full of quality banter and allowed him to belittle the agents who delivered his best results. These were the very same results he presented at the weekly partners meetings where he took all the credit, which he also enjoyed.

Tony put the phone down and smiled proudly. 'That was Dairy Crest, one of my important clients. They want me to take a look at a depot they're shutting, and we need to move quickly to bag the instruction,' he said, as though Ian had not been in the industry for nearly twenty years.

'Actually, Tony, I think you'll find that Dairy Crest is one of the *firm's* important clients. They're coming to the *firm*, not your personal enterprise, to seek advice,' said Ian sharply, nonplussed by the potential fee Tony might eke out by letting a small milkman's depot, probably in Deptford, or somewhere equally unattractive.

Tony laughed nervously. His fee performance last year had been miserable and Ian had little regard for him. Although Tony always put on a brave face whenever Ian invaded his office, the gaggle of partners who had supported his promotion in the firm had largely retired, and there was nobody left to defend his weak performance. His old way of drumming up new business over lunches and golf days had become increasingly redundant, especially now that instructions were commonly tendered and decisions taken by committee.

Ian looked at Tony's third-class-degree certificate on the wall and realised that he lacked the basic skills needed to adapt to a new business environment. He started thinking of alternatives for him – *Maybe doing residential mortgage valuations? Somewhere nice and suburban like Claygate . . .* – but then snapped back to the matter in hand.

'Tony, what do I always tell you?' he asked.

Tony had a think. All he could come up with was, 'Be go-getting?'

'No, Tony. I want you to be honest with me. *Remember?* I pretty much tell you that every week when we go through your fee forecasts.' Even Tony thought he should have got that one; Ian did actually mention it all the time.

'So I'm sitting at my desk this morning when I receive a call from Terry, and I can tell he is pissed off, can tell he's absolutely fuming.'

'Terry . . .?' Tony asked.

'Terry! The senior partner!' Ian shouted.

'Of course, *that* Terry!' said Tony, turning red. He should have got that one too.

'He tells me you've offered someone a job in your team. There has been no approval of any hires and he is certainly not on Terry's list of employees. As your boss, I'm the one who gets it in the neck, and I've been told to look into it. So what do you have to say?' But Tony was shaking his head long before Ian had finished.

'No . . . no . . . no,' he repeated. 'Terry's completely wrong. Our headcount has not changed. There have been no new hires. Zero. And anyway, I would have got your approval for any new hires.'

Ian leant back. Something felt wrong. 'So, just to be clear,' he said slowly, 'I want to get this right. You're saying that nobody has been offered a new contract since the employment freeze was implemented last year?'

'Absolutely not! Well, we're keeping our trainee, Max Hansell, now that he's qualified. He does an okay job, and you know we need manpower to let space in the current market. He's already got a contract with the firm, so it's no big deal.'

Ian closed his eyes and waited for his anger to subside, which it did, marginally.

'You are . . .' he said, opening his eyes, 'a complete and utter tit.' He was so angry that he barely noticed the giggle that came from the other side of the door before Debbie, Tony's secretary, put her hand firmly over her mouth to try and stop laughing.

'How could you be confused by such a simple thing?' Ian shouted. 'Surely you know that graduates are on trainee contracts, which are then replaced by permanent contracts once they qualify? Tell me you know that?'

Tony sat dumbfounded. Ian could see his brain slowly working.

'You idiot, you've promised Max Hansell a job and there's no headcount in your team. Terry has given him the bad news, so you're spared that job, though you might wish to apologise to him for your major cock-up.'

'Ah, that's awkward for me,' Tony eventually replied, '. . . and of course for Max Hansell,' he added.

Ian could see that Tony was frantically thinking how to change the subject. *He's in for a bollocking if he brings up the rating partner who vomited outside the Stars*, he fumed, but instead Tony stuck to business.

'I'm glad you popped in, Ian, as I wanted you to be the first to know that we are finally starting to see some positive signs in the industrial market. Now, as you know, our team is well placed to—'

But Ian was having none of it, and cut him off. 'You're lucky that I'll be calling Roe in Human Resources to apologise for you,' he said abruptly. 'Perhaps if you paid a little more attention to the manner in which you organise yourself, starting with this mess in front of me, you'd find the management of your business a little easier?'

With that, Ian got up and left Tony's office, passing Debbie, who was doing her best to look serious. On his way out, he was pleasantly surprised to see that the Outer London regional office meeting was still going on, and with a slight spring in his step, he went into the meeting room and stopped the conversation instantly.

'No, no . . . please don't mind me,' he said, laughing and raising a hand. 'I'm just a humble listener in the corner,' he demurred, as his stars stumbled over each other to be the first to contradict his affected humbleness. As usual it was Mark, the newly promoted associate, who caught Ian's attention with his bright ginger hair and hilarious Scouse wit.

'Ah, Ian, just in time . . . I was just explaining to Adam that he'll need to up his game if we are going to increase fees this year.'

Adam winced. It was actually he who had raised the topic of boosting fees.

'No, Mark, I think you'll find that Thames Valley Park is now almost fully let,' he replied tersely. 'At least it was when I drove round it with Terry Nighy last week.' Then, turning to Harry, he mentioned, almost casually, 'I'm sure I overheard some agents the other day calling Mark's Croydon Central scheme . . . what was it, oh yeah, *Croydon Mental* . . . some comment about "who in their right mind would build an office there?"'

Harry chipped in before Mark could reply. 'Sounds like you could do with a get out of jail card on that one, mate,' he said, and turned to Ian, neatly bringing him into the conversation. 'What are you hearing from your contacts in the boardroom, Ian?'

Ian stepped up and took the floor, as he had always intended. 'Yes, yes, chaps, that's all well and good, but Harry is right – it's what is going on in the boardrooms that matters,' he said, and then proceeded to share his pearls of wisdom with the eager acolytes looking up at him in their white shirts and bright ties.

The meeting rolled on for another twenty minutes, discussing businesses that were downsizing and subletting space, agents who were still active and picking up new instructions, and the general outlook for the market. Once finished, Ian returned to his office in a buoyant mood. If only the laggards in industrial agency and city office agency would take a leaf out of their book, he would get less white noise from 'Senior Partner Terry', as he liked to call him. Sitting down, he picked up the phone and called Roe. He wanted to be done with the personnel matter.

'Roe, darling, it's your favourite partner.'

'Yes, hello, Ian,' she replied, tolerating but not enjoying his attempt to be charming and witty.

'I understand there's been a mix-up with Max Hansell. I've just spoken to Tony, who has straightened out the whole thing. I mean, terribly nice chap,' he said, lowering his voice a little, 'but I do despair that the lights aren't always switched on upstairs, if you know what I mean?'

'Well, if you mean he's offered someone a job without any approval, then yes, I'd agree.'

'Yes, well the poor chap forgot that trainees are on fixed-term contracts. He'd assumed that Max was already included in his head-count and didn't constitute a new hire.'

'Of all the things—' Ian knew she could not wait to chew his ear off.

'Now, Roe,' he said quickly, interrupting her, 'I've put him straight on this so there's no need to interject. Can I assume this is now with Human Resources and the magic you work there will sort it out?'

Quite incidentally, she was inserting Max Hansell's contract into her typewriter at that very moment. Distracted by the call, she pressed 'release' without properly checking that the paper was correctly aligned. Suddenly, the typewriter bashed out the offending sentence beneath his signature and sloping slightly towards one corner.

'Ian, I'll do my best, as always,' she said, jamming the receiver between her ear and shoulder and unspooling the page. 'I'm not sure there's much magic to it, just good, old-fashioned hard work and keeping on top of things.' She did not want to admit, even to herself, that she had been flattered by his compliment. Ian had no idea that in her eyes the so-called 'magic' consisted of fraudulently amending a contract that had been signed in good faith by a graduate who no doubt hoped to work for the firm for many years.

A copy of the doctored contract, along with Max's notice letter, was put in the post tray, and she then moved on to thinking about the travel agents she would visit at lunchtime. She could do with something to look forward to. A summer cruise in the Med, perhaps. She knew she deserved one in these challenging times.

Walking up Chancery Lane a little later, she thought to herself that *finally* she had arrived where she deserved to be in her career, making important decisions that affected people's lives.

She gave little thought to the fact that the start of 1992 was miserable for most people, and she had little empathy for the experiences of the likes of Max and Tony. The papers were full of articles about the disappointment, anxiety and anger felt by many others across the country and of the people who had lost their jobs, homes, self-esteem and optimism. For Roe, the papers missed the point. It was simple market economics, unstoppable in the country that had been transformed by Maggie's revolution.

The working environment at the firm is so exhilarating right now, she thought, and smiled to herself, dismissing the talk of morale having hit rock bottom. Things were challenging, but she liked a challenge. Passing the Patent Office, she snorted slightly when thinking about the challenge Terry was having with some of the more obstinate partners in the firm. Apparently, they had opposed Terry's decision to close the firm's account at the Wig and Pen club. In defiance they ran up a tab of forty-nine thousand pounds during the year-long notice period. She thought it was a disgrace.

What she *did* accept was that there were now fewer promotion opportunities. The associates who had been working so hard to become partners had seen the prize diminish, as it came with the need to inject capital into an uncertain business. The senior survey-ors were unable to shine in their jobs, unless they were working in insolvency practice, for the market was moribund and companies indecisive. The surveyors and graduates knew that they had just missed the boom years and would have to wait until the next decade before making any decent money. Apparently, the secretaries and support staff were miserable too, but she could not for the life of her understand why.

Arriving outside the Cruise Heaven travel agency, she pushed the door open and greeted the staff with the bubbly smile she reserved for people from whom she wanted something. She was tempted by their Amalfi Coast cruise, but she needed more infor-mation to be able to compare it to a similar one advertised in the *Mediterranean Dreams* brochure.

CHAPTER SIX

Around the same time as Roe was driving away from Colchester with a large encyclopaedia on her passenger seat, Padraig was standing to attention opposite Broadway MBTA station, three thousand miles away in Boston. He was absolutely resplendent in his pipe major uniform. His jet-black bearskin hat was dusted with light snow that was beginning to fall. A sprig of shamrock adorned a green tunic lined with silver buttons, and his chest swelled with pride. Behind him, his pipe and drum band waited patiently to be led out of the holding area and into South Boston.

Adjusting the green, white and orange silk sash that cut across his chest, he raised a large mace, and his pipers began furiously pumping green velvet bags clamped between their elbows and midriffs. A wail rose and floated over the nearby spectators, loud enough, as Padraig put it, 'to raise the banshees from hell'. It triggered a slow, percussive attack on the snare drums that hung off the hips of the drum section, punctuated by an intermittent boom from a large man who pounded a bass drum fixed on a makeshift trolley. Before long, the general melee of sound became a single, coherent marching tune, and Padraig lowered his mace, which was the signal for the group to march slowly out of the holding area behind the embroidered banner of the Department of Correction Emerald Society Pipe Band, held aloft by two men with green rosettes pinned to their beige overcoats.

Light snowflakes whipped around the green, copper-covered bell tower of St Peter and & St Paul's Church as the men filed past, and Father Michael raised his three-peaked black biretta hat, which he always wore when giving absolution at confession. Standing at the top of the stone stairs above West Broadway, he would only raise his biretta to the traditional pipe and drum bands that passed the church. The school marching bands with their modern trumpets, trombones and French horns received just a wave of his hand. The Elvis impersonators were ignored.

The Department of Correction pipe band came to a brief standing march outside South Boston Neighborhood Police Station. Padraig saluted his colleagues whilst behind them the Greater Boston Fire Fighters Emerald Society Pipe and Drum Band began their march down West Broadway. They were dressed identically to the Department of Correction band, other than the brilliant white spats that protected their ankles and shins and the green berets they wore instead of bearskin hats.

And so continued the 91st St Patrick's Day parade organised by the South Boston Allied War Veterans Council on 15th March 1992. This year was going to be a first, though, for 'Southie', as the Council had failed to ban the Irish-American Gay, Lesbian and Bisexual Pride Committee from marching. The rainbow flag would join the ancient banners of 'Louth, Mary of the Gael', '1792 United Irish Men' and 'Armagh, Yellow Forge Battle', held aloft with equal pride and conviction in their right to represent and defend their beliefs. Father Michael had long since disappeared into his sacristy to prepare for evening Mass, as their small contingent passed at the very back of the so-called 'father of all parades' with a police escort.

Rich McDonnell and Neil Elder were sat in J.J. Foley's on East Berkeley drinking stout. The bar was full of people wearing green, white and orange, what with it being 'the day when everyone becomes Irish', as Mick, the long-serving barman, put it. Rich did not need to change his appearance to claim Irish ancestry, but wore a large green felt top hat anyway. With his thick curly black hair, dark eyebrows, pursed lips and pale skin, he was a fine example of that special group of Irishmen who could trace their history back to the Spanish Armada sailors who landed in Ireland and settled with the local womenfolk.

It was Grand-Daddy Andy who had made the journey across the Atlantic, almost four years after the sinking of the Titanic, and the story of what made him leave Toocanagh had been handed down from father to son ever since.

Toocanagh was a small collection of farms in the far northwest of Ireland, most of which have long since disappeared. All that now remains are the crumbling walls of their houses, with nettles for gardens and brambles that push through the wet stone and wrap around the old roof timbers and collapsed fireplaces within. It was here where Andy grew up, until he left for Ellis Island sometime in 1916. The precise date of when he sailed isn't known, but it was what sent him on his way that was the important thing.

It was a glorious late morning in September 1915 and he was walking back from the land at Gorgeen's with his donkey and wicker baskets full of potatoes. Pulling the donkey by its rope halter, he bent slightly to shield the sun and carried on down the Bog Road. Small mounds of turf stood drying in the fields either side, brown water sparkled in the ditches below him and tall reeds swayed gently along their muddy banks. He stopped briefly to watch his neighbour turning turf in the fields and realised that this was the life ahead of him, working in the fields, leading a donkey, cutting turf, laying potatoes. His brother Tom had left to become a police constable in England and was now enlisted and driving lorries in Italy; others had emigrated to America. He knew that he would have to make a decision soon on the course he wanted his life to follow: either stay in Toocanagh or begin a new life abroad.

Arriving back at the family cottage, with its whitewashed stone walls, thatched roof and red-painted door and windows, he began preparing the potatoes for winter laying. Emptying them carefully from the wicker baskets into a straw-lined rectangular hole, he covered them with a deep layer of hay and began shovelling from a large mound of soil to protect them from frost and preserve them through the long winter months ahead. At precisely midday, the Angelus Bell rang out and Grand-Daddy Andy stopped working, as did all other adult men in the fields of Toocanagh and neighbour-ing Bohola. He removed his cap, bowed his head and began the Angelus prayer.

The Angel of the Lord declared unto Mary
And she conceived of the Holy Spirit.

Hail Mary, full of grace,
The Lord is with Thee;
Blessed art thou amongst women,
And blessed is the fruit of thy womb, Jesus.
Holy Mary Mother of God, Pray for us sinners,
Now and at the hour of our death,
Amen.

Behold the handmaid of the Lord,
Be it done unto me according to thy word.

Something made him look up before he started the next Hail Mary. On a low branch of an ancient yew tree opposite stood an angel, pointing towards Gorgeen's land beyond the Bog Road. Andy stood transfixed. The angel was not wearing dazzling white clothes and did not carry a harp but was an angel nonetheless in a plain green robe. No words were spoken, but their message sank into Andy in a wave of consciousness that transcended words. He was to go west, across the Atlantic, to America.

His brothers teased him mercilessly about his vision for several weeks.

'Are you sure he wasn't telling you to forget the spuds and go do some proper work in Joe's field?' suggested Jack.

'I'd say it was the water you were being told to go draw from Croagh Jack's,' said Pat.

'No, to be sure, it has to be the new inn at Castlebar you're being sent to, not America,' added Ned.

Only Ned and his sister Ellen remained in Toocanagh to support their mother in old age. She did not live to see the arrival of electricity in the early 1950s; Ned and Ellen did not live to see running water connected to the village in spring 1979.

Rich and Neil finished their stout and joined the swarm of people in green, white and orange heading down East Berkeley towards the route of the march. Neil lived in Telegraph Hill with his girlfriend, Livvy, and they would be heading back later for their annual St Patrick's Day drinks up on the roof terrace. They had been friends for quite a few years now. Rich's cousin ran a clam chowder stall in Faneuil Hall, and he had got to know Neil when visiting his soccer shop on the top floor of the old market building. Neil was from Speen, a small village in the South of England, and had travelled to America in the late 1980s. He was now living as one of the many 'illegals' that had settled in Boston. He reminded Rich of Grand-Daddy Andy, who had made the same trip up from New York and started a new life in the city some seventy years earlier.

They soon passed Father Michael on the steps of St Peter and St Paul's Church, where Rich had been baptised by Father O'Brien on 29th June 1965. He knew the date as it was the Feast of St Peter and St Paul and a holy day of obligation. His given names were Niall Andrew McDonnell. All male descendants of Grand-Daddy Andy were given the middle name of Andrew, and his initials meant he was known as 'VC' at high school, on account of the recent war in Vietnam.

Richard was the name he took at his confirmation on 23rd March 1977. He had wanted to take the name Fonzie, like the character from *Happy Days*, but Sister Bernadette ruled that there had never been a Saint Fonzie, so he would be Saint Richie Cunningham instead, which was not such a bad thing as Richie was a pretty cool guy as well. He was tired of being called VC, and Rich was a cooler name than Niall, so he started calling himself Rich McDonnell after a few years at Don Bosco's Technical High School, just a few blocks up from J.J. Foley's.

The Department of Correction and Greater Boston Fire Fighters Emerald Pipe Bands were now beginning their return leg of the parade down East 4th, and the Chinese Society band was marching alongside Rich and Neil on West Broadway. They looked frozen in their blue-and-white tabards and matching pixie caps. The men supporting the wide-eyed dragon, which danced behind the band to the clashing of cymbals and kettle drums, were no doubt a little warmer.

This would be Rich's last St Patrick's Day parade for a few years, and he wanted to visit some of the places where he had grown up in the late 1960s and 1970s. As West Broadway turned into East Broadway, they caught up with the Immaculate Heart of Mary School float. The words 'Saint Patrick Bless Us' had been painted across its bright green sides, and a passable imposter stood at the back of the float in a green chasuble and white alb. Framed by a green-and-gold arch, he looked down piously on six girls sitting in angelic white gowns, pawing delicately on gold-painted cardboard harps. A seventh girl stood at the front of the float, dressed all in green. A huge papier-mâché shamrock had been placed on her head, framing her face and her beaming smile.

Pressing on, they reached Flanagan's on East Broadway and K Street. It was a local landmark with its green, white and orange shiplap boarding and large sign advertising 'Harp Lager – Imported from the Breweries of Guinness'. The bar on the first floor was reached via a steep flight of steps squeezed against the shop next door. The ground floor was a dance hall with its own entrance and a small hallway, where the steward, Tommy, collected tickets and kept coats on Saturday nights. During the week, the timber sprung floor and glitter ball were put to good use by Gaelic dancing and judo classes. Flanagan's was the de facto Irish Club for Telegraph Hill where Rich and his family spent many Saturday nights, and Sunday mornings, when he was growing up.

Pushing through the crowd, who were now cheering Boston City PD in their blue uniforms and white gloves, they went up into the bar and breathed a sigh of relief. The streets were heaving, and even though it was busy in there, it was a welcome break from the weather and spectators outside.

'Hey, two pints of your finest, Tommy,' waved Rich as he reached the long wooden bar running down the room.

'That'll be Guinness then?' Tommy nodded, knowing full well that Rich drank Murphy's stout.

Rich grimaced. 'Sure, you'll bring them over then once they've settled?' he replied, and went to sit down with Neil at the only free table at the back of the room. Those at the front had long ago been taken over by people gazing down on the parade.

'So this is where you spent your childhood?' asked Neil, looking around. He hadn't visited Flanagan's before, as it was a haunt of NORAID, or the Irish Northern Aid Committee. Having grown up with the Provisional IRA bombing England, he hated the terrorists and was astonished that an ally of the UK would allow an organisation that funded terrorism to operate perfectly legally in its country.

'Yeah, you know what, I had my first can of McEwan's in the hall and choked on my first smoke in the yard. Me and my cousin lifted a couple of Majors from Uncle Ronnie's jacket. Yeah, well, turned out it was the strongest filter tobacco in Ireland, and we puked all over the yard.'

Rich took a gulp of the Murphy's that Tommy had just brought over. Looking round, he knew he would miss Flanagan's with its Guinness toucans, Irish tricolours and old tourist board posters. His favourite was the one with an ancient round tower covered in mist that drifted away, carrying the words 'Eire, the ancient birthplace of good times'. The Celtic cross poster was also up there, but for some reason the round tower had always fascinated him.

In the background, *Hymns to the Silence* was being played. As this was the latest release from Van Morrison, it had a sort of sacred status, not just in Boston but also in Chicago and New York, where communities of second or third-generation Irish-Americans were intent on retaining their heritage. Rich tapped his fingers to the sound.

By the time Van Morrison got halfway through 'I Can't Stop Loving You', Rich could tell that Neil had something on his mind. He was grimacing, and it wasn't long before he could contain himself no longer.

'Not being funny, but this sounds like the sort of crap music those old geezers would play,' Neil said, nodding at a poster behind Rich.

Rich turned around and looked at the poster advertising the return of Brendan and his Pals for a dance on the 21st March. It promised they would 'play all their favorites', presumably in the matching knitted cardigans they wore in the poster.

'Absolutely, fucking yes! You can scoff all you want, but that hall will be rammed on the twenty-first,' he replied.

Neil just smiled back.

In a funny way, Rich enjoyed their humourless conversations, and they had become good friends. They drank their Murphy's in silence, and Rich watched Neil gritting his teeth as Van Morrison began 'Why Must I Always Explain' and smiled when the chorus made him wince and fidget with his pint.

'So, this new posting. Is it somewhere exotic?' Neil asked, finishing off his Murphy's.

Rich swallowed. 'You know what, I thought it'd be exotic, but I'm not so sure. I took more woodwork classes than geography at Don Bosco's, which figures, as I chose Trinidad over Bogotá, Medellín or Lima. I thought I'd be heading off to the Caribbean, but turns out that this Trinidad is in the middle of Bolivia.' Shrugging, he put his empty glass down on the table.

'Oh, that's brilliant!' Neil replied, chuckling. 'You took the piss out of me seeing "Olivia from Bolivia" until you met her, so there *is* a God after all, and he's sending you to Bolivia!'

'Yeah, well, I've done some reading since. You know that Butch Cassidy and the Sundance Kid were killed in San Vicente in Bolivia?' Rich said.

'I thought they were killed in Argentina. Is San Vicente close to Trinidad then?'

'No, it's nine hundred miles south. Che Guevara also got shot in Bolivia, in La Higuera.'

'Which is, what, nine hundred miles north of Trinidad?' asked Neil.

'No, it's five hundred miles south again, but closer to Trinidad, which is the centre of the Beni region. La Paz, the capital, is four hundred and fifty miles west, up in the mountain range that stretches all the way down South America, sort of like our Rocky Mountains.' He paused and raised his glass. 'You want to get another?' He thought it best to change the subject as he knew he should not be discussing federal business in a bar.

Rich applied to join the Drug Enforcement Administration as soon as he turned twenty-one. He had been inspired by the sacrifice made by DEA Special Agent Camarena, who had lost his life in Mexico the previous March. The murder had received huge media coverage, and 'Kiki', as he was known, was flown back to North Island Terminal, San Diego, with full military honours. Rich had planned on making a long career in Boston PD, but when he saw the footage he knew he had to step up and play his role in fighting the growing drug problem, just as the previous generation had stood up to the communist Vietnamese twenty years earlier.

The DEA had been expanding rapidly since the murder of Kiki, and although he did not have a college degree, Rich's experience in the police force secured a placement on their growing special agent programme. After eighteen weeks' basic training in drug recognition, surveillance, undercover operations and firearms at their new training facility at Quantico, Virginia, he returned to the DEA office in Boston and joined a domestic investigative team.

If Rich were honest, the first few years in the office felt pretty bureaucratic. He was assigned to a team that had set up a new bank, known as Trans America Ventures Associates, or TARA for short. The aim was to lure drug traffickers using undercover agents posing as money launderers. Although he was a very small cog in a big wheel, the operation was a success. The cartels sought similar money-laundering services in Europe, Canada and the Caribbean, and in the process revealed some of the financial machinery of their empires. No doubt it disrupted the flow of criminal proceeds for a short time, but it didn't feel tangible, like the arrest of Pablo Escobar had been in June 1991. This was the sort of action Rich had signed up for. When George H. W. Bush rapidly expanded the DEA's overseas operations, the opportunity to be posted abroad came up and he jumped at the chance.

The previous year, Operation Desert Shield in Iraq had been judged a success, and it allowed the administration to adopt a more aggressive foreign policy. The fallout from the Iran-Contra scandal of the mid-1980s was now history, and with renewed public support, George H. W. Bush felt confident pursuing a more direct approach in the War on Drugs. He saw it as his moral duty to take on the cartels locally, but this time strictly through legitimate channels.

Rich chuckled. Ronald Regan had also justified his behaviour in the Iran-Contra affair on moral grounds. Unfortunately, selling arms to Iran was in direct breach of his own government's embargo, which made it illegal. But the fact that the funds were used to support a right-wing terrorist group aiming to overthrow the Sandinista Nicaragua government was perfectly justifiable as the elected government was socialist. It was also entirely apt – the Sandinistas had resisted an American occupation of Nicaragua back in the 1930s.

George H. W. Bush had both the moral high ground and a legitimate framework through which to win the War on Drugs. For Rich, it was a case of being in the right place at the right time.

He had always been a lucky guy.

CHAPTER SEVEN

Neil went to the bar to buy another round of Murphy's. He was a friend of Rich so Tommy agreed to serve him. There were no tourists in Flanagan's. It was not that they were refused entry, it was just that Tommy would not serve them. If the bar was full, then there were always others to attend to. If the bar was empty, then Tommy would disappear into the back room and leave them standing there until they ran out of patience and left.

'What'll it be then, fella, another two pints of Murphy's?' asked Tommy in a strong southern Irish accent.

'Yeah, another two pints of the same, please, mate,' Neil replied in a strong English accent that was immediately picked up by Tommy.

'You're from England then, by the sounds of it. Are you enjoying the parade?' he asked, drying a pint glass with a shamrock-patterned dishcloth. Stretching up, he got down another glass and started pouring the pints.

'Yeah, it's quite an event, but I live in Telegraph Hill, so I'm used to it,' said Neil, who wanted the bartender to know that he was not a tourist but lived in the neighbourhood.

'Oh, you do, do you. I suppose you're a local then? And how long have you been in Southie?' he asked, looking up from the glasses that were slowly filling with stout.

'Coming on four years now, I guess,' Neil replied.

'And do you have your green card with you, as I need to see it before I can serve the Murphy's?'

Neil frowned. *Is this guy for real?* He had never been asked to show a green card at a bar, or any other place for that matter. A driving licence was normally requested for ID purposes. He had never even seen one of the fabled green cards, and he had no idea if it had a date of birth field. Pulling out his wallet, he passed over his UK driving licence to Tommy, who was just letting the pints settle.

'No, fella, that's a driving licence. It's the green card I need to see. It's the thing what says you're allowed to sit here and drink my beer legally. We're not allowed to serve illegals now, you know.'

Neil began to stammer an excuse about the card being at home when Tommy roared with laughter.

'Be on with you, fella, I'm pulling your leg. If I had a dollar bill for each man sat drinking here without a green card, I'd be retired in County Cork with my feet up in front of the fire by now!'

Tommy was laughing, but Neil felt intimidated and uncomfortable. What had convinced him to go into a NORAID bar in the first place? What did he expect from a place that supported terrorism? He'd pay for the beer, smile nicely and then get the hell out before anything else happened.

Tommy topped off the beers and placed them on the counter. Neil handed him a five-dollar bill, but the bartender ignored him, turned his back and fetched a white bucket and a small cardboard box from between the spirit bottles. Neil stood awkwardly at the bar with his five dollars, but Tommy simply placed the bucket next to the beers and pushed the cardboard box across the bar.

'Take a look in there, fella. You could do with one of those to finish off your St Patrick's Day outfit. All proceeds of sale go to a fine charitable cause, and you'll only see them on sale between Ash Wednesday and Easter Sunday. Tell me, do you English observe Lent back home?' he asked innocently.

Neil looked at the map of a united Ireland stamped on the bucket in green, white and orange stripes and knew that he was not taking the beer until he had made a donation to 'the cause in the North'. He picked up one of the plastic packets that contained a small metal badge of a lily flower. Deep green petals wrapped around a white flower and a bright orange stamen stood in its middle like a burning flame.

'Go on, pin it on your chest. It'll look grand on that black T-shirt you're wearing.'

Neil pinned the Easter Lily on his T-shirt, and Tommy then pushed the bucket at him.

'So, that'll be four bucks for the beer and twenty bucks for the Easter Lily. Put the twenty bucks in the bucket there, and the four can go in my hand.'

In no way did Neil want to pay twenty dollars for a small metal badge that cost the equivalent of ten pints of Murphy's, but the badge was now pinned to him and he felt intimidated by the bartender with the shamrock dishcloth. Reaching for the bucket, he folded two ten-dollar bills and pushed them through a small slit in its lid.

Neil took the pints and returned, somewhat abashed, to the table where Rich was still sitting tapping his fingers to Van Morrison. Rich nodded at the Easter Lily.

'Tommy been practising his sales skills on you? That's a fine Easter Lily you're wearing, but don't go parading it back home unless you actually gun for the IRA. You know it's a Republican badge, right,' he asked, 'worn in memory of those killed in the Easter Rising of 1916?'

Neil grimaced and took a sip of his beer. 'He's a right fucking wanker, that bartender. He pumped me for information, asked to see my green card and then palmed me off with an IRA badge for twenty bucks.' Taking it off, he tossed it across the table and picked up his beer again, 'Come on, let's get these down and fuck off out of this place.'

Rich's face creased into a small smile. 'Yeah, well, don't take it so hard. Tommy's a master salesman and fundraiser. He's been at it for twenty years. I remember the dances downstairs when I was a kid. At midnight, the band would stop playing, the lights turned on and we'd all stand for the Irish national anthem. Once it finished, Tommy and other NORAID members would start at one end and rattle their collection buckets at each table. Not making a donation wasn't an option, unless you wanted this dance to be your last one.'

'What, you'd be executed by the IRA?' asked Neil, genuinely shocked.

'Of course not, you bozo. Tommy wouldn't let you in next time you showed up.' Rich shook his head. 'He was pretty firm on the T's and C's and refused entry to a dance if he felt like it. So, it figured, everyone always made a donation. Anyway, the band would start up again, the lights would go off and the floor would fill with drunks lining up for the Siege of Ennis, which was the evening's grand finale.' He nodded. 'Yeah, that's Tommy.'

Rich had grown up with NORAID collecting for Catholic families discriminated against by the Stormont government. The Catholic minority received poorer housing, were excluded from the best jobs and were actively encouraged to leave Ulster by a Protestant majority who feared the Catholic population outgrowing them and taking the province out of the UK.

A few years earlier a brunch had been organised by NORAID in the hall. Rich attended the feast of white and black pudding, rashers of bacon, tomatoes, sausages, baked beans and scrambled eggs, washed down with endless mugs of tea. Wearing a white apron, Tommy directed a team of ladies in flowery pinafores who kept each table supplied with fried bread and topped up mugs with large white enamel teapots.

That year, NORAID had invited a guest speaker to explain why support was still needed in 'the North', as it was known by everyone in the dance hall. The identity of the speaker had been kept secret. So, when Dolours stood up and was introduced by Tommy, she received a resounding applause and a gasp from some of the older people who instantly recognised her as the leader of an IRA gang that had bombed London in March 1973. Heathrow Airport had been shut just minutes before she was about to board a flight back to Dublin on the morning of the bombing, and she was arrested and sentenced to twenty years in prison. Following a hunger strike, a period in Brixton and then Armagh prison, she was released early in 1981. She was now a well-known figure in the Provisional IRA and a spokesperson for the cause.

Rich did not know who she was, but he was struck by the obvious admiration of the second-generation Irish-American women opposite, none of whom had ever left the US, never mind visited the green, but wet, Emerald Isle. Dolours was indeed an accomplished speaker and explained what drove her to the Republican cause and to notoriety. She grew up in Belfast in a family of sympathisers and part-time members of the Irish Republican Army. Recovering from the injuries she received on a peaceful march organised by the People's Democracy, she swore that the next time she confronted Protestants swinging wooden planks studded with nails and carrying lead pipes, she would be pointing a Webley Revolver at them.

This was her 'Burntollet Bridge moment', as she called it. She joined the IRA shortly thereafter, becoming an expert sniper in the Provisional IRA around the time it split from the Official IRA, and emerging as 'one of the most dangerous young women in Ulster'. She was convinced that someone high up in the Provos had betrayed her and that British Intelligence had prior warning of the bombing on that cold, wet morning in 1973. All ports and airports were shut before midday, and when she arrived at Heathrow for her flight to Dublin, she was met by Special Branch officers and arrested.

She laughed when recalling Reverend Ian Paisley's apoplectic rant on 'the outrageous scandal' that was her release, and how she apparently had 'murder in her heart'. The armed struggle was developing into a political struggle now, and funding was needed for Sinn Féin to push the door open into a more peaceful era for the province. For that reason, more than ever, she was hoping that the good folk of South Boston would support them on their journey to free the Catholics of the North. As Dolours sat down to rapturous applause, Tommy and his ladies swapped their enamelled teapots for white buckets and descended on the tables to collect dollar bills for the oppressed.

On his way out, Rich overheard Dolours and Tommy referring to 'a gesture' that was being planned. Six months later, in February 1991, the Provisional IRA launched a mortar attack on 10 Downing Street whilst Prime Minister John Major was holding a cabinet meeting. He could not be certain, but from then on, he started to give credence to the British government's claim that NORAID was a major fundraiser for a terrorist organisation. Had he known that the IRA referred to the white enamelled teapot carrier as 'Tommy Gun', and that he was a key figure in the export of ArmaLite rifles to the province, then he would have been certain. He decided to avoid being associated with NORAID in future, as he did not want to take any risks with his federal career.

CHAPTER EIGHT

Rich and Neil finished their second pint of Murphy's and left Flanagan's. By now the parade was half over, so they decided to spend the rest of the afternoon out on the streets enjoying it.

Turning down East Broadway, they headed towards Medal of Honor Park, beyond which Rich knew a good spot to watch the rest of the procession. Crossing over L Street, they were overtaken by an old Guinness brewery dray, pulled by eight large dray horses. Up on the driver's platform, two men dressed as leprechauns sat in front of a large rectangular black-and-gold Guinness sign. The dray was full of wooden barrels and the horse's tack was covered in green rosettes. Rich felt a certain pride in being in South Boston that day. It was his town, his roots were here, and he had more right than most to be walking down East Broadway, the route of his old walk to elementary school.

He had grown up in a large public housing scheme called Old Colony on East 8th and Dorchester, on the edge of Telegraph Hill. The walk to Saint Brigid School used to take him twenty-five minutes with his buddy Jimmy, who also lived in Old Colony. The housing scheme was still there with its identical arched entrance doors, part-painted brick walls and air conditioning units hanging out of the windows. The huge sign that was fixed to railings on the roof was now long gone. It had once stood on the corner of the first block on East 8th, towering over the adjoining single-storey hair salon and looking down on the four lanes of traffic passing up and down Dorchester Street.

Rich remembered that sign vividly. In his mind he saw its white background, red-brick wall and cream Celtic cross painted in the centre. The words 'Failte go mBoston dheas' stood out in bold green letters above, and 'Welcome to South Boston' directly beneath. At the bottom of the sign the slogan 'Óglaigh na hÉireann' had been left untranslated. Rich knew this was the Gaelic title of the IRA and roughly translated as 'warriors, or soldiers, of Ireland'. The coats of arms of the provinces of Ireland and the words 'Sinn Féin' and 'NORAID' had been arranged around the red-brick wall. Boston Housing Authority removed the sign in the early 1980s.

Grand-Daddy Andy moved to Old Colony when it was first built in the 1940s. Rich's mother, Eilish, and his father, Jack, still lived there, since they liked it and had never felt any need to move. Jack had served his apprenticeship with furniture-makers Irving and Casson – A.H. Davenport in East Cambridge and worked for them until the factory closed in 1973. As he put it, he was 'following in the footsteps of Our Lord' working at Davenport's. Rich had thought of becoming a carpenter as well, for he enjoyed the woodwork classes at Don Bosco's, but Uncle Johnjo worked in Boston PD and secured him a good position there instead.

According to Uncle Johnjo, he was 'following in the footsteps of the McDonnells' working at Boston PD. Three of his uncles and two of his great-uncles had served in the police force, and one of them, Tom, had risen to the rank of chief inspector in London. He remembered Grand-Daddy Andy telling him he had also served in the First World War in Italy, but he knew nothing else about him.

Rich's early childhood was spent within a triangle that could be drawn between Saint Brigid School to the west, St Peter and St Paul's to the east and Joe Moakley Park to the south. Looking back, it wasn't a privileged upbringing, but it was a good one. Saturday evenings were mainly taken up with dances at Flanagan's. Sundays consisted of morning Mass, Gaelic football practice in Joe Moakley Park and a two p.m.-sharp Sunday dinner at the McDonnell family table. Jack always cooked roast beef, roast potatoes, gallons of gravy and mashed carrot and swede, or boiled cabbage, depending on the month. Dessert varied between tapioca pudding and bread and butter pudding with cremated raisins on top like small pieces of shot.

Before Rich joined the Gaelic football club and had Sunday morning training, he used to love his Da taking out the roasting tray and dipping a slice of bread in the meat juice for him. As Jack put it, 'It's a grand way to excite your taste buds and leave them lingering for the approaching feast.'

Rich had been lucky to attend Saint Brigid's as it was the most modern school in South Boston in 1970. It was no longer run by nuns from The Sisters of Charity of Nazareth, and had been renamed the South Boston Catholic Academy, but the three-storey brick building on the corner of East Broadway and O Street would make a good vantage point, and before long, Neil and Rich were climbing its eleven concrete steps for a better view of the parade in front.

Squeezing past a group on the steps, Rich noticed Declan, an old pal from his Saint Brigid and Don Bosco school days, standing there with some girls.

'Hey, Dec. How you been keeping? It's been a while, you've grown,' he said, looking at his belly.

Declan took a few seconds to recognise Rich, and then clapped a hand on his shoulder.

'VC, buddy, there's got to be a hundred thousand people here. What's the chance of bumping into you? How you been keeping?'

'Yeah, good. This is Neil,' he said, turning to him. 'Over from England.'

Neil winced.

Rich knew Neil regarded himself as living in Boston, not visiting it, but he couldn't bring himself to introduce him as 'Neil, who lives in Telegraph Hill'.

'Oh yeah, the Brit version of VC.' Declan lowered his voice and slurred a little. 'VC told you his real name, right?'

Neil smiled awkwardly – Declan was obviously liquored up.

'You know he was baptised Niall, yeah, like the Gaelic form of Neil? That makes you two kind of brothers, or maybe even twins! So what's your family name? Let's try find you a good nickname as well,' Declan continued, chuckling.

'Yeah, very fucking funny, Dec. You'll miss the *Star Wars* pageant if you use all your energy trying to think up a nickname,' said Rich, nodding towards East Broadway and raising his eyebrows at the girls with Declan.

They all turned round just in time to catch two Emperor Palpatines passing in front, followed by a stream of stormtroopers. A group of Jedi in brown capes waved lightsabers at them, and a funny little man drove past on a speeder bike from *Return of the Jedi*. He had an enormous felt hat on his head and a large grin on his face.

Swaying back to Rich, Declan had more smart remarks to make. 'I heard you were nominated for the Friendly Sons of St Patrick when you turned eighteen and got a shamrock tattooed on your ass as part of the initiation?' Out of everyone, he alone found this funny and laughed out loud.

'Hey, I've no fucking idea where you get your information from, but whoever you've been talking to must have got the Friendly Sons mixed up with Boston PD. As for a shamrock, tell those friends of yours to come take a look and I'll bury them underground,' Rich said, with some menace.

Declan did not pick up on the change in atmosphere and carried on regardless. Turning to Neil, he said, 'I guess Rich hasn't told you much about his elementary schooling? He was a bad kid, and those sadist nuns whipped him most weeks.'

'You want to drop that?' shouted Rich.

'You remember Sister Michael, right?' asked Declan, who was thoroughly enjoying himself. 'My Da used to say that she was given a man's name by her Sister Superior to take away her pride. Apparently, she was "a spirited young girl", but by the time she taught us she was a bitter, vindictive old bitch. That said, she still had some spirit in her right arm, right, Rich?'

Turning to the girls, he staggered slightly, raised his bottle and waved it at the school behind them. 'We both went to this shithole back in the early 1970s. A bunch of nuns ran the place, and Sister Michael's classroom was on the first floor facing East Broadway, where little Niall—'

'Shut the fuck up, Declan, unless you want that bottle rammed up your ass!'

Declan stopped and glared at Rich. Stepping up to him, he burped aggressively in his face and smirked. 'Buddy, you need to show more—' But the words stuck in his throat as Rich's hand locked onto his balls and squeezed them tightly. Rich twisted his wrist and sent excruciating pain through Declan's groin, making him drop to his knees.

'No, *buddy* . . . I'm not your buddy.' He leant down and whispered in his ear, 'The next time you diss me I'll fucking rip them off and ram them down your throat,' and gave them one last squeeze.

Declan collapsed to the floor, the girls gathered round him, and Rich simply walked off down the school steps.

Neil caught up with him back on the street.

'Rich, mate, what was—' Neil started to say, but Rich's glare made him stop.

'Listen, I've got something to do. I'll catch up with you later,' Rich replied, nodding at O Street, which was the cue for Neil to head down to his apartment on the corner of East 7th and generally fuck off.

Rich crossed the street, breathing hard, and looked back up at the school. He had some fond memories, but not of the year he was in Sister Michael's class. In the summer, the sun used to stream in and make the dust rising from its woodblock floor sparkle, but it was the only happy memory of being in that room. Whenever Sister Michael deemed the class to be misbehaving, Niall was summoned to approach her desk. Even though he knew what was coming, he refused to sob, although his legs always trembled slightly.

When he reached Sister Michael she would stand up, smooth the dark blue habit that reached down to her black leather sandals and turn him roughly towards the class. An angelic white starched peak edged her veil and framed the demonic face that made it clear none of the promises associated with heaven's messengers were on offer. She was a tall, angular woman with dead eyes behind silver wire glasses and a small silver crucifix over a hard heart.

As he faced the class, Niall could hear her picking up that wooden ruler, and he braced himself, tensing all his muscles and clenching his fists. Yanking down his sock, she would strike him across the calf as hard as she could, making his leg scream with pain. The reflex to protect his calf was always met with an excruciating blow to his knuckles, before the remaining five strikes were delivered with gusto once his arm had been wrenched behind his back.

Sent back to his desk, the class would watch as he sat down, shaking silently. But to the end, he would refuse to sob.

He knew that Sister Michael ended her days in The Sisters of Charity of Nazareth's motherhouse in Kentucky, where she received better care than that she had provided to the unlucky children passing through her classroom. But he was pleased that she never broke him.

Rich shook his head and turned towards Saint Brigid church, which was just down the road from South Boston Catholic Academy. It was here where he made his First Communion on 25th November 1973. The church had not changed much since then, other than the flower beds at its entrance being slightly smaller and two flagpoles having been erected, on which a papal flag and a Stars and Stripes hung limply. As a kid, he had always thought the sheer brick elevation and pointed gable of St Brigid's gave it the appearance of a ship capsized on East Broadway, with its pointed hull guiding worshippers to heaven above. Many years earlier, the roof extended out over the gable and there was a bell tower, which gave it a far more welcoming appearance.

After the unpleasant reminder of his abuse at the hands of Sister Michael, he wanted to leave that corner of South Boston with a fond memory. His First Communion was a fond memory, as it was the first time he had eaten on a starched white tablecloth, ridiculous though it now seemed. Going inside, he sat down on one end of the wooden pews, next to the aisle. It was down this aisle that he had walked on a bright Sunday morning, almost nineteen years ago. The front quarter of the church was reserved for family members, and as he approached the altar, he passed some of his classmates' parents before reaching 'M' for McDonnell, McDermott and Murphy. Sitting amongst the other parents and all the many siblings were his Ma and Da, proud as could be.

He remembered his stomach rumbling from fasting all morning. He did not remember much about the rest of the ceremony, other than being quite taken with the red sash that he had been wearing over his ill-fitting new suit. He had tried holding on to it after receiving the sacrament, but Sister Deidre was waiting at the back of the church, and she collected them from all the communicants before they returned to their seats.

Shortly after Mass finished, the boys in their cheap suits and bow ties and the girls in their bright white communion dresses were led across the road to Saint Brigid's school. Father Cullinan stood at its entrance. With one hand he shook their little hands, and with the other he directed them to a classroom on the ground floor. It had been set up as a temporary dining room, with a statue of the Virgin Mary on a small table at one end and the desks arranged in one long line leading up to it. They were all covered in starched white tablecloths and had been laid with a glass of lemonade and a plate and spoon for each communicant. Once they were all seated, their mothers served them a boiled egg and toast before their photo was taken next to Father Cullinan and the statue of the Virgin Mary.

Rich, like most twenty-six-year-old Catholics in Boston, rarely attended Mass now. That said, he had a deep sense that there was a purpose to life beyond subsisting. He could not quite pin it to a firm belief in the Scriptures he had been taught at Saint Brigid's and St Peter and St Paul's, but he definitely felt that there was a guiding force behind the events that had shaped his life. He was living in up-market Beacon Hill and about to depart for South America to progress his career. If Uncle Johnjo had not got him the job at Boston PD, he would not have been accepted into the DEA special agent programme. If Special Agent Camarena had not been murdered in Mexico and the DEA expanded, then there would not have been an opening. If Operation Desert Shield had been a disaster, the DEA's foreign expansion would not have happened anyway.

So here he was, a kid from a poor neighbourhood, with this life and its opportunities ahead of him. Looking up at the cross hanging over the altar, Rich smiled. He knew Our Lord was in the church because the Sanctuary Lamp hanging at the side of the altar was lit. At least, that was what Father Cullinan had taught them.

Rich walked away from Neil and Livvy's, down M Street towards the T line at Andrew station. The parade and evening party had been fun in the end, and spending the day in Southie had brought back fond memories of his childhood. As he swaggered down East 8th and past Old Colony, he thought back to the long-gone IRA sign that had once looked down over the city, and just how strong NORAID had become in Southie.

Chuckling, he remembered a story Tommy had told him about a NORAID event back in the late 1970s. The speaker was an IRA commander who ran the division responsible for West Belfast at the height of the Troubles. Jerry, one of the NORAID committee, had told the commander that the struggle needed to be intensified, with all British Crown institutions in the North attacked, not just the Army and the RUC. Astonished, the commander half joked that maybe they should be assassinating postmen, but Jerry replied that 'in all-out war even postmen aren't safe'. Laughing, Tommy said that Jerry turned down the plane ticket he was offered 'to come do the job himself'.

Rich chuckled about Jerry holding more extreme views than an IRA commander. He believed in a cause, but circumstances meant he was prevented from directing his nationalism into personal action beyond the US border. His misfortune of being born abroad should not prevent him from taking part in a just cause for freedom.

Rich was proud of his Irish roots and had never felt the need to reflect on the essence of what it was to be Irish-American. He accepted Ireland was the mother lode out of which the South Boston community grew. He sort of knew that the large Gaelic sign on top of Old Colony would have been gazed on with bewilderment by Grand-Daddy Andy and his fellow immigrants, but it did not matter. For all the Gaelic splashed over buildings and signs in Boston, not one of the Irish immigrants before 1930 would have been able to read it, as the language was virtually dead before its revival after independence in 1922. But the point was that it allowed people to associate with their roots and create a community, and that was what mattered to Rich.

He remembered one of Neil's smart-ass British friends asking him why the old folk did not go back to Ireland after making a decent living in Boston. And why was Boston so full of young, illegal Irish if it was such a good place to be? Like the Irish-American ladies at Dolours' presentation, Rich had never left the US and had only just received his passport. As he had never visited Bohola and its legendary three pubs of Clarke's, McDonagh's and Roche's, he could not describe any first-hand experiences of his heritage, but he smiled when he recalled 'squashing the Brit like a grape' with his list of successful Irish-Americans, starting with the Kennedys.

Now he thought about it, he did not much care for the Brits. Neil was an okay guy, but prone to smart-ass remarks. Most of the other Brits he had met either had bad teeth or a worse sense of humour. Uncle Johnjo had mentioned that they had some distant relatives in England called the Hansards, or Hansells or something, but he had no interest whatsoever in trying to connect with them.

He never believed that Grand-Daddy Andy had seen an angel in that yew tree back in 1915, but boy was he relieved he had emigrated to the greatest country in the world and not followed his brother to England. He also suspected that his Da did not believe the angel story either but would never admit it. The family had relocated to America under divine guidance, which placed a convenient comfort blanket over any hardship experienced, as everything had a divine purpose. Rich's view was that Grand-Daddy Andy had listened to the chatter in Clarke's about conscription being introduced on the mainland in 1916. As it would only be a matter of time before it reached Ireland, nineteen would be a good time to leave the British Empire. Did this make him a coward? If his brother Tom had volunteered and was serving in the Army, what stopped Grand-Daddy doing the same?

With these thoughts, Rich went down into the T line at Andrew. Like Grand-Daddy Andy, he felt sure he was being guided to leave home, and that it was not just by chance. He was determined to do his duty, not least because he had always secretly suspected that, perhaps, his grandfather had avoided doing his. But then, he knew all about the propaganda of the First World War, and shrugged slightly. *Maybe Grand-Daddy was unconvinced by the newspapers and decided that the Great War was not the glorious endeavour it was made out to be?* Luckily he had no such doubts about the War on Drugs.

Tommy had told him that conscription was never actually introduced in Ireland, and the province of Northern Ireland simply came about because the British government felt it owed a duty to the Ulstermen who had freely volunteered for service. Rich shook his head. *If there had not been a war in Europe, then perhaps Ireland would be united, NORAID would not exist and maybe men and women like Tommy Gun and Dolours would be living perfectly ordinary lives?* He shook his head again, stamped his feet to keep warm and wondered if Tommy would ever have lived an ordinary life . . .

CHAPTER NINE

The walk down the corridor of shame that Max had so dreaded on Monday morning had not been the trial he feared. He arrived late on account of the tube strike, by which time people were either busy on the phone or writing reports. They either did not seem to notice him or they gave him a sympathetic smile when he walked past. All of the Outer London regional office team were in their regular Monday morning meeting, so part of the floor was empty anyway.

His fellow team members, Joe Pitman and Dan Willis, stood up when he arrived and offered their support. The three of them were still standing by their desks when Tony emerged from his office. He totally ignored Max, waved a hand at Debbie and shouted, 'I'm going out,' yanking his coat over his shoulders, 'back sometime in the afternoon.' His face was bright red, and Debbie put a finger to her lips, advising Max not to say anything. He later found out that Ian had given him yet another bollocking, and he was gutted to have missed it.

Before long Joe and Dan got back to work, leaving Max to his thoughts for the rest of the day. What gnawed away at him was the fact that he had been singled out for redundancy. What were the reasons for him being rejected, whilst other surveyors like Dan remained employed? In fact, with the exception of Phil, all eight surveyors losing their jobs were more competent than the twenty-four receiving contracts. The incompetence that Phil demonstrated in processing photos had a habit of creeping into his daily work. Max could understand the firm's decision to get rid of Phil, but he just could not understand why Dan still had a job, of all people! He was just lucky to be in the year ahead of Max.

Dan was probably the laziest surveyor in the firm and only moderately able. He had singlehandedly disproved the theory that team sport developed a good work ethic. Even when everyone around him was flat out, he was still too busy planning his weekend hockey travel arrangements to lend a hand. Not only was Dan very successful at hockey, but he also had a very refined voice, no doubt cultivated during his education at Marlborough College. The combination of an elegant voice and a seemingly endless supply of self-confidence would ensure Dan's future success in property. Max's attempts at building self-confidence had long since been crushed by the liberal application of a Dunlop Green Flash trainer on his arse during *his* education at the Royal Grammar School.

Whilst there, Max had studied *Candide*, the 1759 French novel by Voltaire. In it, its eponymous hero is beset by a series of disasters, which he accepts as being 'for the best' as he believes he is living in 'the best of all possible worlds'. He takes to heart the philosophy of his mentor, Dr Pangloss, that all events are interconnected and misfortune for one person allows another to benefit. Sitting at his desk in Chancery Lane, Max empathised with Candide's misfortunes but was grateful that nobody suggested that the meeting with Terry Nighy had been 'for the best'.

Max left the office early and drifted aimlessly up to the tube station. On his way he picked up a copy of *Time Out* with the *Evening Standard*. On its front cover there was a stunning photo of Machu Picchu along with the title 'South America, the next frontier'. Intrigued, he rolled it up with the paper and had a relatively relaxing journey home reading about the Inca Empire that had once spread out from Peru across the Andes.

The following day he had expected to be called in to see Tony, but it was Ian who wanted to see him. For some reason he felt nervous. Ian was head of agency and ran the department. Max was still not reconciled to leaving the firm and felt pressure to appear confident in front of him, even though it was the opposite of how he felt.

The first thing that struck Max on entering Ian's office, which was a large, imposing room at one end of the floor, were the two high-backed red leather armchairs in the corner. Next to them, a walnut-veneered drinks cabinet was arranged alongside a small matching table with a couple of tumblers on it. A slender glass cabinet stood behind the desk where Ian kept his awards, the most prominent of which was a Young Surveyor of the Year (1978) plaque, prominently displayed on top. It was the first time Max had set foot in Ian's office.

Ian was leaning back in his chair. His feet were on the desk and he was facing slightly sideways, somewhat awkwardly, so that he could look out of the window. This was generally how he used the phone. He smiled and waved Max to the seat in front of his desk whilst he finished his call.

'We should be able to get down this weekend for a last inspection,' Ian confirmed to the Padstow estate agent. 'Assuming the work has been completed to our satisfaction, we'll instruct our solicitor to exchange contracts on Monday.' Once the call was over, he put the receiver down, sat up in his chair and smiled at Max.

'Max, as you know, the firm's experiencing unusually severe weather at the moment. The storm looks unlikely to blow over this year, and we're likely to be buffeted by it next year as well,' Ian explained. As he had just been dealing with his new holiday home purchase in Cornwall, he seemed to have unconsciously threaded some nautical slang into his language. Max was trying to keep up with his analogies. 'We're all looking for a safe harbour right now, and the firm has had to trim its sails, as I'm sure Terry explained to you on Friday. We're all in this together though. Whilst I was in Padstow this weekend, I said to my wife that I'd find a way to throw you a life jacket, as I'm determined that a crew member . . .' He hesitated, then corrected himself. 'A team member shouldn't be cast adrift.'

Max looked at Ian and wondered what he was going to suggest. It was not lost on Max that, despite the straightening times, Ian was able to afford a new holiday home.

Ian continued, 'I've made some calls to a few fellow partners, and Mark Herald in insolvency practice could do with a spare pair of hands if you'd be prepared to work in his team on a temporary basis?' Max smiled. He had half expected Ian to refer to 'helping on the rigging'.

Leaning back further in his chair, Ian brushed a hand through his silvery hair and smiled back. He made no reference to Tony's mistake, which had cost Max his employment. He also made no reference to the fact that it had actually been Terry who had called *him* about Mark's opening, as Max later found out.

Max had worked for Mark Herald when he first joined the firm. He was probably one of the most competent and talented partners in the firm and a pleasure to work with. He had appointed Tim, an ambitious associate, to run the insolvency team on a day-to-day basis with support from a couple of Max's contemporaries. Together they made a good team, and Max had no hesitation joining them on a temporary basis. At the very least it would give him some breathing space to find another job.

'I really wasn't expecting that, Ian. Thanks for your support. I need all the help I can get right now. That sounds great,' he said. 'When will the position start, and how long will I be working for Mark?'

'I think it will be for a period of six weeks, extendable at the firm's discretion, but let's call Roe,' replied Ian, picking up the phone.

Winking at Max, he repeated his stock phrase, 'Roe, darling, it's your favourite partner on the line,' and continued, 'I've been discussing the opening in Mark's team with Max Hansell . . . Well, yes, he's got a smile on his face, so I think we can take it that he's happy to join Mark on a temporary basis.' Ian winked again, this time with his other eye.

Max leant forward and whispered as loudly as he could, 'Would you ask Roe to send me my contract, please? It still hasn't arrived.'

'Roe, darling, can I leave it to you to sort out the paperwork for Max? He's asked that you send him his contract as well . . . Oh, okay, I'll let him know.'

Putting the receiver down, Ian told him his contract was posted first class on Monday evening, so it should be with him in this afternoon's post. In the meantime, he could start right away with

Mark, 'Ambitious Tim' and his two surveyors on the third floor. His new contract would be for six weeks, starting upon the expiry of his current contract.

Max left Tony Rowan's team that afternoon. Tony never did offer the apology suggested by Ian, but then Max later discovered that he had bigger concerns – his first-quarter fees only just covered the annual salary of his secretary, Debbie. Max was never quite sure why he had pushed to join the industrial agency team in the first place. Tony had a reputation for being a nice guy to work with and he had left Max with a good impression when handing out the branded sweatshirts at the firm's 'Vision for the Next Decade' conference a couple of years earlier. With his slightly ruddy face and portly frame, he had been a far more approachable partner than some of the others. As it turned out, his jovial appearance had been just that: an appearance. It did not follow him into the day-to-day workplace.

It was Alan, the former head of marketing, who convinced the partners to hold the conference, which was never repeated. Once he was made redundant, the opportunity to harness his musical talent at any future conference was also lost. At 'Vision for the Next Decade', Alan had persuaded the partners to allow him on stage with his silver drum kit. As each of them mounted the steps for their presentation, they were greeted by a roll on his snare drum. By the time it was Terry's turn, Alan had warmed to his task, and delivered an impromptu three-minute drum solo for him. For a hundred-year-old firm of surveyors, this was hugely irritating. For Alan, it was a dream come true. For everyone else, it was clear that Terry had made sure it never happened again.

The sweatshirts being handed out were also Alan's handiwork. A standard joke amongst the graduate surveyors was that they were wonderful for cleaning the car, especially the alloys. None of them would be seen dead in the beige sweatshirt, stamped with the firm's dated 1970s logo.

Mark, Ambitious Tim and the two other surveyors gave Max a warm welcome to their team, and the rest of the day passed uneventfully on the third floor.

When Max returned home, a white envelope was indeed waiting for him on the doormat, as promised. Before taking off his coat, Max tore it open and sat down at the kitchen table to read the clause to which Roe had referred him. She was correct: the contract could be terminated with four weeks' notice upon qualification. The accompanying letter confirmed that his employment would end on 10th April 1992. Unused holiday could be taken as pay in lieu, with the agreement of his manager.

Flipping through the remainder of the contract, Max turned to the signature page and stared in disbelief at the offending 'I hereby agree that I will not make a claim for unfair dismissal under this contract'. Not only was it beneath the signatures and slightly sloping towards the corner, but it was also in a different font to the rest of the document.

Max was absolutely stunned. It was the work of an amateur. Did Roe honestly think that anyone reading it would not realise it was a crude fraud? Did she honestly believe that a contract could expressly remove the statutory rights that the Employment Protection Act gave to all employees? Did she actually despise Max? What was the problem with that ginger-haired, scrawny woman from Basildon?

Standing up, he kicked away his chair and flung the doctored contract into the corner. If she thought she was going to get away with it, she was sorely mistaken. He would find his original contract and she would look ridiculous when her version was compared to it.

The rest of the evening was spent trying to find his contract, but when midnight passed he had to admit defeat. He had no idea what had happened to it. Getting into bed, he felt like he had been given a good kicking, just when he was starting to pick himself off the ground. He slept fitfully. No matter how hard he tried, he could not shake off the feeling of anger, frustration and despondency that came with being treated so abominably.

CHAPTER TEN

Max lay in bed even though his alarm clock had gone off long ago. He just could not summon the energy to get up. *What's the point?* he thought. He really could not understand what he had done to deserve all this.

Fifteen minutes later, once he had torn himself out from under the covers and made it to the kitchen, a wry smile came over his face as he was eating his Scott's Porage Oats. The packet was illustrated with a bright and breezy painting of a man in a tartan kilt, white vest and thick red socks. A shot put was pushed up under his chin the moment before he was about to launch it across a loch bathed in sunshine. His upper body was ripped, and he had a confident smirk on his face, as no doubt he did this every morning. Was this really 'the true taste of Scotland', as the packet proclaimed?

The only men Max had seen in tartan kilts were those irritating bagpipers on Oxford Street. He wondered if they were expressly banned from performing on the underground on account of the atrocious decibel levels their puff bags generated. Or was that to prevent them from being attacked by a stressed-out commuter who would surely be pushed over the edge by the bagpipe's deafening drone?

The Scots that Max had experienced in Glasgow certainly did not wear kilts. They did not smile much either. Last year, one of them had opened the door of the public telephone box that Max was using in Buchanan Street. Mid-sentence, he was interrupted by a dour man asking for money. Presumably the man knew he had money because he was spending it on a call in the phone box, so that seemed perfectly reasonable?

Looking at the cereal box a little longer, Max suddenly realised that the shot-putter appeared to be giving a fascist salute. Max had never noticed that before. He sat back and reflected on how the mind wanders when under pressure, as though protecting the brain from more pressing matters. Max was certainly struggling to focus on the matter in hand, which was deciding what he should do. Should he tell the firm to stick their temporary contract? Should he consult with a solicitor and see if there was any chance he could take the firm to an employment tribunal? Should he raise the matter with Ian, who had said to come to him with any problems?

Max felt his anger return as the painful memory of spending the whole evening pulling out cardboard boxes and emptying drawers came back. Maybe he should just have one last look? Fuck it, there was no point. He didn't have a copy of his contract.

He grabbed the nearest thing to hand and flung it against the wall. It happened to be a green, unripe banana that gave no satisfaction at all, for it bounced off the ceramic tiles and hit the floor perfectly intact.

I mean, why did she do it? he asked himself. *Why would she risk her job just to spite me?* He knew that even if he could not produce a copy of his contract, the firm would soon realise that his contract was different to those of the other graduates, and therefore must have been doctored.

Max began to think about the best way to deal with Roe. He was sorely tempted to confront her directly but realised he would get nowhere without Ian. Despite his reputation for being a bit of an arsehole, he actually seemed to be a decent guy, and he was known to get things done. When he said he would sort out any problems, Max believed him. With Ian's support he could expose Roe's duplicity and maybe the firm would offer him a permanent position to keep him quiet. And if not that, then at least some financial compensation for the way in which he had been treated?

But why was he even here in the first place? *What a complete bunch of wankers.* The thought of spending just one more day in the office made him wince, and he realised that his heart was no longer in it. The *Time Out* article on Peru had really fired his imagination, and the thought of going travelling again really appealed. *Who knows, if things don't work out, maybe I'll go for it*, he thought, getting up and clearing away his breakfast things. He felt his mind wandering again and tried to remain focussed. He would need to concentrate on finding a new job, as he knew deep down that even if offered a permanent position, there was no way he could carry on working at the firm. The next couple of months would be made more bearable, though, by seeing Roe caught out and dismissed for gross misconduct.

The first thing he did when he got into the office was phone Ian from the privacy of a closed meeting room. It was embarrassing enough that he had been made redundant. He certainly did not want people to know that his contract had also been fraudulently amended. When he called Ian and explained what Roe had done, there was a stunned silence on the other end of the phone. Ian genuinely could not believe what he had heard, and told Max to come and see him at five thirty when he would have an answer for him.

Once he had left the meeting room and sat back down at his desk, Mark put him straight to work on a large instruction he had secured earlier in the year. It was probably the most prestigious instruction in London and had been won by Mark's competence, professionalism and trustworthiness throughout the pitching process. The case concerned a larger-than-life newspaper owner who lacked all of Mark's qualities, as discovered by members of the staff pension scheme that he raided. Max would be working with Ambitious Tim, who had also played an important role in the pitch to the administrative receivers. Whilst Max would never be one of Tim's close circle, he nevertheless respected his judgement and had learnt a lot from him when he had worked in Mark's department during his training.

The newspaper group owned a lot of property around Fleet Street and further east into the City. Tim was dealing with one of these, which was an office block just north of Broadgate, named after the newspaper owner. It was awaiting redevelopment, having previously been occupied by HM Customs and Excise. Little could the Customs and Excise officers have imagined that Maxwell House was owned and named after someone who would become one of the most notorious British criminals of the decade. Its basement was adapted for use as a holding centre for suspected drugs mules. Once arrested at Heathrow Airport, they would be driven straight to Maxwell House, down a secure ramp and held in basement cells, each of which had a large, transparent WC bowl made of glass. After a few days, the passage of nature would reveal the contents of a suspect's stomachs in those glass WCs. In almost all cases the X-ray machine at the airport had been correct in its assessment that drug packets had been swallowed. It was deeply ironic that the newspaper mogul was also rumoured to have a large WC in the privacy of his palatial office. Apparently, it was not glass but gold-plated. The contents of *his* stomach found their way out not whilst a customs officer was near at hand but whilst he sat on a gilded seat and held business calls with all and sundry.

Max's first task was to access the single computer terminal shared with asset valuations. Angus, one of Tim's gang, was struggling through one of its black screens with green lettering, whilst making wise cracks to anyone who was listening about getting a great *Space Invaders* score. Angus was a Scot with a good sense of humour. Max thought about raising his Scott's Porage Oat musings with him, but decided against it. He knew Angus wouldn't appreciate the reference to a stereotypical Scot any more than Max would appreciate being asked if he wore a Morris Man outfit at the weekend.

The rest of the day was spent researching transactions for Tim and retrieving files from the firm's archive system. He also managed to squeeze in an hour or so looking at the job adverts in the *Estate Gazette* and *Chartered Surveyor Weekly*. Although the section was quite slim, there were nonetheless a few jobs out there. The problem was that they were all for qualified surveyors with a minimum of two or three years' experience, which Max did not have. A number of the adverts stated that 'Agents need not apply', which was a sad reflection on the number of agents out of work and seeking employment.

He decided that he was unlikely to find a position by replying to an advert, or through being registered with an agency. So, even though he would not rule out these options, he had to find another route if he were to land a permanent job. As he did not have any relations in the property industry with a network of contacts, he would have to make his own. Starting tomorrow, he would spend each lunch time writing letters to property companies whose activities were being reported in the press. Maybe he would strike lucky and one of them would invite him in for an interview?

Max felt better now that he had a plan, and if that did not work then maybe Peru would be a good fallback? With that in mind and a good feeling about a financial settlement, he went up to Ian's office on the fourth floor with somewhat of a spring in his step. Ian's door was shut as his secretary had left for the day, so Max knocked gently and peered around it.

Ian was in phone position again with his feet on the desk. This time, though, there was no smile, just a cursory glance and a cautioning finger telling him to wait by the door. Finally, he finished his call and asked Max to close the door and sit down.

Taking his feet off the desk, he leant forward and replaced them with his elbows. 'Max, I took the allegation you made this morning very seriously. I've sat down with Roe and discussed it,' he said, 'and I must say we're both shocked that you could make such a claim.'

'But it's true, you just have to look at it,' said Max, completely thrown off guard.

'Max, I imagine you feel that Roe is in some way responsible for you failing to be offered a new contract with the firm, but let me assure you, these decisions are taken at a far more senior level. You gain nothing by accusing her of amending your contract, other than making yourself appear foolish.' Ian's reply was both patronising and dismissive.

'Well, that is just not the case. My contract has had that wording added, and Roe knows it.'

'The fact remains, Max, that Roe assures me your contract is no different to any other of the graduate contracts. I've worked with her for almost fifteen years. If she tells me there are no grounds for your allegation, then I believe her.'

What then followed was a battle of stares that Max quickly lost. Turning red and with an acute sense of embarrassment, he reached for his last line of attack, which was pretty flimsy.

'You do know that you're getting rid of some of the best graduates, don't you?' Max proffered.

Ian leant forward further, clearly affronted. 'That could be regarded as quite an arrogant thing to say in the circumstances. I suggest that we leave it there.' And with that, the meeting was closed. Max stood up and walked out of the office without saying a word. Ian jumped up. 'Close the door, you stupid—' he began, but stopped himself swearing. Striding over, he slammed it shut just as Max was booting open the door to the stairwell.

Max stood there and glared at the stairwell emergency exit sign. *So that was the firm's response?* There was to be no offer of a permanent contract, no financial compensation and definitely no consequences for Roe, unless he took the firm to an employment tribunal. The spring in his step was gone, and he was furious. He had worked hard for a company where he clearly did not fit in, which had been entirely unbeknownst to him until last week.

Walking down the stairs, he shook his head and wondered what unspoken rule it was that he had broken. Perhaps not wearing his suit jacket when out one lunchtime was his downfall? Tricky Dickie had cast him a disapproving glance when he walked past, but it *had* been during a heatwave, for fuck's sake! *Maybe it was when—* 'Fuck it!' he shouted, and stopped dead. *I'm not taking that for an answer.*

Turning round, he took the stairs two at a time and swung around the metal banister, back up to the fourth floor. Yanking open the door, he emerged from the stairwell, strode across the floor, grabbed the handle of Ian's door and launched himself into the office.

'You must think I'm a complete and utter fucking—' he started to shout, but the words stuck in his throat. Ian was nowhere to be seen. Max closed the door and checked he was not behind it.

Puzzled, he opened it again, stuck his head out and looked up and down the floor, but again Ian was nowhere to be seen. He turned back into the office and this time checked behind the walnut drinks cabinet, but the head of agency had completely disappeared.

'Max, mate, he's left for the evening,' Joe said, placing an arm around his shoulder. The noise of slamming doors and shouting had aroused the interest of the whole fourth floor, and he had come to the rescue of his old mate, Max.

'Come on, let's grab a beer,' he said, and he led him out of Ian's office.

That evening both of them sat in a booth in Ye Olde Cittie of Yorke pub. With the help of several pints of Stella, Max's anger gradually eased, and the two of them chatted through the options that remained for him. Either he could walk away, letting Mark and his team down in the process, or take the firm to an employment tribunal. He had too much respect for Mark to do that, and a further six weeks' salary would be of help. But then taking the firm to an employment tribunal would mean he would never again work in the property industry, irrespective of the tribunal's decision. He had spent three years at university and a further two years working towards a professional qualification. There was no way he was prepared to sacrifice that.

On his fourth pint, Max came up with the idea of breaking the story to the press anonymously.

'Max, mate, you're getting ahead of yourself. I don't want to put you down, but you're hardly a player in the market!' Joe said, laughing at the suggestion. 'There may well be a time and place for your story, but I can tell you it's not in the latest edition of the *Estates Gazette*.'

He took a gulp of his Stella and added, 'What you could do, though, is speak to Rodge. He's been around the block and will give you some advice. I can't guarantee it will be *good* advice, but he'll certainly have a view.'

Max and Joe had both worked for Roger Wolsey-Burton as trainees. He was one of the old guard, but, despite having been at the firm for over twenty years, he was no more than a junior associate. His explanation was that he 'refused to sacrifice himself on the firm's altar', whereas rumours were that he had put his hand down a secretary's blouse and it had caught up with him. Apparently, when leaving the office a few days after the groping, out of nowhere a sharp right hook connected with his jaw and a large boot ground his fingers into the pavement. Sprawled on the ground, whimpering, Roger stared up at the face of a furious boyfriend and, even worse, the gaze of Johnny Cupboard, a newly promoted associate. Details of the altercation somehow reached the partnership, and Roger ended up being branded as unsuitable partnership material from that day on.

Max knew it was a bit left field speaking to Rodge, but he had few options and, in the circumstances, agreed it was worth a try.

By the time the evening drew to a close Max had decided to take the money and work out his contract. But he was not finished with Ian and Roe, and together, he and Joe came up with a scheme that seemed both fitting and hilarious over their fifth pint of Stella. Joe agreed to bring his socket set into the office, confident that it could loosen even the most stubbornly tightened bolt. Max would buy a tube of lubricating grease and spend the next few weeks practising Ian Dodds impersonations.

With the matter settled and resisting the temptation of a last pint, they left their empties strewn over the table and stumbled into Holborn, delighted in equal measure with their creative plan and the revenge that awaited Ian Dodds and Roe Tarburt.

CHAPTER ELEVEN

Three weeks later Max stood captivated by a column of bubbles that sprang to the surface and bobbed down a small stream in Trewsbury Mead. The Head of the Thames was in Lechlade, fifteen miles away, but it was here that the river emerged and started its journey. He had spent the morning sloshing through water and across fields to reach the spot where he was now totally mesmerised. Something struck him about the gentle ripple and calm flow of the water that drifted away from the spring into the distance; for a brief moment he reflected that he too was at the start of a journey, and maybe he should worry a little less about its precise details and where it would take him?

Eventually he left the spring to wade through the dips and flat sections of a field that would be dry in the summer but for now was covered in the water that trickled down from the flooded meadow above. The river got him thinking about Peru again, or more specifically, the Amazon River. The article in *Time Out* had a short section following its journey from high up in the Peruvian Andes to the Atlantic Ocean, seven thousand kilometres away. Peru sounded like a fascinating place, and Max was increasingly tempted to buy a one-way ticket to it. His life in the UK was going nowhere. The letter writing had produced no results, his job applications had been unsuccessful, and he was truly sick of working at the firm. Even trying to speak to Rodge had been a complete waste of time. He had not been in the office for a few weeks now, something about 'a nasty virus', when everyone knew he had booked into a clinic for the treatment of alcohol abuse.

Back in the office, the days dragged on until precisely twelve minutes past three on Thursday afternoon. That was the time when the single bolt remaining on the sliding rail of a large seat succumbed to the strain of two weeks' worth of 'feet-on-desk activity'. At least that was the time circulating around the secretaries, one of whom witnessed it first-hand.

It only took twenty minutes before the rest of the building were aware of the event. The screaming siren that swept up Chancery Lane was not unusual, but the blue flashing light outside reception meant something was up. The windows became crowded with curious faces, and before long their prize was delivered up, strapped on a stretcher and covered in a red blanket. It was still light, and Ian Dodds could be seen with a large bandage round his head and matted blood in his grey fringe. He was bundled into the ambulance, its back doors were slammed shut and he was whisked up Chancery Lane, the siren blaring once more.

It took another fifteen minutes before Mark's secretary could reach Ian's secretary. Her phone was red hot. When she finally connected, everyone crowded around her desk.

'Tina, we saw him carried out on a stretcher . . . Ah, well that would explain it . . . No! You were just bringing him in a cup of tea?' she said, trying not to laugh. 'He did what? And it just shot back! You're joking? What . . . on top of his head!' she replied, waving away the laughing surveyors. 'No, not the one right at the top?' She stifled a laugh with her hand. 'Broken glass and blood everywhere, oh dear. Of course, I'll let you go . . . Yes, yes, we must have lunch sometime soon.'

She put the phone down giggling uncontrollably, and they all had to wait impatiently before she could relay the story, which she finally managed after a couple of false starts. Apparently, Ian had been sat with his feet on the desk talking to Throgmorton Estates. Something had made him take his feet down and lean forward abruptly. Tina was not sure, but she thought he had said something like 'the tenant can't just walk away' or 'the tenant can't get their own way'. Either way, he looked furious, placed the heels of his shoes on the edge of the desk and pushed back aggressively, probably to spin the chair backwards.

But then, what happened was unbelievable. Rather than *push* the chair backwards, Ian *shot* the seat clean off its rails and launched it at speed into the cabinet. He smashed through its glass doors like a battering ram, destroying most of the cheaply made awards inside. His Surveyor of the Year Award wobbled precariously on top of the cabinet, but it was heavy marble, and it would have withstood the assault were it not for the phone he was still holding. The cord of the receiver whipped the handset off the desk like a boomerang and crashed into the award, sending it plummeting straight down onto his head.

Max left the group and walked back to his desk with an enormous grin on his face. He needed to confide with his partner in crime. It was just such an incredibly wonderful result for them. Picking up the phone, he called Joe whilst everyone else was still busy laughing.

'Joe, mate, I can't believe how well it went,' he whispered into his cupped hand.

'Yeah, me too. Best to keep a low profile though. If he ever finds out, I'll be sacked as well.' Joe paused as he was starting to laugh. 'The best bit of it is . . . most of his awards are . . .' – and he had to stop himself again – '. . . smashed to pieces,' he finished, allowing himself a good belly laugh.

Max waited for him to calm down and managed to control himself enough to reply. 'Mate, that's not a problem – we can replace them with some new ones from Poundland . . .' He paused. 'He won't notice the difference.' At which he roared with laughter, which attracted the attention of Angus the Scot.

'Got to go, Joe, Angus is on the prowl,' Max said, putting the phone down and sharing a wide grin with Angus. Everyone in the office seemed to be either smiling, laughing or just plain happy; even Mark was finding it hard to keep a straight face whilst pretending to be concerned about the plight of his fellow partner. Max had never realised just how unpopular Ian was at the firm, and he had no doubt that several pints would be raised later to that strangely defective seat bolt.

*   *   *

The week finished on another high note when Max received a message from Roger's secretary apologising for not getting back to him. Roger could meet him for lunch the following Friday and suggested the Cock Tavern on the Strand at one o'clock. Max was sure Roger would have an alternative view on what to do, which he needed right now as he had run out of options. The date was fixed and Max ground through his work the following week until the day finally arrived. Roger was standing outside the Cock Tavern smoking when Max crossed the Strand.

'Come on, Max,' he said. 'I can't stand here all day.' He looked awful, like he needed a drink. Max just nodded and followed him inside.

'Right, young man, two pints of Pride coming up,' said Roger as they approached the bar. Not that Roger had asked him what he wanted.

'Actually, I'll have a pint of Carlsberg,' said Max. Roger looked at him coolly before turning to the bartender. He did not care if Roger disapproved. He had long ago decided not to pretend to like bitters, stouts and IPAs just because the rest of the office did. Max knew the truth: a crisp, chilled lager was far more palatable than a lukewarm bitter.

'I thought you were on the wagon, Rodge?' he asked.

'Who told you that?' Roger replied, clearly irritated. 'If you must know, I'm cutting out spirits during the week, but beer is perfectly fine.' With that he took his change from a fiver, and they headed over to a table with their pints and a large packet of cheese and onion crisps.

Lighting up a cigarette with a trembling hand, Roger took a deep drag, released the smoke over Max and drank a third of his pint straight down, as though he was not just thirsty but hungry too.

'I've been looking forward to that all morning,' he said, holding his shaking glass up to the light as though it were a fine wine. He stuck it back down on a beer mat, took another drag and exhaled. 'So, how are you finding it, working for Mark and Tim?' he asked.

'It's been okay. I just feel lucky to have been given some breathing room to find another job, but I really don't think there's much out there.'

'Ah, well you should have come back to us rather than industrial agency. We were a little disappointed you didn't approach us, but we've offered Alison and Tina contracts now and our headcount's used up.'

Max was surprised to hear this. He had no idea that Roger had thought so highly of him. If only he had given him a hint that he wanted him on his team; maybe that would have changed everything. As Tony had already offered him a permanent job, Max had not bothered applying for any other positions. It was too late to do anything about it now. Max just raised his eyebrows in resignation.

'The likes of you will be fine,' pronounced Roger. 'You'll find something in property. You've got a bit more drive than some of the other graduates.'

This was not particularly comforting. Most of the other graduates had secured a job. Nothing at that moment suggested he would be fine.

'Thanks, Rodge, that's nice to hear. But what would you do now if you were in my position?'

Roger was not listening. He was now totally focussed on his pint. He finished it off and waved the glass at Max.

'Another one?'

Max shook his head. His glass was hardly touched. Roger shrugged and disappeared to the bar.

When he returned, he lit another cigarette, took a deep drag and asked, 'What was that?' Pausing for another drag, he added, 'What would I do in your place?' and blew more smoke over Max's head.

Roger had been in the industry during previous recessions and Max saw him as someone with experience. If anyone would know what to do, it was Roger.

'You know what I'd do in your place . . .?' he said, staring at Max.

Max leant forward.

'I should have done it years ago,' Roger said.

'Go on,' Max replied, impatient to hear what he had to say.

'Yes, I think I would have done *rather* well in that line of business,' Roger added.

'Yes, yes . . . so what should I do?'

'I certainly would have been following my natural instincts,' he continued.

'Rodge!'

'Patience, young man.' Roger took a drag, leant back and announced with a flourish of his cigarette, 'If I were in your position, I'd get myself into the sex industry!'

'What?' spluttered Max.

'Don't grimace,' Roger replied.

'You are kidding me, right?' Max exclaimed.

'No, I'm not!' Roger replied with a leer. He counted out on his fingers: 'Where else are you going to get amazing job satisfaction, unlimited paying punters and wild parties . . . certainly not in the property industry, which is totally screwed!'

Roger smacked the table with one hand and leant back, laughing and coughing alternately as only a thirty-a-day man can do. His wheezing lungs struggled to cope with the laughing fit, and his red face turned purple before he calmed down and managed to take a small sip of his Pride.

Max watched his mentor recover and felt there was something poetic about discovering, in that moment, that the Sage of Orpington, with all his experience and wisdom, really had nothing to offer him at all. He finally accepted that he really was on his own. Nobody was going to mentor him, to take him under their wing. No one was going to save him. Rather than go straight back to the office after the pub, he continued up Chancery Lane and went into STA Travel. He then walked straight up to a free desk, took out his credit card and booked the first available flight to Lima, departing the week after his contract ended.

He was leaving the UK on a one-way ticket to Peru, where he would trek to the source of the Amazon River. He was going to start afresh in South America, and his life was going to grow into something meaningful like the stream that tumbled down from the Peruvian Andes. But first, he had one last score to settle at the firm.

'Joe, we're on,' Max said, putting the phone down.

He waved goodbye to everyone on the third floor and disappeared into the lift. Mark was happy for him to leave early as it was his last day at the firm. When handing his pass in at reception he leant over the desk and placed all his weight on the firm's logo. But not even the slightest bit cracked off – it was indestructible! *No problem*, he thought as he jangled a couple of fifty-pence pieces in his pocket and pushed on the revolving door, smiling.

Crossing over Chancery Lane, he pulled open the door of the telephone box on the corner of Carey Street and took out his fifty pences. Roe picked up the phone, the first coin disappeared into the payphone and Max put on his best Ian Dodds accent.

'Roe, darling, it's your favourite partner.'

'Yes, Ian, how is your head now?'

'Oh, fine thanks. I'm calling you from the phone box on Carey Street as there is something very private I need to say to you.'

'Okay.'

'Your ginger hair is *so* erotic.'

'What!'

'Your scrawny neck reminds me of a turkey – ready to gobble me up!'

'Ian!' she shouted.

'Your gnarly fingers remind me of a spider, ready to crawl all over my aching body!'

'Are you mad?' she asked.

'Yes, madly in love, my temptress, longing for just one kiss.'

'Ian, I'm putting the phone down now,' she replied.

'No, my love, blow me a kiss from your fifth-floor tower. I will await its caress on my forlorn cheek.' Max could barely contain himself. 'Come, my princess, approach the window. Your servant awaits you on Carey Street.'

Roe's curiosity got the better of her, and against her better judgement she got up and looked out of the window. At the same time the entire third and fourth floors crammed against their windows to see Max drop his trousers and give Roe a full moon of his bare cheeks. Giving them a wiggle, he pulled up his trousers to resounding cheers and stuck the Vs up at the old bag.

'Good riddance!' he shouted, turning round, zipping up his flies and sauntering up Carey Street for the last time with a large grin, and almost a swagger.

CHAPTER TWELVE

The engines of the Iberian jumbo roared and the plane thundered down the runway with Max strapped into seat 32A. Dry scrub shot past his window and then disappeared as the plane climbed and banked sharply over the arid Castilian plain. Max ramped up the volume on the track '8 Times 8', and the vocal loop 'You must be leaving me, my son' swept over him and sent a tingle through his chest and up his throat. He leant back and closed his eyes; it was the perfect track to play flying towards Miami, where it had just been released by Monochrome Records.

The next ninety minutes would be back-to-back house music, some of which was bought from the cash Mark and his team had tucked into his leaving card. The next track was 'Kiss the Sky', released by Frequency on The White Label, followed by 'Elevation' on React and 'The Ride', produced by The Hypnotist and released on Rising High Records. He ran out of music with a travelling theme by track seven, and settled down into a medley of Detroit house, starting with Derrick May's 'Salsa Life'.

Flying from London to Madrid that morning, he had read about the bankruptcy of Olympia and York. The entire front page of the *Daily Telegraph* was devoted to it. The Canadian developer of Canary Wharf was declared bankrupt on 30th May 1992. Its demise was announced in the Sunday papers, alongside a photo of One Canada Square, its iconic office tower in Canary Wharf. Once more Max thought about his Great-Uncle Tom, who had left Ireland to become a police constable in London, late in 1913. After his First World War service, he worked for the Port of London police force in West India Dock.

During his service, he would have seen the dock expand and reach its peak of activity around the time of his retirement in July 1955. It seemed a shame that he never saw it regenerated as the Canary Wharf development and emerge as a rival to the City of London's office market.

Max smiled when he thought about the commendation Sargent McDonnell received fifty-seven years earlier. His service history noted 'his good work in a case of larceny of bananas from "A" shed, West India Dock'. In April 1935, when Great-Uncle Tom was preventing banana larceny, No. 32 berth was being built as a new facility for Fruit Lines Limited. It would become known as Canary Wharf, on account of its trade in bananas imported from the Canary Islands. Most likely the pinched bananas in question were being lifted from Fruit Lines' old warehouse.

He wondered what emotions he would have experienced when West India Dock was being bombed in the Second World War. Max had seen his commendation for 'devotion to duty and setting an inspiring example in hazardous circumstances during enemy action on 19th and 20th April 1941'. Maybe he recalled the assurance made in spring 1915, that he and his fellow recruits were signing up for 'The War to End All Wars'? Did he wonder how an Irish boy growing up in the remote northwest of Ireland could end up amongst exploding bombs in the East End of London? If he had, then he certainly did not share any of these thoughts with Max.

Perhaps the Sage of Orpington was right when he said that the property market was screwed. Reading about the demise of the visionary Olympia and York as he flew over France, Max felt confident he had made the correct decision. What was the worst that could happen? Maybe he would run out of money. Maybe he would not be able to reach the source of the Amazon. Maybe he would have to return to London and start looking for work again. But maybe, just maybe, he might find himself on a new path and begin life afresh in South America. One of his university mates knew someone who had gone to Brazil in the 1980s and ended up living on, and ultimately running, a cattle ranch. What he did know was that he turned twenty-seven next month, and rather than spending his birthday feeling miserable in the UK, he would instead be somewhere in Peru.

When the Iberian plane ticket arrived in its red, white and gold wallet, the trip suddenly became real. Up until a few weeks ago, all that Max had known about everyday life in Peru was that groups of men wearing stripy ponchos frequently got together and played panpipes in their plazas. It also was famous as the country where Paddington Bear was supposed to have been born. He thought that perhaps he should buy a travel guide and do some proper research before visiting, as those two facts would not exactly come in handy when he got there. WH Smith had a good selection of guidebooks, and he chose the latest edition of *An Adventure in South America – On the Cheap*.

The front cover of the guide had an illustration that could only have been drawn by one of the editor's children. A large *campesino* lady filled half of it, but she looked like she came from Central America, not South America. Alongside her, the tiny figure of someone with a backpack stood on the head of what looked like an Aztec statue, again from Central America. In the background, the city of Rio de Janeiro spread out onto the Nazca Lines and was overlooked by the Christ the Redeemer on Corcovado. Opening the cover, Max was even less inspired by the photos of three bearded men who were listed as the authors. One of them was bald and looked about sixty. The next was sitting holding his baby in a photo from the early 1970s. The last of them was a Polish guy called Krzysztof who looked like he dug progressive rock bands like Genesis and Emerson, Lake & Palmer, both of which were now extinct. Rather foolishly, Max had chosen the *On the Cheap* guide before doing any research in the local library. He had used their guide in Southeast Asia, which he thought was very good, and at £12.95 it was quite a bit cheaper than *The South American Handbook*.

It was apparently 'the most thoroughly researched practical guide available' and contained 'essential information for every independent traveller', but it had absolutely no information what-soever on the source of the Amazon River. As it is probably the most famous river in the world and the most visited natural feature in South America, the publisher Lively Places made up for this oversight by including a helpful section on the native Quechuan language in Peru. It extended to two pages, and luckily for Max, he could now say 'please repeat' in Quechuan if he so chose. Max reflected on the fact that 99.9% of the people buying the guide would never understand any Quechuan, no matter how many times it was repeated, and wondered if perhaps he was missing the point.

More luckily for Max, he had read the *Time Out* article and did not buy a flight to Rio de Janeiro or Sao Paolo in Brazil, being the country where most people would assume the Amazon started. Rather, he knew that the Apurimac River was generally accepted as the source of the Amazon, springing from Nevado Misti, a 5,590-metre-tall mountain in the Peruvian Andes. Arequipa, in the south of Peru, was the nearest city, and it had a good bus connection from Lima. Max had decided to spend a few days in the capital and then travel straight there.

He had also read that Peru was in the grip of attacks by Maoist guerrillas, the Sendero Luminoso, or 'Shining Path'. Several tourists had recently been murdered and the US and the Australian governments now advised their citizens not to visit the country. By April, the death toll from the twelve-year conflict had risen to eighteen thousand at the same time as its congress was dissolved and its autocratic president, Alberto Fujimori, began crushing political dissent. In a bizarre twist of fate, the Chief of the National Intelligence Service responsible for defeating the Maoists was baptised Vladimiro Lenin Ilich Montesinos by his communist parents. Quite coincidentally, he was also born in Arequipa, where Max was heading.

Max had come to realise that this was not the best time to visit Peru, but worrying about it would have spoilt the memory of that dreamy day alongside the Thames, deep in the Cotswolds. Besides, he was working hard at not worrying about things he could not change, and he most certainly could not change anything right now, thirty-six thousand feet over the Atlantic Ocean. With that in mind, he mixed some of the tangy sauce with the grilled chicken, rice, carrots and sweet corn in his silver-foil container and settled back to watch Robert De Niro in *Cape Fear*.

In just over eleven hours he would arrive in Lima.

PART TWO

Private misfortunes make for the general good,
so that the more private misfortunes there are,
the greater is the general good.

Dr Pangloss

CHAPTER ONE

Rich McDonnell sat under the shade of a large red umbrella watching the traffic circling around the plaza in Guayaramerín. He had arrived in Bolivia ten days ago and was still adapting to the differences with Boston, one of which was the fierce tropical sun that had given him a bright red patch down one side of his face.

'How's the sunburn, mate?' John asked in a broad Australian accent. John Rogers was a Queenslander that Rich had met in Hotel Litoral a couple of nights ago.

'Sore,' he answered, raising a hand to his cheek, all too painfully reminded of the previous day he had spent skulking around the port without sunblock.

'Best avoid the midday sun with your pale skin,' John replied. 'Those baseball caps aren't great in strong sun either!'

Rich did not need it pointed out that he had pale Irish skin and the fact that his Nike cap was unsuitable, but he tolerated the friendly Australian, whom he had chosen as an unsuspecting partner for his mission.

The two of them were in an ice cream bar with four rickety metal tables and a selection of yellow, green, blue and purple plastic seats arranged on the road outside.

'This ice cream's pretty good,' Rich said, nodding in approval. He was really missing decent chocolate in Bolivia, but the ice cream had been a revelation. The venue had been John's choice, although in practice there was little to choose from in the small town of Guayaramerín and the purple seats had caught their attention.

'Thanks. We won't be getting any of this on the boat, so best enjoy it now,' John replied.

Rich had persuaded John to join him on a journey upriver to Trinidad rather than cross into Brazil, which was John's original plan. He needed an authentic travelling companion if he were to be convincing as a backpacker, and it was ideal that John was Australian. He felt that two Americans travelling together might arouse suspicion. Rich could not guarantee his safety as all DEA operations came with risk, but this one was 'low risk' and he had therefore decided that it was suitable for his unsuspecting partner.

Opposite them, the enormous plaza in Guayaramerín was like a magnet, drawing in the town's scooters, spinning them around its four corners and then shooting them off one of its side roads in a cloud of dust. Almost all the traffic that afternoon consisted of either red or blue scooters, although the occasional car with dusty Brazilian number plates could be seen, having come across from the neighbouring town of Guajará-Mirim. The rhyming towns were separated by the Rio Mamoré and were contrasted by a big difference in the standard of living, with most of the Brazilians simply crossing over to Guayaramerín to stock up on cheap ciga-rettes and alcohol before returning later across the river.

Rich was still coming to grips with the new country in front of him. Bolivia was a cacophony of noise and colour where even the ordinary appeared exotic, like the small buses that swung around bends with luggage half strapped to the roof, the street vendors pushing ancient barrows that bumped and jarred on the road but somehow stayed in one piece, and what seemed like builders on every street corner, clinging precariously to wobbly-looking ladders inches from racing traffic. Every street also seemed to have a build-ing that was either half built or falling down, but for the life of him he could not figure out which one it was.

He was still thinking about some of the half-built places in Guayaramerín when John pointed out two guys wobbling on a scooter. It looked like the driver was struggling to steer, probably because of a large steel beam that protruded from its handlebars and restricted its movement. As they sped towards the corner, Rich noticed that the men wore hard hats and heavy boots, and it looked like they probably worked on a nearby site. He was just about to turn back to his ice cream and watch the men pass when suddenly the passenger grabbed the driver's arm and waved frantically at something ahead. It was a large pothole, and Rich knew that they were going way too fast to avoid it. He winced as the scooter's front wheel plunged down and smashed against the edge of the hole, throwing the men sideways but still clinging on to the scooter that now bounced across the corner and careered straight towards the ice cream bar.

'Shit,' Rich shouted, jumping up. 'They're coming into us!'

The scooter shook and veered violently out of control, bearing down on them with its lethal battering ram. Rich lurched across the table, knocking the umbrella down and smashing their ice cream onto the floor. John stood rooted to the spot in panic before Rich grabbed his arm and pulled him away. Both of them watched in horror as the driver wrestled with the scooter and somehow managed to hold on and swing it away from the ice cream bar, back towards the safety of the wide road.

The sound of crashing furniture brought the owner rushing out into the plaza, where he shook his fist at the scooter, but it was a futile gesture for it simply took off and disappeared down a side road. Despite the risk to life and limb, it seemed a perfectly normal occurrence as nobody else took any notice.

Rich and John turned round and helped the owner, who was now clearing up the mess.

'That guy should be banged up in a fucking prison, not loose on the streets,' Rich said, helping to rearrange the tables.

'Yeah, he's a fucking lunatic,' John replied, picking up a purple seat.

'You know what, that plaza is pretty goddam ugly when you look at it,' Rich added, stopping and pointing at the square in its centre.

John looked up at the kerbstones, which were painted alternatively yellow and black.

'That's a road safety measure,' he said.

'No, I mean the desiccated palm trees, scrub for grass and those ugly park benches,' Rich replied, missing John's weak attempt at humour.

Once the furniture was upright, they thanked the owner of the ice cream bar, gathered their things and walked up Calle Mariscal de Santa Cruz, past the Cathedral of the Immaculate Conception, which in practice was not a cathedral at all but an ordinary church. They were going to the port of Guayaramerín, ostensibly to see if there were any boats sailing to Trinidad, but Rich already knew that there was one such boat; it was called *Tondy* and it departed tomorrow. The streets on their way up to the port were either named after famous military figures or commemorated significant dates in the Republic's struggle for independence. Rich approved of the pride taken in Bolivia's armed struggle and wondered why Southie had such ignominious names like 'K Street' and 'O Street' when Boston was at the heart of American Independence.

After three blocks, they reached the Capitania office on the edge of the Rio Mamoré. It was a tidy, whitewashed concrete building that looked down on the timber gangways and colourful boats that littered the riverbank. A large blackboard fixed to its wall listed the name, date and size of the boats leaving Guayaramerín that week. The remaining space was taken up with a huge mural of Jesus with his arm around a sailor, above which the words 'Jesus is my guide' were written in peeling blue paint.

Checking out the blackboard, Rich soon found the boat that he was looking for, *Tondy*, and by a stroke of luck, it was leaving for Trinidad the following morning. Inside the dark, cool office of the Capitania, they woke up a half-snoozing man and got him to point out the boat for them. It was at one end of the port, hidden behind a larger vessel. Feigning innocence, Rich commented that it looked pretty new and the captain seemed competent, so why not just go for it? John agreed, and they each paid two hundred bolivianos, or around fifty dollars, for the seven-day journey up to Trinidad with evening meals included. On their way back to the town centre, they checked out some provisions for the trip and grabbed a pizza for dinner.

That evening, Rich sat in his room and reflected on his journey so far. He had arrived in Trinidad on a C-130 Hercules from Howard Air Force Base in Panama, where he had spent the previous month, first on a US Army Ranger camp and then on a Marine Corps Reconnaissance training programme. Another nine special agents were on the flight, but all of them were travelling onto Chimoré, the base for DEA operations in the Chapare Valley.

The DEA's Trinidad hub, where he would be stationed, was initially set up in 1986 to provide logistics and intelligence support for an initiative called Operation Blast Furnace. It was now the centre for all intelligence and operations throughout the Beni region – a largely uninhabited area of around 215,000 square kilometres, roughly the size of Idaho, or the whole of Great Britain. In practice, transport around the region was only really possible by boat or by the light aircraft that flew in and out of Guayaramerín and Riberalta in the north, Reyes in the west and Santa Ana del Yacuma in the east. The roads that carved their way through the lowlands were largely treacherous, especially in the rain.

On his arrival, Rich had been assigned to DEA Grade 14 Supervisory Team Leader Jim Wernham. Jim was on his sixth tour and was one of the original agents who had signed up for Operation Snowcap, the US counter-drug initiative launched in 1987. Rich's first few days in Bolivia had been pretty relaxed, during which he boarded in Residencial Loreto on Calle La Paz. Jim would visit and run through details of his first operation in the field. The rest of the day he was free to saunter around town and read books, but as Trinidad resembled a frontier town with dusty, dirty streets and rundown buildings, Rich ended up spending a lot of his time in Residencial Loreto with other Westerners, drinking Tropical Pilsner Extras and playing pool.

Jim had explained that the DEA base at the airport was full of informants, especially in UMOPAR, or the Mobile Police Unit for Rural Areas, which was the national force set up in 1983 to eradicate the cocaine trade in Bolivia. It had been bought by the drug cartels several years earlier. For this reason, he had received permission for Rich to be temporarily stationed off base and remain unregistered with its network of informants.

Apparently, Rich would be a perfect undercover agent, which he needed for a mission on the Rio Mamoré. Information had come in that the Beni cartel were moving a shipment of coca paste south to their laboratories in Santa Cruz Department; once processed into cocaine hydrochloride, it would then most likely be sold in Brazil or the US. A boat named *Tondy* would be leaving Guayaramerín, ostensibly to pick up cattle from a ranch close to Santa Ana del Yacuma, but around two hundred three-metre-long planks would also be loaded, and this was the cargo that interested Jim. If the intelligence were correct, they had been hollowed out and filled with containers of coca paste with a projected weight of one thousand kilograms.

Were Jim to seize the coca paste, it would be one of the biggest ever hauls in Bolivia, and the equivalent of last year's total seizures from the lowlands laboratories. All that Rich had to do was be on the boat, observe whether or not the planks were loaded and then notify the DEA. Using a high-frequency ground-to-ground radio on the boat would be impractical, so it had been agreed that he would wear a yellow neckerchief if the cargo was on board, and a spotter would pick this up beyond the Santa Ana ranch. Rich's instructions were to relax and play the American tourist, ideally with another unsuspecting traveller, and enjoy the trip up the Rio Mamoré. He knew that convincing John to join him on the journey was a good start, and he was confident that he could pull off his role as a backpacker.

Lying back on his bed, he really could not believe his luck. The other DEA agents on the C-130 would be supervising UMOPAR and the local police force, as they destroyed illegal coca plantations with machetes. When not doing this, they would be assisting at road checkpoints or following up intel on deliveries of cocaine precursors such as sulphuric acid, cement and soda crystals. Here he was, booked on a seven-day, all-expenses-paid trip up a tributary of the Amazon in a largely uninhabited region of Bolivia, where he would wake up in a hammock with the sound of the river drifting past, listen to birds waking at sunrise and watch wildlife on its riverbank, undisturbed. His choice of Trinidad as a posting might have been accidental, but it was also inspired.

CHAPTER TWO

Rich and John arrived at *Tondy* in good time for their midday departure. That morning they had bought hammocks, mosquito nets, bottles of Double Cola and drinking water, bananas, tomatoes, processed cheese, crisps, biscuits, bread rolls, beer and lots of sweets. The bread rolls were to be filled with mortadella, a processed meat bought in a roll the size of a small marrow. It was pinkish with white lumps of gristle. The cheese and tomatoes would make it mildly edible.

Rich looked a little preppy in his tailored shorts, Nike trainers and sports shirt. John balanced this out by looking like a bum and helped give the impression that they were just a couple of ordinary Western travellers. In fact, it was pretty clear that he could be narrowed down to a region of Australia where time had stood still since 1976. He wore a faded dark blue vest, which he called a 'singlet', and a tight pair of skimpy khaki shorts with a slight rip, through which his underpants, or 'dunders', could be seen. On his feet were a pair of black sandals that he called 'thongs' and on his head was a crappy old hat, which he fondly referred to as his 'Akubra'.

The bank down to *Tondy* was muddy, and as John descended, his right thong failed to grip on to a particularly muddy patch. Luckily, the crew missed the sight of him slipping on his arse and 'snagging his nuts on his dunders', as he put it, which was clearly quite painful. Boarding *Tondy* across a couple of old planks, John gave a flourish with his Akubra when greeting the captain, revealing a mullet that was styled gracefully around his forehead and ears but tumbled recklessly down the back of his neck. Rich joined him, and together they took a look around the boat where they would be living for the next seven days.

Tondy was twenty metres long and made entirely of wood, as were all the boats passing up and down the Rio Mamoré. Her engine room roared all day and night on the river, and stank of diesel. In a small room opposite, a large plywood box with a jagged oval hole was used as the WC, emptying directly into the river below. Luckily, the washing facilities were towards the front of the boat, as the water to be scooped from it looked murky enough and the communal bar of soap oily enough without the need for further detritus to increase the risk of a nasty skin condition. That said, hanging off the side of the boat on a wooden platform and scooping water in a coconut shell seemed like a cool way to wash, even if it was only one-handed.

The crew's hammocks were strung out next to the engine room, and the captain had his living quarters above. Food was prepared in a small kitchen behind the captain's quarters, directly above the engine room, which they later discovered meant their meals always had a slight aftertaste of diesel. At the front, the bridge had a comfortable deckchair next to the helm and allowed the captain to both relax and direct his crew beneath the shade provided by a tin roof that extended the length of the boat. Other than being painted bright red, blue and white, *Tondy* was pretty much identical to all the other cargo boats in Guayaramerín.

Tondy also had two barges attached alongside and one tied to its front. The front barge had a tin roof with steel reinforcement bars fixed to pillars that protruded from its deck and allowed the area to be used for additional storage. Rich and John fixed up their hammocks in this barge, above some grain sacks and oil drums. The other barges were empty, apart from some agricultural machinery parts.

Just after three o'clock, *Tondy*'s moorings were released and it drifted into the middle of the river. With black smoke billowing out of its engine room, Rich and John dangled their legs over the prow of the barge as it slipped past the blue concrete wall and white balustrade of the promenade high above the muddy water.

'Well, mate, this is the life,' said John, kicking his dangling legs. 'I'm glad you convinced me to come to Trinidad, although I've got to say I was looking forward to visiting Brazil.'

'Yeah,' replied Rich, who didn't think it would be sensible to mention that he had originally confused Trinidad with Trinidad and Tobago in the Caribbean.

'What are we going to do when we get to Trinidad?' John asked. 'Is there much to do there?'

Rich shrugged. 'Who knows? I haven't thought that far ahead.'

John turned and looked at him. 'But you've got a decent guide-book, right?' he asked. 'With some information on Trinidad? I've only got *An Adventure in South America*, and it's shit.'

'No, I haven't,' Rich replied tersely. He could sense that John was irritated, but he was going to have to learn to live with his decision. Rich was not going to get suckered into revealing that he knew Trinidad, and moreover, that it was a dump. He might accidentally expose his real identity and his mission would be compromised.

John had also tried to catch him out a few days ago, asking how he had got to Guayaramerín. Rich had given him an evasive answer as he was not going to admit that he had caught a Lloyd Aero Boliviano flight down from Trinidad. His patience was beginning to wear thin though; the next time John stuck his nose in he would tell him to butt out in no uncertain terms. As a DEA special agent, he was especially wary of strangers that took an unhealthy interest in his business, and John was taking an unhealthy interest.

The conversation inevitably petered out, and they were left to their own thoughts whilst the muddy river and its steep, grassy banks slipped past and the impenetrable forest became contiguous and unchanging. Before long, dusk arrived, and with it the first of many tasteless meals. An evening meal was included in their passage, but the captain's wife was no cook and Rich and John would learn to treat anything that came out of her kitchen with extreme caution.

That evening she served up boiled rice and fried *plátano* on cream-coloured enamel plates with cracked green edges, but Rich and John could only stir the food around as they had no appetite for such a bland meal. Then swarms of mosquitoes appeared, forcing them out of the barge and up onto its tin roof, but not before they had flung the savoury banana meal into the river and replaced it with sweets and tins of Tropical Pilsner.

Up on the roof, the gentle breeze halved the number of mosquitoes. The tin was still roasting from the sun, so they balanced two planks between some rebars and sat down to watch the sunset turn the forest black, cast a blue hue across the river and finally send an orange tinge across the wake stretching out behind them.

'Take a look at that wake,' Rich said, pointing at the dazzling colour, but John was not interested.

'Mate, I've seen better sunsets on the Burnett River,' he replied dismissively, and raised his tin of Pilsner. 'This beer's too warm. We should have packed some ice.'

'What? Oh yeah, ice would have been good,' Rich replied.

'The guys in the Billabong Inn wouldn't drink this, I can tell you.'

'What?'

'My local pub in Mundubbera. They wouldn't drink beer this hot.'

John then launched into a diatribe about the maximum temperature at which Australian beer could legally be served whilst the boat slowly crept up the Rio Mamoré in the arc of light cast by its powerful navigation lamp. By now, it was pitch black and fireflies swarmed around it, dazzling in the total darkness that seemed to swallow them whole just a few metres away from the boat. Rich was mesmerised by the phosphorescent beetles, and he tried to change the subject from warm beer to that of the beetles that were desperately seeking a mate with their brilliant display.

'Yeah, nice light show, but I'd enjoy it more with a cold beer—' John suddenly stopped talking and leapt off the wooden plank as if he had been shot. He cracked his hand across the side of his neck, yanked his Akubra from his head and waved it in the air. 'Shit!' he shouted. 'These mossies are giving me the bollock ache!'

Rich looked up at John and wondered why he had to talk incessantly. He was not at the Billabong Inn now but on a boat meandering up the dark, endless Amazon basin that stretched out before them. Overhead, a multitude of stars spread out over the sky and an occasional satellite cut across the glistening patchwork before disappearing into the distance. It was timeless.

Rich began to point this out when John interrupted him again.

'Have you used the dunny yet, mate? I nearly cracked my arse open on the edge of the plywood.'

'What?'

'The toilet. Sorry, that's Aussie for toilet. It's a bloody health hazard! Take care when you use it.'

'I will,' Rich replied.

And whilst the Rio Mamoré drifted past and the vast scenery enveloped the tiny boat, the conversation continued on the same mundane theme. Inevitably, John got onto the subject of Australian rock music and its most famous band.

'I'm guessing you don't know that AC/DC are Australian?' he asked, as if he already knew the answer.

The nationality of this 'amazing band' had been revealed to Rich many times, but he replied anyway, 'Really? I never knew that,' and waved goodnight as he disappeared off the tin roof and went down to his hammock.

The following morning, they were both covered in mosquito bites. The captain had assured them that there were no mosquitoes out on the river, so when he appeared above them on the bridge they decided to climb up onto the roof and see what he had to say.

John waved up at him. 'What about all these mosquitoes? We were bitten alive last night.'

The captain leant over the railing and cupped a hand to his ear.

'I was saying,' John repeated, 'you told us there would be no mosquitoes, but there are swarms of them.'

The captain shook his head and pointed at the engine room.

John was not to be put off. 'Mosquitoes! Lots of them. Lots of bites!' he roared, and ran his hand up and down the blotches on his leg.

The captain shrugged and disappeared from the railing. A moment later he returned, gestured at John and threw him a bar of soap.

'No, mate! I don't need a wash – I haven't got a rash from being dirty – I've been fucking bitten to pieces.'

The captain looked surprised but indifferent to his reaction, and he gave them a casual salute before disappearing again.

'Fucking—' John was lost for words.

Rich chuckled slightly and remembered that he had seen several mosquitoes on the captain's back when they were still in the port. He was probably immune to them and no longer noticed they were even there.

The scenery crept past them the following day, and the day after that. Apart from an occasional black curassow and caiman dozing on the riverbank, they had seen little wildlife since leaving Guayaramerín. On the third morning, they moored at a ranch and watched the sailors prepare the front barge for some cattle that were being held in a large bamboo pen alongside the river. Once the barge was ready, the cattle were herded using long bamboo poles, and the sailors got to work loading a supply of hardwood planks onto the barge behind.

Whilst this was going on, Rich and John got off the boat and joined the captain, who was enjoying a cold Sprite under the shade of a tree. A few minutes later, a small woman came out of the ranch with a plate of *salteñas*, a small savoury pastry crammed full of vegetables in a little sauce. They had been baked first thing that morning in an onion-shaped mud oven next to the ranch, and were delicious.

The captain turned to them with his mouth half full of *salteña* and waved the other half at them.

'Thank God for some decent food!' he remarked.

They all laughed at the clear reference to his wife's cooking.

'What do you think to the Rio Mamoré? It is beautiful, no?' he asked.

'The mossies aren't beautiful, mate,' John replied.

The captain shrugged. 'They bother you soft-skinned gringos, but not us *marineros*,' he said. Ramming the other half of the *salteña* into his mouth, he mumbled, 'What are your jobs back home?'

Rich tensed up. It did not seem like a natural thing to ask.

'I'm a true Aussie,' said John, 'working on the family farm with my brothers. We've got a thousand acres of grazing land and a flock of sheep that extends—' But the captain cut him off.

'And what about you?' he asked, looking at Rich.

Rich could tell that the captain was more than merely curious. He really wanted to know what Rich was going to say.

'I live in the city and have done various things, you know, office jobs, deliveries . . . that sort of thing. Nothing special,' Rich replied.

The captain nodded. 'In Boston?'

Rich stared at him and felt his suspicions give way to a rising anger. 'How do you know I come from Boston?' he snapped.

'It's listed as the place of birth in your passport. I was just wondering if you still live there,' the captain replied innocently.

Rich realised that he had shown his passport when paying for the boat, and he relaxed a little, but the captain had noticed his irritation. Getting up, he raised his bottle of Sprite and said, 'Good luck with your journey ahead, *señores* . . .' Walking off, it sounded like he added, under his breath, 'wherever it takes you'.

Rich watched him head back to the boat and felt uneasy. Maybe he was being paranoid, but instinct told him that the captain could see through the role he was playing.

After several hours, the sailors finished loading the timber planks. Once they had been covered with tarpaulin, *Tondy* swung back into the river as black smoke billowed once again from its engine room, and Rich stood at the front of the barge tying a bright yellow neckerchief around his neck. The barge next to him was full of bony cattle, and the rear one was full of timber. It looked like the DEA were going to make a huge seizure after all, and he was proud to be at the very centre of it.

John came out of the dunny and joined Rich at the front of the barge. The first thing he noticed was the bright new neckerchief around his neck. It was impossible not to – it was almost fluorescent.

'Mate – is that your sister's hankie! What are you trying to do

– catch someone's attention or something?' he asked, laughing. 'If the blokes back home in Mundubbera saw you, you'd never hear the end of it.'

Rich squared up to him. 'Well, you can tell those *blokes* back home to fuck off the next time you see them. The sun's burning up my neck. I'll wear what I want,' he blustered, realising deep down that he had been discovered.

'Easy, mate. No harm meant,' John replied, stepping back, clearly puzzled by Rich's aggressive reaction. 'Why do you think we Aussies all have the same haircut? It's because it's practical for the blazing weather we get back home. The short fringe and cut above the ears keep us cool but the long hair at the back protects our necks from the sun,' he said, turning his head to show off his mullet. 'You could do with growing out the back of yours, mate,' he added, in an attempt to make light of the moment.

Rich didn't say anything but just glared back. Was he for real? Was he in league with the captain? Were they both plotting behind his back? How had he blown his cover? Was he in danger? The thoughts were swirling round his head when he sensed the captain behind him. Spinning round, he ducked slightly and raised his arms to protect himself from the impending blow, but it was just one of the sailors climbing into the barge with the cattle.

Relaxing a little, he reminded himself that it was *he* who had chosen John, not the other way round. John was just a stupid farmer from Australia. He had said so himself. Rich felt his paranoia ease a little, but the damage was done. John left Rich and went up to the tin roof on his own.

A few minutes later, Rich watched two sailors drag one of the cattle to the back of the barge and place a four-inch blade on its temple. Animal instinct made the other cattle huddle at the front of the barge as a sharp strike on the knife's hilt made the cow stagger and then collapse. The sailors spent the rest of the day butchering the fresh carcass, hanging huge strips of meat over wooden poles, slinging the intestines into a couple of buckets and filling some old cooking oil drums with chopped-up bones that rattled when they threw them in.

Anticipating some steak that evening, Rich was disappointed to receive a watery soup with long strips of grey meat floating in it. The cook surpassed all expectations that night and created a meal that was not just inedible but truly revolting. She had cleaned out the cow intestines and stewed them in salty water and stock. Rich retched when he realised that the rubbery strip he was chewing was a piece of colon, and he jumped up, throwing the contents of the bowl overboard in disgust. Unfortunately, the cook watched the soup and its metal spoon spin into the Rio Mamoré, and for the rest of the journey his food was served with cheap plastic cutlery. He was also forced to eat it in silence as John refused to spend any more time with him.

Over the next couple of days, the river narrowed and sandbanks started to appear just below the surface, forcing the boat one way and then the other as it squeezed past them. On one occasion they passed a boat stuck in the soft sand. Its sailors were straining to push it free with long bamboo poles and waved for help, but *Tondy* simply sailed straight past without stopping. Rich knew this could only have been on account of the valuable cargo they were carrying. On another occasion, they stopped beside a boat going in the opposite direction. Rich was worried that the timber barge was going to be transferred and regretted not having a radio to alert Jim, but it was a simple exchange of dried meat for some fresh vegetables from the approaching town of Trinidad. After that, he began to relax a little and enjoy the remainder of the journey, for it seemed that they were going to reach their destination with the cargo intact after all.

The last few days on the boat were by far the most scenic. The river narrowed even more and filled with wildlife. Beautiful, soft pastel pink–coloured Andean flamingos stood next to caiman that were sunning themselves on the riverbanks. Black curassows with bright yellow beaks perched on partly submerged tree trunks, and families of large capybara rodents wandered across the small sandy beaches. Where the water pooled, brilliant blue-and-golden king-fishers darted around, and blue-throated yellow macaws screeched overhead when crossing between the forest either side of the river. It was magical.

On their last morning, the boat turned off the Rio Mamoré and wound its way up the tiny Rio Ibare on its approach into Puerto Almacén, the disembarkation point for Trinidad, which was five miles beyond. Rich was lucky to be up on the tin roof when two pink dolphins joined them in the clear water below, tracking the boat on the last part of its journey. Pedro had also been tracking the boat from vantage points nearby, and UMOPAR were waiting when *Tondy* finally arrived.

One of the sailors leapt out, the captain swung the boat across the river and then positioned *Tondy*, ready to dock. Waving his hands, the sailor guided it up to a run of wooden planks that formed a rudimentary jetty on Puerto Almacén's riverbank. Meanwhile, three Toyota Land Cruisers crept out from a gap between a row of rundown buildings and slowly descended the muddy riverbank. They were full of UMOPAR officers and a single DEA agent, Jim Wernham.

The sailor leant down and expertly tied the boat to a large post, but jumped when a voice behind him shouted, 'Raise your hands, *cabrón*, and get back to the boat.' Rich watched him walk back whilst UMOPAR officers swarmed around *Tondy*, pointing rifles in their direction.

And yet, up on the bridge, the captain seemed perfectly unconcerned by the unfolding drama. He was wearing a white hat with gold braid and black piping, which he raised and then waved at the men.

'Welcome, *señores*,' he shouted. 'To what do I owe this pleasure? We already have transport arranged into Trinidad – surely you have not come to collect us as well?'

Rich could not believe the balls of the captain. One of the UMOPAR officers, who he would later find out was called Alfonso, shook his pistol at the captain and told him to come down from the bridge.

'Of course,' the captain replied, giving him a bold salute.

Rich noticed Jim amongst the UMOPAR officers but was unsure whether he should attract his attention or not. It did not seem his help was needed, so he decided to remain incognito up on the roof.

Some of the officers were now in the rear barge pulling the tarpaulin off the incriminating timber planks. Jim joined them. Rich could not understand why the captain was so relaxed. Maybe he thought the lumber was so well prepared that the officers would be unable to detect that it contained coca paste?

The barge was then untied, and one of the men waved at another boat to come and remove it for a detailed examination. Rich was impressed by the smoothness of the operation and felt proud to have played such an important role in its implementation. Without realising, he ran a hand down the edge of his fluorescent-yellow neckerchief to where his DEA badge would usually be found.

A strange thing then happened. As the captain was being led down the gangplank, he suddenly stopped, turned his head and looked Rich straight in the eye. Waving his hat, he shouted up, 'Good luck with your journey ahead, *señor.*' But it sounded more like, 'Good luck with your fucked head.' And then he simply walked over to one of the Land Cruisers and got in without another word.

He couldn't have said that, could he? Rich thought, puzzled and slightly worried that maybe he *was* a little paranoid.

CHAPTER THREE

The light was fading when Rich McDonnell and Jim Wernham met at Kivon's, their favourite ice cream bar in Trinidad. Jim had been busy all afternoon helping UMOPAR process the coca paste they had seized, and Rich had gone to his hotel to shower and change clothes. His companion on *Tondy* had made his own way into Trinidad to find a hostel. The friendly Australian did not have a guidebook to help him find a good place to stay, but as far as Rich was concerned, that was one of the risks of travelling in a foreign country. He did not give it, or John, a second thought. Rather, he reflected on how successful his operation had been.

Almost ten days ago he had been sat in a smaller ice cream bar wondering if his mission would succeed. Now he was in the self-proclaimed 'Rey de Heladerías' eating one of their *ricos sorvetes* and he was ecstatic. He had foiled the cartel's plan to process, package and ship a large quantity of cocaine, and he had done it in their own backyard; it may well be a strange country, but he had no doubt that he was going to change it.

Rich had arranged to meet Jim at Kivon's at six o'clock, an hour before they were to join some senior UMOPAR officers for an informal debrief. They would want to know everything that Rich had discovered during 'Operation Tondy', as he was calling it. In turn, he wanted to meet his colleagues in UMOPAR now that he would no longer be working undercover.

Kivon's had a prime position on the plaza, as befitted the 'King of Ice Cream Bars', and their 'delicious sorbets' were indeed delicious, as Rich could confirm. He spooned some of their raspberry sorbet into his mouth and watched the traffic grow on the highway that encircled the plaza. The policemen that had been directing it from timber platforms on each corner were now gone, and the scooters swirled continuously around the plaza unhindered. The increasing noise of their engines and the parakeets screeching from palm trees in the square started to get on Rich's nerves, and he could feel his temper rising.

Jim was quiet, playing more with his pink *toronja* sorbet than eating it. He seemed distracted to Rich, as if his mind were somewhere else. Rich did not know him well, but he was surprised that he was not more excited about the seizure. It was probably the noise of the scooters that was bothering him, as it was Rich. *Fucking pieces of shit*, he thought as his irritation grew. *What a shithole . . . Nothing to do but ride round and round its plaza for entertainment.*

'Those scooters are fucking annoying,' he said to Jim.

'Yeah,' Jim replied. Rich had expected more than a one-word answer. He tried again.

'How's the grapefruit sorbet?'

'Good,' Jim answered, spinning his spoon around the slush at the bottom of the tall glass. Rich noticed an expensive-looking TAG Heuer on his wrist and was about to comment, but he stopped himself for Jim was clearly not in the mood for small talk.

The sound of a particularly loud scooter forced him to look round. A bright fluorescent-yellow scooter was approaching, with smoke billowing from its exhaust and a large man sat on it, grinning. As he got closer, he began to wave to Rich and then saluted as he passed. Rich looked again and recognised *Tondy*'s captain.

Motherfucker!

But then a woman squeezed past and returned the wave. *Of course, he was waving at her.* The captain was being held by UMOPAR, so it couldn't possibly have been him on the scooter. Rich realised that he was still on edge, but there was every chance that the drug cartel was smarting from the seizure, and he felt he needed to be alert to any danger. Turning back to Jim, he decided to get straight down to business, even though Jim still seemed distracted.

'How many kilos were seized?' Jim appeared a little uneasy with the question, but said nothing and spooned the last of his sorbet into his mouth, leaving Rich puzzled by his continued reticence.

'Did we break all records then?' he asked.

'No, we didn't break any records this time,' Jim replied.

'Come on then, how large was it?'

'We were misinformed. The lumber wasn't hollow. It didn't contain paste. The operation was a failure,' Jim answered, with a slight shrug.

'What!' Rich shouted, pushing his chair back. 'Fuck off! You telling me a cattle ranch has all that lumber? They trade in cattle, not lumber, right? Help me out here if I'm missing something?'

'Calm down, Agent, remember where you are,' Jim said, looking around, irritated.

Rich realised that he was out of line. Leaning back on the table, he said in a lower but intense voice, 'There was coca paste on that boat. I saw it being loaded up with my own eyes. I know it wasn't swapped before we reached Puerto Almacén. UMOPAR must have swapped it afterwards.'

'Did you actually see the coca paste?' Jim asked.

'No, of course not. It was hidden inside the lumber.'

'I was there when the lumber was sawed open. There was no coca paste inside.'

Rich sat back, crestfallen, but Jim seemed unusually calm about it.

'Listen up. You're going to have to get used to the way things are out here, or you'll lose your mind. It only takes a simple mistake or a bit of bad luck for an operation to yield little or no results. That's the deal. This is the front line. This is their country, and they have the advantage. Remember what I told you happened in Operation Tandem? If the cartel can outsmart the combined force of UMOPAR and every DEA agent in Bolivia, don't think they can't protect a coca paste consignment.'

Jim had described the failed operation to Rich when he first arrived. Over three hundred UMOPAR officers and thirty DEA agents had failed to capture Yayo despite the help of three Bolivian

Air Force C-130s and nine UH-1 Iroquois helicopters. The head of the Beni cartel had escaped from his hacienda in San Ramón before they even got close to it. He had obviously been tipped off, and the DEA no longer trusted their partners in UMOPAR. For that reason, it had been explained to Rich that operational protocol was such that the target was now only disclosed once airborne, and details of the operation were restricted to the commanding officer.

Rich said nothing. He could not believe that Operation Tondy had been a total failure. Someone in UMOPAR must have alerted them to the danger. He realised that it must have been the captain on that scooter, and he sprang from his seat, scouring the plaza for any sign of his foe. It was not lost on Rich that the colour of the scooter matched his neckerchief. *But*, and it was a very firm *but*, once he found Captain *Tondy*, the 'boot would be on the other foot', literally, and the captain was going to find out how a 'fucked head' could inflict excruciating pain.

Jim stared at him.

'Sit down!' he hissed, clearly annoyed by the brash agent who was drawing attention to them, now glaring at all the scooters as if he were a mad dog.

'Don't take it personally, Special Agent. It's something you've got to adjust to out here. Act professionally,' he said firmly. 'It's all part of the battle with the narcos. They win some, we win some. Overall, we're winning the battle, but it's going to be a long, drawn-out conflict. Now, calm the fuck down!' Jim pushed away his glass and leant forward. 'Bush is ex-CIA, right? We're fine. Those guys don't fu—' He stopped dead, as if wrestling with a memory. Taking another breath, he continued, though more to himself than Rich. 'We've just got to hope that the liberals don't gain a voice in DC, otherwise we'll be kicked into the long grass again, just like we were in Vietnam.'

Rich could see that the memory of the Vietnam War energised him far more than his failure to seize the coca paste, and he was surprised by his sudden loss of composure. He decided to tread carefully.

'When did you see action?' he asked.

Jim snorted, and replied dismissively, 'I signed up on my eighteenth in sixty-eight, just before McNamara stood down as Secretary of Defense. Fucking waste of time. I did two thirteen-month tours but left the Marines once the pinkos lost their stomach for the fight.'

'So, how was it? You were scared?' Rich asked, wondering if a more direct approach was needed to discover what had provoked Jim.

'Listen, anyone who tells you they weren't scared is full of shit. Either that or they weren't there.' Jim paused, as if collecting his thoughts and wrestling with what to share with Rich.

He then leant forward further and looked Rich directly in the eye. 'The thing is, once you commit to something, you've got to follow it through. If for nothing else, you've got to do it out of respect for the guys who've lost their life fighting for it. You get that, right?' Rich nodded, and he was actually relieved by Jim's reaction. His casual acceptance of the failure of Operation Tondy had planted seeds of doubts about his commitment.

With their sorbets finished, they got up from Kivon's, found a way through the scooters and walked across the dimly lit square of the plaza. It was full of old women with ancient wooden barrows selling *pomelos*, a dark green citrus fruit the size of a football, bananas, bottles of water and stale-looking *salteñas* arranged in small glass cabinets illuminated by tiny fluorescent lights. The parakeets overhead still screeched and the scooters zoomed around, but Rich was now totally focussed on the job in hand and no longer noticed them. He was on his way to outsmart the UMOPAR officer who had betrayed him. For Jim, the meeting with UMOPAR was simply to discuss the operation. And it could stay that way as far as Rich was concerned, but for him it was now all about uncovering the informant. He was sure that he would be there, laughing behind his back, but he knew he only needed to provoke the smallest reaction to uncover him, and he knew he could do that.

They crossed to the other side and headed off to El Bar Tábano, or 'The Horsefly Inn', several blocks up from the plaza. It was not long before the street lighting disappeared; there were fewer people around, and it was so dark that Rich could not make out any of the road names. He was glad to be following Jim as he had never been in this part of Trinidad. He only knew that they were somewhere north of his hotel. There were fewer and fewer cars on the roads, and the town felt less and less welcoming. He knew he stood out in his Western clothes, and he could feel the eyes of every Bolivian shopkeeper following him as he walked past. He was sure that he was being followed, but whenever he looked around there was nobody there.

Eventually they reached an unremarkable two-storey concrete building that had two signs – 'Coca Cola Siente el Sabor' and 'Ducal el Rey de Cerveza' – hanging outside. It was painted mint green with 'El Bar Tábano' written across it in bold black letters. Jim pushed open the door and Rich followed him inside, relieved to have finally arrived in the half-lit bar, which was empty, except for four men who were sitting at a table in the middle.

Colonel Alfonso Vargas García stood up to introduce himself and his three colleagues, none of whom looked in the least bit threatening. But Rich knew that he was in the same room as the very serpent that had betrayed him, a person so low that he was prepared to undermine the War on Drugs for his own gain. He shook hands and returned smiles, when all he wanted to do was crush digits and twist wrists, but the crash of a heavy bolt locking the door caught his attention and brought him back to his senses.

CHAPTER FOUR

Rich scanned the room for another exit; there was none. It felt like a trap, but when he looked over at Jim, he seemed perfectly relaxed. *Of course the bar has been closed, to keep the meeting private*, Rich thought, and with relief pulled out one of the chairs.

The six of them sat down and the bartender brought over a bottle of *aguardiente* and some shot glasses. The bottle had an illustration of a large horsefly on its label and the words 'beware the bite' underneath. Rich smiled to himself. This was El Bar Tábano's signature spirit, and UMOPAR were going to try and out-drink him; the machismo was unsubtle but familiar. He had experienced it many times in Flanagan's over a bottle of poteen, but Tommy's illegal liquor was eighty per cent proof, and he knew that he could keep up with the smaller men.

Jim turned to Rich.

'This is the elite UMOPAR unit. These guys risk their *cojones* every day facing the cartel in the Beni, unlike their compadres in the Chapare, eh, Coronel Vargas? The biggest risk in the Chapare is tripping over uprooted coca bushes. Out here we face Uzis and AKs, isn't that right?'

Alfonso just rolled his eyes, as many of the Chapare officers were his friends. Rich recognised the short but powerful-looking man who had commanded respect from his men at Puerto Almacén. He had an air of confidence and experience, but Rich was already suspicious of the man in charge of the failed operation. He had no evidence, yet he suspected that the cartel would have attempted to corrupt the head of UMOPAR in Trinidad. He would find out soon enough just how successful they had been.

'*Salud*, gentlemen,' Alfonso replied, raising one of the glasses filled by the bartender. Turning to Rich, he said, 'Welcome to Bolivia. I hope the next time we meet it will be in more satisfying circumstances.'

Rich raised his glass and downed the *aguardiente*. Slamming it back down on the table, he replied, 'You bet. The next time those cockroaches crawl out I'll be waiting to crush them.' His bravado did not go unnoticed by the UMOPAR officers, one of whom refilled his glass.

Meanwhile, Jim turned to Alfonso. 'What did you get from the captain?'

'Nothing. We had nothing to hold him. His papers were in order.'

'What about other boats on the Mamoré. Did he see anything unusual?' Jim asked.

'No, although he mentioned a suspicious-looking character checking out the port a couple of days before he sailed.'

Jim leant forward, his interest piqued. 'Could he describe him?'

'No, other than he had pale skin.'

Rich tossed the *aguardiente* down his throat and looked for the hint of a smile around the table. There was none. He badly wanted to find the captain and slowly torture him. His eyes took in the faces of each of the men at the table. One of them was in on what had happened, of that he was sure, and Rich was going to flush him out by forcing a reaction. He jumped in.

'The lumber . . . it was switched at the ranch and picked up by a different boat,' he said with confidence. 'That captain knew you were waiting for him at Puerto Almacén. He was playing with us the whole time. As for that ridiculous captain's hat he put on when you arrived, that was a fucking joke . . .'

All eyes turned to him, including Jim's, who looked a little surprised at his outburst.

Alfonso replied calmly, 'I doubt the lumber was switched. We probably just received some bad information. Maybe there was a shipment from another *estancia*. Maybe we had the right *estancia* but the wrong boat.' He shrugged. 'These things happen. Maybe we missed something, maybe we missed nothing.'

'You're telling me that the cartel weren't tipped off in advance?' countered Rich.

There was now a deadly silence at the table. All of them knew that he was referring to UMOPAR. It had always been a given that the DEA distrusted them, yet the subject went unspoken. The silence continued for several seconds before Jim interjected.

'Hey, Rich, buddy,' he said, trying to defuse the situation. 'You've spent too much time behind a desk in Boston. Out here we work with small, and usually imperfect, scraps of intel. Sometimes the dots join up, most of the time they don't, but we certainly don't doubt the security of our operations and the invaluable support of the Bolivian authorities.'

There was a slight easing of tension, though it needed Alfonso to really calm things down.

'We can't rule out the cartel having paid informers,' he eventually replied, with some irritation. 'My guess would be there was never a cargo of coca paste being shipped up the Rio Mamoré. Most of the paste from the Beni goes north to Peru and Colombia for processing in their labs, so maybe we received some misinformation to divert us away from another shipment. Or maybe, as Jim suggested, we just joined up the wrong dots.'

But Rich was not going to let it go that easily. Downing another shot of *aguardiente*, he upped the tension once more.

'No, that captain knew exactly what was going on. He *absolutely* works for the cartel. They knew we were on to them. Someone tipped them off. We all know that only the DEA and UMOPAR knew about the operation . . .' He left his words lingering for a reaction. But the reaction he got was not what he expected.

Jim stood up. 'Gentlemen,' he said to the assembled men, 'this is not the DEA's position. I must apologise for my agent's comments. He is young, inexperienced, and El Tábano's *aguardiente* has given him a sore bite.' The men across the table laughed loudly. This only further incensed Rich.

Jim sat down and whispered loudly to him, loud enough for everyone to hear, 'Shut the fuck up,' and then waved at the bartender.

With perfect timing, the bartender approached the table carrying his speciality dish, *pollo a la broaster*. The Bolivians cheered when the huge platter of roast chicken and chips arrived, and Rich knew that he had lost the opportunity to uncover the informant. Jim had humiliated him. Right then and there he would have busted his ass at the slightest opportunity, ex-Marine or not. Another shot of *aguardiente* went down, and he tucked into the food, suspicious of the way that Jim had cut off his line of questioning.

After the meal finished, Rich got more drunk and relaxed a little. The UMOPAR officers were just ordinary guys like him. One of them, Eduardo, had explained how UMOPAR were not only despised by the national police force but also hated by the locals for collaborating with the gringos. He could relate to his own experience working in Boston PD and being regarded with suspicion by the community. Rich decided that he would try and elicit some information from Eduardo in confidence, so when he got up from the table, he followed him into the bathroom.

A light flickered in the damp, pungent-smelling lavatory, and water pooled on the floor beneath the dripping waste pipe of a small sink. Rich knew he would not be able to spend long in the foul room and got straight to the point.

'What's your theory on Operation Tondy?' he asked Eduardo.

'What?'

'What went wrong?'

'Oh, the failed operation,' Eduardo replied, zipping up his flies. He had not heard it referred to as Operation Tondy. 'I don't know,' he said, going over to wash his hands.

Rich joined him. 'But you have your suspicions, right?' He could tell that Eduardo had something on his mind.

Eduardo dried his hands on a grubby strip of cloth nailed to a pole over the sink and left. Rich followed him, but he had lost the chance to get him to talk. On his way back, he noticed the bartender pass some money to Jim that was quickly stuffed into his pocket.

He was a bit drunk, but he trusted his judgement. It was a suspicious thing to do.

The hours passed with more *aguardiente*, and then vodka, before the door was unbolted and the bartender ushered the men into the humid night. The sudden heat made Rich's head spin, and the din of racing cars and barking dogs disorientated him. He fell slightly against the wall as the men ahead of him disappeared into the night with lots of laughter and back-slapping.

Rich wandered off with the vague idea that he needed to head south to Calle La Paz and the drunken conviction that he would recognise some of the streets closer to his hotel. Around him, groups of people were emptying out of bars and restaurants, and he careered towards them, forcing them to one side. Another, darker figure emerged from the shadows and followed him as he staggered down the street.

Giving the finger to a group of men that were mocking him, Rich missed a loose paving slab, crashed to the ground and rolled across the pavement to the edge of the kerb. Sprawled there, he realised just how strong the *aguardiente* had been, and he regretted using it to prove his machismo. Getting up slowly, a sharp pain shot up his ankle and made him fall against a parked car and bang his head, but he knew he had to get up, and he pushed hard against its door, levering himself up and bringing his eyes level with a man half hidden in the gloom of a small alley.

As if from nowhere, some blinding headlights shot round the corner, and Rich turned to see a car race down the street and nearly run over a skeletal dog. Enraged, it scarpered between the parked cars and emerged baring its teeth and barking aggressively. Instinct told him to leave the street fast, and he lunged at the dog, waving his arms and shouting loudly. Fortunately, his bluff paid off and it cowered long enough for him to limp past, but turning round to check on it, he saw that the man was now tracking him and making no attempt to hide.

Hauling himself around the corner, Rich tried to gain some distance before the man noticed. His ankle screamed, but he pushed on and focussed on a brightly lit shop at the end of the street. Twisting his head round once more, the man was now walking faster, almost running, and he had something obscured in his hand. It was either a cosh or a gun. Rich could not tell, but he turned back nonetheless, for he knew that he had to reach the safety of the lights. And then, just as he got closer, a car screamed past and drew up in front of him. Rich stopped in his tracks, panting. The driver's window wound down with a judder and a powerful arm appeared, ready to spring out and bundle Rich into the car that was blocking his path.

Behind him, the sound of running steps echoed on the pavement, and he knew that the moment had arrived to confront the man. Spinning around with his weight on his good leg, he placed the other leg forward and raised his fists in a fighting stance, for he needed to land the first blow on his approaching assailant if he were to stand any chance. The man slowed down, sized up his opponent and brandished a dark object at him, but instead of launching into Rich, he gave him a wide berth.

'*Puta borracho*,' he spat as he hurried up to the waiting car, where an arm shot out, grabbed the bottle of wine that the man was holding and roared off with him in the back seat. Only then did Rich realise he was safe, but a wave of nausea gripped him and he retched, splattering some of his *pollo a la broaster* onto the pavement. A hand grabbed his arm, and he looked up to see Eduardo. *Maybe it was Eduardo following all along*, he thought, but then another violent retch shook his body and the rest of the meal shot over the pavement. He remained there unable to move, held up only by Eduardo's tight grip.

The next morning, he awoke fully dressed on his hotel bed with a splitting head. Rolling off his mattress and trying to stand, he instantly felt the pain in his ankle and collapsed to the floor. He had no idea how he had hurt himself, and he crawled to the bathroom, where he groaned several times before retching into the toilet. The smell of his revolting shirt was making him gag, and he twisted and struggled to get it off his back; finally it was torn off and flung into the corner, and he rolled into the shower, where he sat with water pouring over him. Bit by bit he began to feel a little better, and tiny glimpses gradually came back of the night before.

Hobbling across the room, he crashed on the bed and lay staring at the ceiling. Eduardo had helped him back to the hotel; of that he was sure, but he had no idea how he had got to his room. The thought of the horsefly *aguardiente* made him shudder, and he struggled to recall what had happened in the bar. He knew that he was no further uncovering the informant, but he had found out something important. Try as he might, he could not recall what it was, and he lay dead still and groaned loudly.

He must have fallen asleep, for the sun was no longer shining through a gap in the curtains. Sitting up gingerly, he checked his watch and saw that it was three o'clock. He jumped with a start when he realised that he had been expected at the DEA base that morning.

'Shit!' he shouted, struggling to pull the leg of his trousers over his ankle. He still had no idea how he had sprained it.

Collapsing back on the bed with his trousers only half on, he grabbed the phone and dialled a number written on a scrap of paper. The call connected, but Rich slammed the receiver down just in time. *Thank God!* At the last minute his brain had whirred just enough for him to remember that it was the weekend.

Night finally arrived, and with it some of what happened the previous evening. He began to remember snippets of the journey home with Eduardo. At one point they must have stopped because he saw himself sitting with Eduardo and him making a casual remark about 'looking for the informant closer to home'. Something about 'expensive watches', but he could not remember anything else, try as he might.

Rich only managed to get himself up and fully dressed once it was pitch black outside. Leaving Residencial Loreto, he wandered up Calle La Paz to find some food. The plainer the better. His head was less sore and his appetite was slowly returning, along with his memory. He clearly remembered Jim taking money from the bartender, and what's more, he knew that he had been totally humiliated by his partner.

With a feeling of bitterness, he went into Restaurante Ranchero and found a quiet table in the corner. Only half looking at the menu, Eduardo's comments went round and round his head, and bit by bit they began to come together. The inference was clear – it wasn't an UMOPAR officer who was the informant. It was DEA Grade 14 Supervisory Team Leader Jim Wernham. *But it can't be Jim, can it? The DEA is his life, isn't it . . .?*

CHAPTER FIVE

Rich pressed his forehead against the tempered-glass window and tried to make out something, *anything* . . . It was like an inky-black curtain had been dropped over the land below, smothering all light and movement, for he saw nothing and stared into an abyss. Above him, the engines of the high-winged Casa C-212 turboprop made the plane vibrate and shake slightly, pushing it deeper into the void ahead.

He was surrounded by men dressed in the same fatigues as he was wearing, but he couldn't trust a single one of them. The informant of Operation Tondy was still at large, and it could be any of them. He had taken on a particular distrust of Alfonso, and even his own partner was not above suspicion. Clenching his fist, his knuckles tapped gently against the glass, and he winced slightly as the memory of his humiliation in El Bar Tábano returned.

All he needed was a bit of luck . . . He had snooped on telephone calls, read papers left on desks and listened to conversations, looking for any attempts made to discourage a particular line of enquiry. But he was still no closer to finding the informant. For now, he had decided to immerse himself in the day-to-day business of the base and wait for a clue to emerge.

It had taken a few weeks for Rich to familiarise himself with the DEA set-up. At first, the flow of intel from the CIA, the national police and DEA snitches had been overwhelming. Luckily, his training at Quantico and in Boston PD had helped him to develop a system for sifting through and finding promising leads in the mass of papers he received. He had started to get on well with Jim, who also had a police background, and their inauspicious start and the disastrous evening at El Bar Tábano were never mentioned.

Rich turned away from the window and faced the Bolivians, who were sitting opposite him with their backs against the fuselage. He was going to demonstrate to them that the US was not just a consumer of cocaine, fighting its war from cushy offices on the east coast. It was an active participant on the battlefield, and Rich was one of the select few sent by the greatest nation on earth to help co-ordinate, cajole and command their efforts on the narcotics playing field. He was proud, calm and prepared for his first operation.

Only ten of the sixteen passenger seats were occupied. The remaining space was taken up by a couple of two-hundred-and-fifty-gallon rubber bladders which would refuel the UH-1 Iroquois helicopters they were flying towards. Rich and Jim knew what was planned, as did Alfonso, but none of the seven non-ranking UMOPAR officers had any idea what lay ahead. They looked tense, and none of them spoke. The anxiety on their faces felt good to Rich. It meant that the narcos would not be expecting them this time.

His eyes wandered around the cabin and up to an array of lights in the cockpit. Green, orange and blue dials shone on the control panel, and the cockpit window had a slight green shimmer from the pilots' night-vision goggles. He knew that the goggles had only recently been supplied by the US Department of Defense, and he hoped that the pilots had received proper training in their use. A couple of years earlier, another DEA agent, Rich Finley, had been killed when a Casa C-212 crashed into a mountain at night. With a maximum flying altitude of ten thousand feet, the lack of any ambient light made navigation at night dangerous in the unpressurised plane.

Fortunately, the Beni is relatively flat, and Rich knew he had no need to worry. Looking back, his attention turned once more to the engines humming overhead and the vibrations that rippled across the side of the rubber bladders, but then, and without warning, the bladders jumped and the plane plunged downwards. Rich grabbed the edge of his seat as a violent patch of turbulence threw the plane across the sky and made his stomach turn and his heart race. But none of the men opposite him looked rattled, and they remained perfectly composed. Another wave hit them, and he clung on before the plane eventually stabilised. Rich reluctantly acknowledged that the men opposite had more operational experience than him, and that hurt. So far, his posting had not worked out as he had imagined, but he was about to put that right.

A few minutes later the plane began a rapid descent towards a faint strip of sparkling lights. The Casa C-212 was designed for short landings, and it shot down into the dark expanse, through a narrow corridor cleared of trees and across a rudimentary grass runway surrounded by dense forest. The tri-wheels of the plane bounced several times before the pilots could angle the pitch of the propellers and slow it down. Rich breathed a sigh of relief when the brakes were finally applied and the plane taxied into a holding area at the end of the runway.

Outside, a faint tree-line could be made out as dawn approached, but the forest beneath was still indistinguishable. It was nearly six thirty and daylight would not penetrate its dense canopy for a while longer. Rich checked his kit, looked down at the solid stock of his M4 assault rifle and prepared himself for the next stage of his journey. After a couple of minutes, the propellers of the Casa C-212 came to a virtual stop and the men jumped out of the side exit of the plane, just in front of the turbo prop engine. The fuel bladders would be unloaded later through the rear exit.

Rich stood there and breathed in the damp air that rose from the grass around him. He felt slightly numb, but also exhilarated. He was about to embark on his first mission, and he was going to nail it. Then a hand tapped on his shoulder, and he turned to find Eduardo, smiling.

'How are you feeling, *hermano*, excited or nervous about your first operation?' he asked.

Eduardo had been on annual leave immediately after the evening at El Bar Tábano, and after he returned to the base there never seemed to be the opportunity to discuss what had happened. Rich's instincts told him that Eduardo was trying to get details of the operation.

Rich began to follow the other men with their rifles and small packs, and Eduardo joined him.

'Calm,' Rich told him. 'I'm going to knock it home. Those motherfuckers won't know what's hit them.'

Eduardo nodded in approval, and another officer joined them to listen in on the conversation.

'How many "motherfuckers" are we up against?' Eduardo asked.

Rich nodded towards Alfonso, who was walking in front of them.

'Ask your CO buddy, you know the protocol.' He paused, and then added, 'What I can say is . . .' He hesitated a little. 'It's a heli-borne operation.' He knew that he at least owed Eduardo that piece of information. Besides, they would arrive at the helicopters soon enough.

'Hey, Rich, you can trust me,' Eduardo said. 'Information is a two-way process. Don't forget the lead I gave you on your inform-ant?' Rich did not want to be in anyone's debt, but his primary focus came rushing back and he knew he needed more help to catch the rat.

'Listen, this is off the record, but it's a raid on a pozo pit, just the ten of us.'

Rich watched the UMOPAR officers breathe a sigh of relief. From the scale of the operation it was obvious that it was a low-key one and only four or five people would be at the pozo pit at most, and they would be lightly armed.

Rich had broken protocol and the need to uncover the inform-ant had clouded his judgement. It was obvious that the DEA agent had a blind spot, and Eduardo took advantage of it.

'You might want to check out your partner's watch today,' he said cryptically.

Rich looked at Eduardo and realised that he had made a mistake. He could not afford to be distracted, and he regretted having been so easily coerced into revealing the nature of the operation.

'Sure, I'll do that,' he replied, and quickened his step to catch up with the men heading into the forest.

Up ahead, a narrow path dimly lit by lanterns disappeared into a dense wall of trees. Turning on his flashlight, he followed the men into the forest that now rose up and towered over him, casting sinister shadows that made it feel threatening and impenetrable despite the path carved through it. Rich gripped his rifle and focussed on the man ahead, but Eduardo's comment swirled around in his mind and bothered him. Right now he should be concentrating on the operation, not having his suspicions raised. *Maybe I'm being played by Eduardo*, he thought, just as a root caught his foot and sent him crashing into one of the lanterns, knocking it over. Feeling stupid, he cursed Eduardo's mind games and recovered quickly – but he realised that he could not afford to let his mind wander today.

Finally, the lanterns ended and the path opened out into a large oval clearing. Dawn was just breaking, and Rich could make out a small white hacienda at one end with a fine mist drifting over its veranda. The sun was brushing the top of the trees behind it, and two UH-1 Iroquois helicopters stood on a concrete apron in front. The rising sun cast a long shadow across the grass, and it drew Rich's eye up to a Bolivian flag painted on the tail of one of the helicopters where it was poised ready to spring from the apron with its blade cutting through the air in a fast, percussive beat that exuded power and speed. Alongside it, a thick cloud of black smoke burst from the turbine of the other 'Huey' and its two huge rotating blades came to life, slowly gathering momentum as the whine of its turbine grew louder.

It was as though the forest had been rudely awoken by the sound of the helicopters, for as Rich walked down its dirty yellow path the noise of screaming birds and scratching insects swirled around the man-made arena and made it feel close, immediate and threatening. Luckily, the *estancia* was only the pre-stage for their operation and they were not staying there.

Rich approached the group of men assembling at the helicopters and joined Jim. It was then that his senses went into overload and a wave of panic hit him.

'You okay?' asked Jim.

His heart was beating furiously, and he gulped in air to control his breathing. 'You bet, let's hit them . . .' he gasped.

'You sure?' Jim said, looking closely at his partner.

Rich nodded with a weak smile. He had never suffered a panic attack before, and this was not the place to have his first.

'Looks like you could do with some food. It was an early start,' Jim added. 'Grab some water and something in the Huey,' he said, pointing to the nearest helicopter.

Rich climbed in and collapsed on the bench seat. He breathed hard several times and managed to slow down his racing heart. The reason for the attack left him dumbstruck. Surely he was expertly trained, young and fearless? The environment had unsettled him, but it must have been the pressure of searching for the informant that pushed him to his limit. It reminded him again that he could not afford to be distracted.

Picking up an energy bar, he tried to focus on the operation. The Bolivian Air Force had discovered the pozo pit on one of their spotting exercises last week. They were always built near a river as large quantities of water were needed to convert coca leaves into coca paste. Eventually, the precursors used in the process slowly seeped into the ground, leaving a distinctive sheen on the surface of the river, which was exactly what the pilots had spotted.

The target was located about forty miles north of the pre-stage, close to the edge of the Rio Beni. Aerial photographs would guide them from the landing zone, and the acrid smell of macerating coca leaves would pinpoint the pozo pit on the ground. Yet doubts filled him that, despite the planning and experience of the men with him, a bullet might yet smash into his skull and send him home in a body bag. He breathed deeply, and slowly counted to himself as Jim and three officers jumped in.

Jim gave the signal and the Huey rose sharply into the air with its doors pinned back. Rich was relieved to see Eduardo still standing below with Alfonso; he would concentrate better away from him. Putting on his headset, the distinctive *thump thump* of the rotor blades was muffled, the nose of the helicopter dipped and he was pushed back in his seat as it powered over the forest that soon became a green blur just a few hundred feet below.

It was only then that a growing sense of patriotism hit Rich, and his anxiety began to ease. Here he was in a Vietnam-era Huey shooting over the jungle like the soldiers before him, defending his country from the insidious forces that would tear it apart given the chance. Looking down on the scenery rushing below, the feeling of being one of the 'elect', one of the chosen few, returned once more. It was thanks to the sacrifices of men like him that his country would have a secure future. He was confident that the drug trade would be defeated, just as communism had been destroyed before it, and swapping the barrel of his M4 rifle into his left hand, he placed his right hand over his heart and gently hummed 'The Star-Spangled Banner' to himself. When he got to the third verse, he realised that he did not know the rest of the national anthem, and he turned back to see Jim staring, as if he were reading his thoughts. Rich quickly removed his hand and wondered if his patriotism had been that obvious.

Avoiding Jim's stare, he noticed that the two UMOPAR officers alongside him were still tense. *Maybe the operation really is dangerous?* He began to worry, and tapped at the headset of the man next to him.

'Did you guys get a briefing outside the Huey?' he asked over his crackly set.

The man shook his head.

Rich waved at Jim to turn on his headset. 'Jim, these guys haven't been briefed.'

Nodding, Jim gestured for everyone to turn on their headsets.

'Gentlemen, forgive me, I should have briefed you earlier,' he said with a slight shrug. 'This morning we will deliver a message to the cartel that they aren't going to forget in a hurry. We are acting on intel received from the Diablos Rojos on a pozo pit sixty-five klicks north of the pre-stage. The usual sweep is going be employed, with Coronel Vargas leading. Once the lab has been secured and the narcos arrested, we will destroy it under the terms of . . .' He hesitated, struggling to find the right words. 'Under the terms of . . . Operation Burning Anger,' he said, as if the name had suddenly come to him.

Rich watched the officers' shoulders relax and grins appear as they realised that the operation was low key. Their reaction also helped Rich relax. Nonetheless, he thought Operation Burning Banger sounded like they were about to tackle a barbeque out of control rather than destroy a pozo pit. But he thought better of raising it and replied, 'Roger, let's get to it. Those guys have it coming. Operation Burning Banger's going to bury them underground.'

Jim gave him a high five and held back a chuckle at his unfortunate mistake.

CHAPTER SIX

The Rio Beni appeared in front of them, glistening in the early-morning sun. Rich knew that it would be a murky brown colour on the ground, but from the air it looked magnificent flowing through the rainforest. On either side the forest stretched as far as he could see, with no evidence of roads or villages to indicate that it was inhabited by anything other than exotic wild-life – but he knew their target was down there somewhere. The helicopter followed the river for a few miles and then slowly descended onto a gravel spit that had been chosen as the landing zone.

Once on the ground, four of them jumped out and helped the fifth down with his M2 flamethrower. Rich looked back and saw the second Huey appear in silhouette against the low sun, bearing down on them with its shimmering blades and powerful search light. All of them stood and watched as the sound of its huge rotor blades echoed around the forest and the helicopter dropped onto the LZ, bouncing slightly on its skids. Jim had forgotten to brief the men at the pre-stage and left early; otherwise, they would have flown in tandem, as was the plan.

Alfonso leapt from the door and beckoned to the officers standing by Rich. The other men jumped down, and all seven of them lined up in front of their CO. Once the combat plan was confirmed, the DEA agents joined them and they set off in single file past the second Huey, whose rotor blades were still slowly turning and blowing a light mist across the river. Rich prayed that the sound of it had not reached the pozo pit. The element of surprise was critical if they were to avoid a serious exchange of fire, and he was anxious to push on.

There was a natural thinning of the scrub at the end of the gravel, and they went through it, leaving the river behind. The terrain by the riverbank was full of thorns, ferns and shrubs, and the going was slow. But they pressed on, eventually reaching an area where the forest's dense canopy cut out the sunlight needed for undergrowth to survive, and walking became easier. The men fell into a quick-time cadence, and Rich just about managed to keep up with the officer with a large AN/PRC-77 radio on his back.

The terrain beyond was wild and care was needed to find a course through it. Alfonso had selected one of his men as the guide, and it was he that chose their path and regulated the marching pace. The two men behind Rich and Jim were the flank guard, and the men at the head of the column were alert to any oblique fire. They pushed deeper and deeper into the forest before eventually reaching a small stream that was their phase line. Aerial reconnaissance showed it ran north-northwest and would lead them to within a hundred metres of the pozo pit. Most likely it carried a residue of the precursors that had exposed the laboratory.

Rich knew that their target would soon be reached, and he tried to stay focussed on the task ahead, but his hands were sweaty and the adrenaline was making him jumpy and edgy. Following the man in front, he waded into the stream, and the team moved quietly through the clear water that reached their knees, each of them watching the man in front in case he stumbled. Rich also kept a keen eye out for snakes, for he knew that they could be near the watercourse and they were notoriously dangerous when disturbed. Gripping his assault rifle, it was only then that he realised the firing selector was on 'Fire' and not 'Safe', as it should be when in the middle of a column. It was quickly flicked into the correct position, and he pushed on.

Finally, the acrid fumes of coca leaves macerating in gasoline could be smelt, and it was clear that the laboratory was nearby. This was the signal to slow down and move as quietly as possible. The guide raised his hand and the column halted. On their left flank, a wisp of smoke rose from the forest and the pozo pit could be seen a short distance beyond a slight dip in the terrain. Alfonso selected two men for reconnaissance, and the column left the river whilst they scouted the area.

Rich's nerves now switched to a heightened sense of alert and he felt numb. His initial excitement at the Casa C-212 was long gone, and he began to have real doubts about what he was doing, and whether he would survive. Sweat trickled down the back of his neck and he really needed to pee, but it was too late for that. He glanced at Jim, who had a fixed stare and looked wired. Around him, the other men waited in a combat-ready stance, either for the patrol to return or for the sound of gunfire. The tension was unbearable, and his heart was thumping so hard that the veins in his throat felt ready to burst.

The patrol soon reappeared. There were two men eating breakfast outside and a further two or three inside a rudimentary laboratory, but none of them were carrying weapons and there were no guards. Alfonso listened and confirmed that there was no need to adjust the plan of assault, which was a V-formation advance with a shock action overrunning the camp. He would lead from the front. The right flank would peel off and secure terrain north of the zone; the left flank would cover the south sector after the raid. To the west, the river was a natural barrier preventing escape.

Rich and Jim were in the right flank with Eduardo and two other officers. They pulled into formation and Alfonso gave the signal to advance. They were on! Rich crept through the forest. Adrenaline pushed him forward and his fear vanished. His vision became tunnel-like, and he felt almost detached from the person about to annihilate the narcos. At the dip, Alfonso gave the command to attack and the men launched themselves towards the camp, crashing into it with a volley of bullets that cracked in the air.

Alfonso was the first to reach the centre, and he rushed across to a man scrambling to his feet. The kick he delivered sent him sprawling across a large fire and he rolled on the ground, screaming. His nearby compadre was motionless, in shock, with a spoon frozen by his mouth. Two men dashed from a wooden building and lunged for guns hanging nearby, but threw up their hands when confronted by the officers. A fifth man tried to escape out the back before being captured. And like that, it was over.

Rich had not fired a single shot, but he was victorious, empowered and confident. The operation was a success and the feeling of failure from the previous mission vanished. He was at the start of great things, and his spirit soared.

Then, as he walked off to explore the camp a little more, he turned a corner only to find himself face to face with a narco scrambling out of a hammock. Both men stared at each other for a brief second, before the man pounced for an AK-47 hanging nearby. Rich raised his M4 to release a burst of warning fire, but the trigger barely moved! Looking frantically at the body of the rifle, he cursed violently at the fire selector, which was still on 'Safe'. Flicking it to 'Fire', he lost precious seconds, and the man now had the AK-47 in his hands. He turned to Rich, but a stream of bullets passed over his head and he threw the gun down. Eduardo brushed past and smashed the butt of his rifle into the man's thigh, making him collapse to the ground.

'Fucking piece of shit,' Rich shouted, throwing his weapon to the floor. 'The firing mechanism jammed,' he added to Eduardo, who now had an M4 in one hand and an AK-47 in the other. Eduardo turned round and shrugged.

'I'd rather one of these any day,' he replied, raising the AK-47. Jim joined them, and Rich hurriedly picked up his rifle, without acknowledging Eduardo's help, for he did not want Jim to realise that he had made such a basic mistake.

Eduardo took the narco back to the camp, and Rich, Jim and another officer finished a sweep of the area. It was clear that they had successfully overrun the camp and the area was secure, so the officer walked back to his colleagues, leaving the DEA agents to stroll over to two pozo pits at the back of the laboratory.

Rich was baffled by his mistake. For a brief moment he was worried that perhaps he was not up to it. If anyone had the nerve to criticise his work back home, his favourite retort went something like: 'I'm the guy who gets the job done. You must be the other guy?' It was pretty clear that today he had been the other guy. But it did not last. Instead, he quickly blamed the weapon and the fact that the fire selector had been designed with poor visuals.

Jim stood over the pozo pits and began explaining them as Rich nonchalantly unzipped his flies and peed over the residue of the mash below. Some of it splashed up and dripped slowly down the polythene sheet, but Jim was too busy explaining the chalky powder in the adjoining pit to notice.

'That's cement and fertiliser covering the leaves that have been cut with a strimmer,' he said. As the process had already been explained to Rich, he was not really listening. 'That red drum contains gasoline, and the others are full of water,' Jim continued, pointing to some drums balanced at the top of the pit. 'Looks like we got here just before the narcos got to work.'

Rich cast a glance at the barrels and the pits below. Zipping up his flies, he replied, 'If anyone needs proof that the coca leaf is a filthy crop that needs eradicating, just come take a look at one of these.'

Jim agreed. 'Sure, it's indigenous and pays a whole lot more than a crop of bananas and coffee,' he said, 'but unless they find a better way of controlling it . . . the *cocaleros* are going to lose it,' he finished, waving his hand as if he knew something he could not share.

Something caught Rich's attention. Try as he might, he would never remember whether it was the silver strap or the sun reflecting off its bright yellow face, but whichever one it was, it made him stop and stare at the large Breitling on Jim's wrist. In fact, he was surprised that he had not noticed it before. It was such an ostentatious and expensive-looking time piece.

Jim caught him staring. 'Nice, isn't it?' he said, and turned his wrist towards Rich. 'It's my lucky combat watch . . . wear it on every mission.' Rich was reminded of Eduardo's comment back at the pre-stage, and the thought lingered as they returned to the camp.

By now all of the narcos had been handcuffed and were lying face down on the ground, opposite some blue barrels that had corrosive-warning labels on them. They no doubt contained sulphuric acid, which was needed to convert the coca leaf mash into cocaine sulphate, or *agua rica*, which was the next stage in producing coca paste. The officers were taking serial numbers from the barrels to trace their providence, and Rich's focus switched to the acid inside. *Some of that could so easily accidentally spill over their feet*, he thought. The narcos would not be threatening his country again, but he would still like to have given them something more painful to remember than just a jail sentence.

The camp was swarming with officers taking photos and collecting evidence. None of the narcos moved or talked, but Rich noticed ants crawling across the white vest of one of them. It looked like he had only just got up as he was barefoot and still in his yellow polyester boxers. The rest of the men were in various stages of dress, and some of them were also without footwear.

Jim watched him staring at the arrested men and beckoned to him.

'Hey, come take a look at this,' he said as he took him over to them. 'Take a good look at the soles of their feet. The feet always give them away. Those sores are from trampling in the pozo pits.' Rich could see the slight swelling and red ulcers that covered all their feet, with the exception of a couple of the men who wore sandals. 'The Viet Cong were always given away by their feet,' he added. 'All of them, to a man, wore identical black combat sandals with straps covering the tops of their feet. So, it was simple – all we did was look down at their feet when they came into the market, and boom, we knew we had one of those Viet Cong scumbags standing right in front of us.'

'So they were dumb enough to wear the sandals?' Rich asked.

'Of course not, but they couldn't hide the tell-tale cross that the sun had burned into their feet. We always caught them, and they squealed innocence – until the ARVN persuaded them otherwise, that is.'

'Smart,' Rich replied, nodding.

As Jim led him over to the laboratory, they passed two rusty green drums supported on thick, heavy wooden frames; holes were neatly punctured in them from top to bottom and a large metal spout caught all the grey liquid squeezed out from their stinking insides.

Jim waved. 'This is where the mash is pressed and the *agua rica* collected. We'll find soda crystals and coca paste inside,' he said.

The officers were already carrying out packets of coca paste from the laboratory, along with pots half filled with a yellowish mixture. A large bench made of branches stretched down one side of the building, beneath which the soda crystals were indeed stored. Rich went up and looked inside a large tin cauldron sitting on one of the gas burners arranged neatly on the bench. It contained some of the yellow-coloured paste he had seen the officers remove.

'That's where the *agua rica* and soda have been heated,' said Jim. 'That gooey stuff will dry into coca paste and be parcelled up along with the rest.'

Stepping outside, they watched Alfonso directing his men. The narcos were now on the edge of the camp, next to the parcels of coca paste, where they were being guarded by two of the officers.

'How much paste have we got?' Jim asked him.

'Maybe a week's work for these guys. Twenty kilos. Will that give Señor Ferrarone a small smile?' Alfonso replied. Don Ferrarone was the DEA chief in Bolivia, renowned for his coolness towards UMOPAR.

'He's going to be grinning from ear to ear,' Jim said.

Alfonso just smiled and changed the subject. 'I think we're about ready for the group photo,' he said, waving his officers to a spot in front of the laboratory. Passing a camera to one of them, he gestured for the others to line up in front of its black tarpaulin roof and wooden posts. In his enthusiasm, the man with the camera stepped back too quickly, knocking over a pot of coffee by the side of the fire, and they had to wait until the fire stopped hissing and the steam blew away before the photo could be taken.

Alfonso stood in the centre and raised his rifle, which was the cue for his officers to do the same. There was no laughter; rather, each man stared sternly at the camera and the moment was captured for future display in UMOPAR's briefing room. Rich and Jim stood at either end, and Rich pushed his chest out when the photo was taken. He knew that the DEA were simply tolerated by the Bolivians, but none of them would be standing in front of that laboratory without the help of his country.

The man put the camera down and the officers cheered and shouted with their customary back-slapping and wide grins. All of the evidence was now secured, and the men got to work emptying the gasoline and sulphuric acid barrels and jamming the propane gas cylinders open at a safe distance from the camp.

The man with the M2 flamethrower then appeared to resounding applause. Taking a small bow, he strode forward and stood, legs apart, facing the laboratory, turned a small dial on the side of the tanks and waited for the pressurised fuel to reach the big squeeze trigger that was gripped in his right hand. With his left hand, he pointed the barrel of the flamethrower at the centre of the laboratory and then pulled hard on the gun trigger. There was a loud click, the ignition cartridge spun, a puff of smoke and a small flame exploded from the barrel and then a stream of liquid fuel burst across the camp and a fireball engulfed the laboratory.

Rich watched the camp go up in flames and black smoke spiral through the trees, making the wildlife scream. This was exactly where he wanted to be, on the front line of the war, not stuck behind a desk in Boston. He was hurting the cartel in their own backyard, and the best of it was that they were powerless to stop him. He had destroyed one of their laboratories, but this was just a taste of what they had coming. Standing proud, he knew he had the divine right to be there and to exercise the power entrusted in him by the government of the United States of America. Anybody choosing the side of the Colombian cartels against its people deserved to be marched out of the jungle barefoot in just a vest and yellow boxers, as one of the narcos was about to find out.

He loved this. How could he not?

Jim stood next to him, watching the camp blaze. 'This is what you signed up for, right?'

'Fucking yes. Point me at the next one, wherever it is. I'm ready to go right now. I'm going to destroy every single last one.'

'That all depends on our informants and some successful spotting exercises,' Jim replied. 'You never know, one day we may find a better way of finding and destroying these labs,' he added, walking off to collect some of the evidence that needed taking back to the Hueys.

Picking up his allocation, Rich grinned at the narcos being marched into the jungle. He knew that the red scabs on their feet would be torture when walking back to the Hueys. It was only then that he noticed the yellow boxers were covered in small Mickey Mouses. *Fucking cheek*, he thought, irritated at the irony of the narco's ass being covered in an icon of the very culture that he was so intent on destroying.

CHAPTER SEVEN

The following day, Rich drafted his report from some rough notes whilst phones rang, voices echoed around the office and people dashed to and fro with a real sense of urgency. The national police would collect the narcos later that afternoon, but first Alfonso would lead a debrief and then UMOPAR would extract some information from the men. It was all so different to the failed mission on the Mamoré.

Rich wandered over to Jim's desk to see if he wanted a coffee. His back was turned and he did not see Rich approach. Had he done so then maybe his drawer might not have been open. Inside, at least three expensive-looking watches were laid out carefully on a neat velvet cloth.

'You've got to be fucking kidding me!' The words burst out, making Jim swivel round in his chair. When he saw Rich looking at the drawer, he quickly slammed it shut. It had been obvious that Rich had been watching him closely on the base, but from his reaction he knew he had to move quickly.

'Rich, buddy,' he said, locking the drawer, 'let's grab a coffee and I can fill you in on the next steps.'

Rich stared at his partner – both of them knew that he had been caught out. Rich had finally got the bit of luck he needed, and the evidence was indisputable. Jim was receiving more than his federal salary and buying watches with the bribes. *Clever, keep the money out of a bank account.* He shook his head. *No doubt the money at El Tábano had gone on one of them.* Returning to his desk, he picked up his Glock. He knew that he had to confront his partner and he had no idea how it was going to work out, but he sure as hell wasn't going to find out unarmed.

Jim suggested a coffee bar just off the base, and as they walked over, Rich felt the tension building. Jim tried to engage him in small talk, but he was having none of it. He was going to expose his partner's duplicity, no matter how senior he was. *All that horseshit about believing in a cause.* Rich ground his teeth. *Laughing at me, busting my ass on that boat.* He stopped dead when Jim asked him about his plans for leave.

'Cut the crap, buddy, you don't give a fuck what my plans are,' he snapped.

Jim stared at him for a second, and then broke out into a laugh.

'No, you're right,' he replied. 'I don't. You think you saw something that you didn't, and I needed to get you off the base to explain it.'

Jim's suggestion that Rich had made a mistake enraged him even more, and he had to stop himself from grinding a fist into his partner's face; instead, he shouted back at him.

'Your ass is grass and you're looking straight at a big fucking lawnmower, buddy. You've got five minutes, then I'm back in there.'

Despite the threat, Jim just smiled. 'Come on, at least give me my five minutes,' he said calmly. 'By all means return to the base afterwards and do whatever you want.' Pointing at the bar, he said, 'Look, we're almost there.'

They sat down, and Rich glared at his partner as he ordered the coffee. How anyone could undermine the trust and opportunity granted by his country sickened him. He could understand an UMOPAR officer being tempted to accept bribes. They received a low salary with no pension, but federal agents were well paid. They had absolutely no excuse.

'Rich, stop glaring at me, you motherfucker. You'll wear out those Irish eyeballs,' Jim said, finally losing patience. Luckily, the coffee showed up and provided a distraction, but Rich visibly bristled as he stirred his espresso. 'You think I'm on the take. You think you saw watches bought with bribes. You think you saw me receive money in El Bar Tábano. You think you informed on the operation.

Guess what? You are totally fucking wrong, *hermano*,' Jim continued, losing his cool a little and unconsciously slipping into some of the language used by UMOPAR. Leaning forward, he matched Rich's stare. 'Alfonso and I have suspicions that Eduardo is the informant. I'm trying to gain his trust to see if he reveals himself. There's no fucking way we can succeed in this country unless we have the advantage of surprise. Eduardo, or whoever it is, needs to be found quickly. I've got Don on my back for a big win after the failure of the Mamoré operation.' He waited for Rich to respond, but he was still too incensed to say a word.

'Do you really think I would stand at a bar and make a show of stuffing money into my pocket? Come on, give me some credit,' he said. 'I was waiting for Eduardo to come out of the restroom. It just so happened that you followed him out.' Jim laughed when he saw Rich glance at the watch he was wearing. 'You're wondering about the watches, right? They're for show.' He took it off and handed it to him. 'I wear a new one every month or so. They're not worth shit, and come from a very good counterfeit shop on the Kowloon Road in Hong Kong.' Rich looked at it closely. 'They look fine from across the room, but up close there are little imperfections that give them away.' Rich's shoulders sagged when he realised his mistake. 'Give me some credit, buddy,' Jim added. 'Would I really be stupid enough to wear flashy watches if I were taking bribes?'

Rich remembered the passion he'd witnessed at Kivon's, and the same look of conviction was now on Jim's face.

'You go back in there to try and expose me,' Jim said firmly, 'all you'll do is delay us. You'll undo months of work, and in the end you'll look foolish. You wouldn't want to be the one who fucked this whole thing up, would you?'

Rich sat back and realised that it had been Eduardo who had encouraged him to suspect Jim. It was no coincidence that he had found Rich in the street that night. He must have been following him all along and chosen his moment.

'Fuck,' he said, placing the watch on the table and pushing his hands through his hair in anguish. 'I fucked up. Coming here has been harder than I thought—' He stopped himself from admitting any more. 'The mind plays tricks around here. I followed up on the wrong lead . . .' he quickly added.

Jim grinned and stuck his hand out, which Rich shook.

'I know how hard it is. I was new here once too. Come on,' he said, picking up the watch and strapping it back on his wrist. 'Let's get back before the debrief starts.'

In fact, it had already started, and they sneaked in quietly and found some seats at the back of the room. Alfonso stood at the front with chalked arrows and lines laid out behind him on a large blackboard. A Bolivian flag hung on another wall, alongside a gallery of successful operations that would shortly be joined by the photograph taken during Operation Burning Anger.

The operation was deemed a success. Even though a relatively small amount of coca paste had been seized, the cartel's production had been disrupted, if only for a short time. Everyone knew that pozo pits were cheap and quick to construct and that a new one would soon spring up to replace the one they had destroyed. But they had six men in custody who would not be working on it, and that was the prize.

'The lab was secured without receiving fire. But we were still surprised by the extra man in the hammock. We got lucky,' Alfonso said. 'Eduardo, you disabled him, but not before he had an AK in his hands. Next time, you need to be in his face before he's out of that hammock.'

Rich looked at the back of Eduardo's head. *A hard, tight hook would send him crashing to the ground*, he thought as he clenched his fist and simmered. He did not hear the rest of Alfonso's presentation, for his mind had wandered to a filthy prison cell where Eduardo sat convicted of treachery, shivering in a bitter wind blowing in from the freezing *altiplano*. Together with Jim, he would catch him, and that prison cell would soon become a reality.

Alfonso eventually sat down, and Jim got up to address the group.

'I would like to thank everyone here on behalf of the DEA and the US government. This is a long war we are engaged in, but every small success leads to victory. You can be sure that Operation

Burning Anger has been registered by the cartel and they know we are here for one reason only, to drive them out of business. That's accepted, but we all know we need to win the hearts and minds of the population before we can really drive the narcos out of Bolivia. To that end, I am pleased to be able to announce the decision of the government of the United States to build a new school in Santa Ana, where the land has been donated by the Bolivian government, and the school will be handed over on completion to its *ayuntamiento*.'

The officers gave a polite applause. A new school would be very welcome in Santa Ana, but everyone knew that it was ultimately a public relations exercise and would not go far in bringing about lasting change. The US government was fixated with the town since six thousand of its residents expelled one hundred and fifty US soldiers and UMOPAR officers back in 1986, at the conclusion of Operation Blast Furnace. The operation hardened local attitudes to the counter-drug forces and the US were now viewed as unwelcome intruders. A common rumour had even been circulating that the gringos were seizing laboratories to fund the Nicaraguan Contra rebels, such was the distrust stirred up by the local papers after the heavy-handed operation. One of the officers thought that *his* local village, just south of Sucre, could also benefit from a new school. He had to pay for his two daughters to attend school, an hour away by bus. If he did not supplement his salary, he could only have afforded for one of them to receive an education. Why should he be forced to choose between his two daughters?

'Thank you,' Jim continued. 'I know the Army engineers in Fort Bragg are delighted to be able to help improve the lives of the children in Santa Ana. All being well, they'll be on site later this month. On a more mundane note, on Saturday evening I'll be presenting the winner of the Trinidad half-marathon with the prize of a new mountain bike. So, you're all welcome to turn up at the Plaza Central and watch me make a fool of myself in Spanish.'

The officers laughed as Jim returned to his seat.

Rich looked around and felt proud of his country's commitment to Bolivia. *You know what, this is my destiny*, he thought. *From small beginnings come great things. Destroying pozo pits is like chipping away at the foundation of a huge, rotten structure. Soon enough the whole thing will collapse and the country will be liberated from the narcos.* Maybe it was his Catholic upbringing that had showered such good fortune on him? In a way, the War on Drugs was a bit like a crusade. Not quite the Holy Inquisition, but still a calling to destroy people who have taken the wrong path in life. Good, honest values were being trampled on by evil and needed stopping. Luckily, his strength of character, and the intensive training received from the most powerful country in the world, allowed him to do something about it. He had a purpose in life, and it felt good.

Some of the officers left the room to look in on the narcos, and Rich made sure to join them. They were held in a room identical to the briefing room, except it had bars across its windows and two buckets of water for a latrine in one corner. The men were sitting on the floor and the remains of a meal lay on a table in the middle.

Rich was struck by just how young some of the men looked. Most of them were in their early twenties and one was so fresh-faced that he must have been a teenager. But *el jefe* was clearly older, and it was he who was sat on the only wooden chair in the room. This was the man in whom UMOPAR had a particular interest, the very same man who had confronted Rich. They did not have long to question him before the national police would arrive for the men, and he sat there staring at them when they entered. Rich watched in amazement as the officers sat cross-legged in front of him and spoke almost reverentially. One of them gave him a cigarette and lit it; another poured a glass of water and handed it to him.

Rich turned to the officer standing guard at the door and whispered, 'What's this shit? This ain't no party!'

The officer laughed and replied, 'Of course not, but, after all, we're all Bolivian in spite of our differences.'

Rich shook his head. He could not believe what he was seeing. *El jefe* laughed at something said by one of the officers, and cigarettes were now being passed to any of the other narcos who wanted one.

'I didn't realise he was going to be getting the star treatment,' said Rich to the officer. 'He is meant to be under arrest, not a guest in a hotel. You need to get him out of here for questioning – and he can stand up when interrogated.'

'Why, would that make him answer the questions more honestly?'

Rich grimaced but said nothing. Turning his attention to the younger men on the floor, he asked, 'What's the story with these guys? They from La Paz street gangs or something?'

The officer waved at one of his colleagues to guard the door and went over to them. The prisoners displayed no animosity. They seemed to understand that this was their situation and simply accepted it. One of the men looked like he had recently been in tears as his eyes were red and swollen. The others just sat there, deflated and resigned to where they found themselves.

Rich's irritation grew as he watched the officer treat the men with compassion and respect. After a few minutes, he returned to Rich.

'They're not hardened criminals,' he said. 'They're just innocent kids.'

Rich shook his head. Wiping some sweat from his forehead and running his fingers through his thick curly black hair, he scanned the prisoners' faces.

'No, I can't see that. I'd say they've been involved in the drug business for maybe two or three years. Most likely they're from farming communities in the Yungas and thought growing coca and processing paste would be more lucrative than doing some hard work in the fields, like the rest of their family? Either that, or they're from La Paz street gangs.'

The officer laughed, which really irritated Rich. He did not like being laughed at.

'No, you're wrong. Of the five young men, three of them are second-year students at the Universidad Católica Boliviana in Cochabamba, all studying civil engineering. The money their parents send isn't enough and they need to work to pay their way through college. The offer of two weeks' work in the Beni came up, paying the equivalent of a year's work in a bar. They chose a pozo pit over a bar, and now they find themselves behind bars,' he replied, without a smile.

Rich was a little stunned. He could see students wanting to make some extra money, but never imagined them getting dragged into the drug business. He knew some students at home dealt in marijuana, and of course the temptation of making a lot of money quickly is attractive, but surely they would have realised the harm they were doing to their fellow students in the US, some of whom would drop out of college once they became addicts?

The boy in the Mickey Mouse boxers had especially irritated Rich, and he had taunted him on their way back to the helicopters. Back then he saw him as a villain, bent on destroying his country back home. But now he was starting to see him as just that, a boy, who had happened to have taken the wrong path in life. Luckily, Rich thought, he had personally halted his life of crime before he was ever able to become a *jefe* himself. A few years in jail would give him time to repent and to see the error of his ways.

After a long pause, Rich finally answered, 'You've got two outcomes in life – you either succeed or you fail. Who knows if they would have succeeded as civil engineers? They failed as narcos, that's for sure.'

The DEA would later discover that the young men were from the *altiplano*, not the Yungas. Their parents were mainly shopkeepers, although one of their fathers was a bus driver. They were all studying for a qualification that would land them one of the most prestigious jobs in South America. Rich knew that their parents would be destroyed by the shame of their arrest, but he blamed them for allowing their sons to study at the city closest to the Chapare and the Beni businesses in the first place.

Rich left the room and went outside, where Jim was standing with Alfonso. Seeing Rich approach, Alfonso quickly broke off the conversation and headed back to the office. It was obvious that he had something to discuss with his partner.

'Good job, Coronel,' Rich said as they passed each other. Alfonso simply waved a hand.

Jim nodded, clearly pleased to see Rich.

'I've just watched UMOPAR questioning the narcos,' Rich said. 'Seems like they are more into bonding than interrogating. What's the deal?'

'It's the Bolivian way,' Jim replied. 'Why fight something that ain't going to change? They do their job well, as you saw, but their hearts tell them they are not on the winning side. They believe Bolivia would not exist without the trade in coca leaves, and no other country is going to step in and help them if they abandon it. No other country supported them when they lost their ports to Chile and when Brazil took land for its rubber boom, so why would they this time?'

'Yeah, but the world is a different place now. Our government wouldn't abandon a country that has supported the War on Drugs, and look at all the dollars we pump in here. We don't just walk away from that sort of investment, right?'

'Sure, but you try convincing UMOPAR that we are here for the long term,' Jim answered. 'They know we walked away from the South Vietnamese and abandoned them to communism. It's a tough one to dispute when they raise it. They may want the drug trade to end, but they can't see it happening.'

'Yeah, well, UMOPAR need to realise that "the wanting" and "the doing" aren't the same thing, not even close,' Rich eventually replied. Turning back towards the building, he added, 'Come on, let's grab a cool soda. It's cooking out here.'

Jim smiled at the patriotism of the DEA agent and stopped him just before they reached the door.

'Listen, I can't say much at this stage, but I think you and I should have a meeting with Don,' he said, lowering his voice. 'We know we can't beat the narcos working with UMOPAR. This is strictly off record, and I don't need to remind you of your duty to protect classified information, but we have finally found a way to destroy the cocaine trade here once and for all without them.'

Rich turned to Jim with a part-disbelieving, part-quizzical look. The official policy was that the US government was assisting the Bolivian anti-narcotics forces to eradicate the drug trade, and

UMOPAR were the essential link between the military and the national police force. If what Jim was suggesting was correct, the US government would be breaking the conditions of their permission to operate in the country, which would make the DEA agents criminals in the eyes of the Bolivian government.

Rich thought for a split-second, then looked Jim in the eye. 'I'm ready to dig ditches if I have to,' he said.

Jim clapped an arm around his shoulder. 'Great. Let's get that cool drink,' he said, heading inside. 'I'll set up a meeting with Don and his military advisers, but things are likely to move quickly, so don't go planning any leave to visit the mines at Potosí or the salt lakes at Uyuni, or some other tourist attraction.'

'I'm no tourist, okay?' Rich replied, irritated by the comment. 'I'm here to win a war,' he said, slotting some coins into the large vending machine.

Jim realised that Rich would fight the war singlehandedly if necessary, before a can of Coca Cola crashed loudly into the dispenser and the young guy swaggered off.

The air conditioning was turned up high and music reverberated loudly around Jim's apartment. It was a basic place in a quiet part of town, but its private sanctum was one of the few privileges that came with being a Grade 14 special agent. Jim grabbed a beer from the fridge and went through to the lounge where side B of *L.A. Woman* was spinning on an old turntable, filling the room with the haunting guitar on the track 'L'America'. He picked up the record cover by the turntable, collapsed on a faded sofa and took a large swig of beer to The Doors' last ever recording.

Reaching down for an old boot, he picked it up, flipped it between his legs and slid the bottom of its heel open. A small packet popped out, the heel snapped back, and he threw the boot back into the corner. Some Rizlas and a cigarette were pulled out from behind a cushion, and Jim got to work with the blues track 'Crawling King Snake' crackling from two speakers fixed to the wall.

The four members of The Doors looked up at him from the iconic sleeve cover balanced on his lap, framed in a yellow rectangle over which the cigarette papers were deftly joined and the tobacco spread. A generous portion of a yellow-brown material was added, the papers rolled together and finally a small filter slotted in at one end. Jim then leant back, lit the twisted end of the papers and took a deep drag. The hit of *basuco* grabbed and shook him, sending small pulses down his fingers that tingled in time to the accompanying bass line and crashing thunder of 'Riders on the Storm'. He closed his eyes.

It was mid-week, and he was determined to have just the one smoke, otherwise he would be jittery in the morning and he could not take the risk of being suspected of using *basuco*. The smoke of coca paste would give him a thirty-minute high, and the day and its challenges were already slipping into a distant haze. Taking another slug of beer to cool his throat, he pulled hard on the *basuco* and exhaled slowly, directing the smoke up to the speakers. *Trying to destroy cocaine is like trying to push back waves*, he thought, *and that ain't happening anytime soon!*

It was Jim who had alerted the Beni cartel to the risk of their coca paste being seized. It had been collected a couple of days earlier by another boat and swapped with the planks picked up by *Tondy*. Alfonso was right: most coca paste found its way to Peru and Colombia, but the cartel now had laboratories in Huanchaca in northern Santa Cruz that were processing the paste into cocaine base and then cocaine hydrochloride. From Santa Cruz it was taken across Brazil and shipped out of Asunción, in Paraguay. The country was not identified as a source of cocaine, so flights to the US were less well monitored.

It was the catastrophic failure of Operation Tandem that had made him realise that no counter-drug effort would ever succeed in a system that had been bought by the drug cartel. Coca delivered too much money into Bolivia for it to be replaced with yam and banana exports, and he knew that hundreds and hundreds of families in the enforcement system relied upon its profits to provide the education and health care they believed their children deserved.

Jim received a monthly supply of *basuco* from the cartel and $30,000 for each operation foiled. The Rio Mamoré deal had netted him an additional $20,000 in a Paraguayan bank account, as the coca paste saved had a value approaching $250,000. He would never endanger another DEA agent or an UMOPAR officer with his information, but he did not see any reason why he should not enjoy the same sort of retirement as the cartel's clientele on Wall Street. In his eyes, they were simply paying him a small token for the luxury of an uninterrupted supply of affordable cocaine.

He finished the *basuco*, swapped *L.A. Woman* over to side A and sat back down to enjoy the music with the last of his beer. Raising the bottle, he laughed loudly. 'Here's to Operation Moses!' he said, and then downed it. The mission would inevitably fail, and moreover, Jim knew that the consequences of its failure would finally kill off the DEA in Bolivia.

Getting himself up, he went back into the kitchen and picked up a *pomelo*. Chopping the top off one end, he squeezed the dark green skin and let the slightly sour juice cool his throat, which had become a little sore from smoking. Slinging the empty husk into the sink, he leant back on the counter and thought about the cool tiled floor and the ocean breeze that would blow through his retirement condo in Boca Raton. He knew that the sun always shone in Florida and that the Coors beer was served ice cold all year round. It gave him a deep feeling of contentment, and anyway, the DEA's days were already numbered in Bolivia. All he was doing was hurrying up its inevitable end.

CHAPTER EIGHT

It was nearly ten o'clock when the express to Trujillo edged out of the depot and pushed its way into the busy traffic that streamed past Expresso Internacional Ormeño's office. Spotting a small gap, the driver swung the bus around the corner and sent a thick cloud of exhaust over a huge wooden sign that was black from years of Ormeño buses leaving the depot and beginning their journeys across Peru. It lingered there for a brief moment and then drifted through the open door of a nearby bus whose exit had been blocked by a taxi. The driver and an approaching official were shouting at a woman scrambling out, but she ignored them both and simply leapt onto the bus with a big grin. Only then could the express to Arequipa start its journey.

Max watched the woman pass his window seat, and he was grateful that she did not take the aisle. A twenty-one-hour journey to Arequipa was going to be hard enough without someone pressed up next to him. Before she had found her seat, the bus was already turning out of the depot and accelerating past an ugly office with peeling mustard-coloured spandrels and a large fluorescent-lit frame hanging in one of its windows. Judging by the set of dentures and a large molar on display, it appeared to be a dentist's surgery, but Max wondered how on earth anyone could be convinced to visit a dentist in a place like that.

The bus continued down Carlos Zavala, past clothes shops, confectionaries, hardware stores and small kiosks selling roast chickens and rooster broth. Turning up Jirón Leticia, it blasted some fumes into a covered market, almost ran over a street vendor and then aggressively pushed up against the traffic before reaching the Pan-American Highway at the start of its twenty-one-hour journey south.

Max settled back and felt excited about what lay ahead. Here he was bumping along on a bus through Lima, in the middle of Peru, in the middle of South America, thousands of miles away from Ian with his floppy grey fringe. He was surprised just how quickly Ian had faded into insignificance, someone who, until very recently, he had held in such contempt. Good luck to him letting office buildings for the next few years, before taking early retirement and moving to Padstow where he would bore the local barman in the Old Custom House pub. Max was absolutely convinced that he had done the right thing. Here he was at the start of his journey to the source of the Amazon. He did not envy Angus the Scot or Ambitious Tim in the slightest. In fact, none of them mattered in the least to him.

Once they reached the Pan-American Highway, the driver put on some salsa and the passengers had to listen to a Colombian singing about how he was never going to leave Barranquilla, where the girls are as beautiful as his country and where he always found hope in life. Max reclined his seat slightly, put a Chiclet into his mouth and chewed away to the syncopated piano and bass line that were pumping out of some old, crackly speakers built into the ceiling of the bus. The noise made listening to his own music on his Walkman impossible.

Before long, the bus was racing down the highway, past block after block of grim concrete and bare brick buildings, broken only by an occasional billboard, factory entrance or petrol station, one of which drew Max's attention, with its graceful jet-black canopy and tasteful orange, white and red logos displayed around its service area. His eye was particularly caught by the elegant rectangular column that advertised the price of fuel, the design of which put the ugly irregular structures behind it to shame.

Three hours later and the highway was still hugging the coastline, squeezed between the sea and the barren hills that stretched up to the *altiplano*. The capital's architectural influence extended down the Pan-American Highway, although its brutalist design was occasionally softened by an owner painting their bricks white, which made wonderful canvasses for the local graffiti artists.

A new salsa tape was now playing, and the same crooner was singing about riding in the mountains and serenading his lover; apparently his heart had melted and he almost passed out when she smiled down at him from her bedroom window. By now, the bus had also picked up some additional passengers and stopped for food, where Ormeño supplemented their revenue with a fee from the restaurant owner. Max's meal of chopped steak in onions, rice and fried vegetables was not bad for a couple of soles, and he grabbed some of their delicious, heavy Peruvian bread pudding for a snack later. The bus was now almost full, but the aisle seat was still free. There was another Westerner on the bus, but he avoided striking up a conversation at the restaurant: not because he was feeling particularly unsociable, but rather to avoid him grabbing his precious spare seat.

Just before six o'clock, they rolled into another service area outside Nazca. The sun had now set and it would be dark in another thirty minutes, so it seemed a sensible option, both for the passengers, who were hungry, and for Ormeño, who needed all the extra revenue they could get. The food option was either pizza or chopped steak in onions again, so Max tucked into a pizza and a Cusqueña beer. To his horror, when he got back on the bus an elderly *campesino* woman in several large skirts was sitting in his seat, presumably because she preferred the window to the aisle. He would have to get her to shift over. *Dammit!* He had travelled for almost ten hours with the seat free, but now someone would be next to him for the hard part of the journey.

Approaching the woman, he showed her his ticket for seat number five with a smile and gestured towards the aisle seat that was hers. To his surprise, she just grinned back and waved her ticket.

'Er, no, *señora*, this is my seat. You'll have to move to this one,' he said, pointing at the aisle seat.

She shook her head and smiled broadly. The distinct smell of *chicha*, a homemade maize alcohol, wafted over Max, and he realised she was most likely topped up for the long evening journey ahead. *Well, that's just great*, he thought as he wondered how he was going to get her out of his seat, never mind manage the next eleven hours or so next to her.

Max showed his ticket once more but was met with more *chicha* breath and a wave of an Ormeño ticket. *Okay*, he thought, *I'll point out her ticket is for seat number six and then maybe she'll move.* He gestured for the woman to hand over the ticket, which she did with an even bigger grin.

'Ah, *señora*, your ticket is for seat number *fifty*-six at the back of the bus. These are seats number five and six,' he said, chuckling, realising that she had got it completely wrong. It was only when the driver intervened that the woman finally got up and wobbled to the back of the bus, leaving Max to wonder if the helpful Quechuan language section in the Lively Places guide had anticipated the situation he had found himself in. *Ah, señora, even though your seat number has two digits, this doesn't entitle you to two seats. It's a little unfortunate that you have been drinking chicha, as double-digit numbering can be confusing at the best of times.* He did not bother digging out the guide from his daypack to check if this particular situation was covered.

Settling back as the bus left Nazca, he took off his money belt and put it in his daypack, which was wrapped around his arm and would be his pillow for the night ahead. A second, smaller cotton bag with his passport, a credit card and two twenty-dollar bills was secured safely down his boxers. Now that the salsa tapes had run their course, Max attached himself to his Sony Walkman and watched the stars twinkle as the highway rushed under him and the bus descended into the pitch black of the coast road towards Arequipa.

He dozed in and out of sleep for the next few hours, safe in the hands of the salsa-loving driver, who was concentrating on the long, dark stretch of highway ahead. He had finished off the bread pudding earlier and was now settled comfortably across the two seats.

The bus slowed just after midnight as it approached some road-works. A large barrier blocked the highway and a group of men in high-vis jackets shone spotlights and waved at the bus to stop. One of them instructed the driver to open the door and half stood on its step so that he could direct the bus across a temporary route at the side of the road. Max awoke as the bus lurched across a particularly rough patch of ground, and he assumed that they were in for yet another Ormeño revenue stop, even though it was in the middle of the night. That said, they had only stopped a few hours ago, so maybe it was just a passenger drop-off in the middle of nowhere. Either way, he decided he was not getting off and closed his eyes again before the bus eventually came to a stop.

The man in the high-vis jacket was now joined by one in army fatigues who clutched a menacing-looking submachine gun. The bus lights came on, and Max peered up over the seats. *Oh, for fuck's sake. It must be a police check-point or something, but at this time of night?* He checked his watch. He knew that the Sendero Luminoso were based in Ayacucho up in the *altiplano*, but since last year they had spread down to the southern coast and the highway was an important north–south transport route, so maybe the police were checking papers and the like? They would probably ignore him, being a Westerner. The man in the fatigues walked up into the bus and looked down at the faces staring back at him. His eyes fell over Max, and he pointed his gun and gestured for him to get off the bus.

Max sighed. 'Do you really need to go through my papers?' he asked.

It turned out that this was not a sensible question to ask, as the man grabbed his arm and roughly pulled him up, cursing loudly.

'Okay, okay,' said Max. He picked up his daypack and made his way off the bus whilst the man with the submachine gun continued down the aisle and selected other passengers to disembark. The Westerner at the back of the bus was soon up from his seat, but Max could not see the *chicha* lady being disturbed. Maybe she was blind drunk and the officer was letting her sleep it off?

Stepping down, Max was pushed hard from behind. Tripping slightly, he looked up and saw that the bus was surrounded by people in fatigues and black masks.

'Oh shit!' he mumbled to himself. It quickly dawned on Max that these were no policemen. Only a few of them had weapons, but even the ones who didn't were seriously intimidating. A bright light then approached Max and shone straight in his face, freezing him to the spot. Expecting a blow, he cowered, but when it reached him, it was simply another push, this time towards a long bench lit with three paraffin lamps. Stumbling over, he joined a Peruvian couple that had been sitting right at the front of the bus.

The lady was emptying her handbag onto the table and sobbing. Her partner had his arm around her. Three smaller people in masks, who Max presumed in the dark were probably women, stood opposite them. Just as another passenger was pushed into Max, he was gestured by one of the women to approach. Nothing was said, but it was obvious what he had to do. He handed over his daypack and watched its contents fall onto the table. Anything remotely of value was put into one of two plastic boxes. He lost his brand-new Pentax ME Super SLR camera and wide-angle lens, and his beloved Sony Walkman went into the box, along with his favourite Colin Dale tape. His money belt was of particular interest, especially the large wad of American Express traveller cheques and the hundred dollars in Peruvian soles.

Anything considered rubbish was thrown over her shoulder, which largely consisted of a rain jacket, a day diary and his Lively Places travel guide. As he watched it fly through the air, he wondered if it contained a helpful section on what to do in the event of a long-distance coach being held up. Once he had been made to empty his pockets and pull up his shirt to show he had nothing hidden underneath, he was done. Or maybe, he thought, done for.

Max shuffled over to the other passengers who had already handed over their belongings. Three queues were now formed in front of the bench, probably half of the entire bus. None of the *campesino* passengers had joined their fellow *mestizo* countrymen. He was *fairly* sure that he was not going to be killed and tried to convince himself that he would be dead by now if that were their intention. But despite the reassuring thought, he was nonetheless gripped by a terror that made his legs shake uncontrollably, for he knew that his life was in the balance. Death faced him for the first time in his life, and he realised that he would only escape if the terrorists so chose, for it was obvious that he was in the hands of the Sendero Luminoso. *Who else would hijack a bus in a military-style operation?*

How come the other men and women are not shaking? Do they know something I don't? Maybe the papers don't report it, but these terrorists don't just ransack buses, they kill people!

He tried to stop his leg shaking, but the hand he placed on it was also trembling.

The luggage from the bus was now unloaded, and the men with torches were tipping out the contents of the cases and ripping open the carefully wrapped packages that were spread out on the ground. It looked like the *campesinos* were not to escape their luggage being rifled through after all. Max noticed a large backpack being emptied of clothes and saw a sleeping bag being stuffed back into it. Presumably this was the other Westerner's pack? To his horror, he saw that his pack was being used as a depository for other items selected from the luggage. His heart sank. He was going to need a pack if he was going to trek to the source of the Amazon, and good ones were difficult to find in Peru. He would get his traveller cheques replaced and had only lost a hundred dollars in cash, but he needed a backpack to start his journey proper.

Then his hiking boots appeared underneath a pile of clothes, and he decided to try and grab them when no one was looking, except a moment later the man with the other backpack took a liking to them and picked them up for himself. Max bowed his head and let out a large sigh. It was then that the other Westerner placed an arm on his shoulder. He would later find out that his name was Sol, but now was not the time for introductions.

'Don't sweat it, dude. We're going to get out of this fine, trust me,' he whispered. Max shrugged. He was still alive, so that was good. All of the passengers were now standing together, and the women at the bench had picked up the boxes full of valuables, so maybe it would soon be over?

But just as Max began to feel more hopeful, a command rang out and three men with submachine guns rushed forward and lined up in front of the passengers. Max stared into a pair of blank eyes behind a sinister mask and began to shake violently. *What the fuck is going on? I can't die here, in the middle of nowhere!*

On a second command, the men raised their firearms, and Max squeezed his eyes shut. He was reconciled to the impending rush of pain that was about to rip through his chest and explode his lungs, but he just wanted it to be quick. There was an interminable pause, and then suddenly a burst of bullets shook his body and forced his eyes wide open. In the shadowy light of the paraffin lamps, he saw the terrorists lower their guns, and only then did he realise that they had discharged a volley of bullets into the night sky. It was simply a crude display of paramilitary power. With guns now at their side, they each raised a clenched fist and shouted.

'Long live the people's war! The people's war towards communism!'

The assembled Peruvian passengers also raised their right fists and repeated the slogan, as though they were well rehearsed and they knew what was expected of them. Max followed Sol's lead and joined in enthusiastically. This was the most sensible, and possibly life-saving, option. *Please let me be a communist, I love communism and hate death*, Max thought as he tried his best to repeat the unfamiliar words.

And then, as if on cue, the terrorists dispersed and started up motorbikes parked behind some bushes whilst the passengers were still screaming: 'Long live the people's war!' The motorbikes emerged with the women riding pillion, clutching their boxes, and the men with guns jumped on behind their comrades. Max watched with delight as his pack disappeared on the back of one of the men in the group. As if the curtain had been dropped on a performance, the passengers were left in silence, stunned, with only the oily smell and shadowy light of the paraffin lamps to remind them that they most definitely were not dreaming.

But it felt like a dream to Max. Had this really happened? He only half heard Sol next to him.

'What was that?' he asked.

'I was saying that everything always works out for the best. We just need to understand the *purpose* of what happened.'

'The purpose? Well, it looks like you lost your pack and valuables as well. Bad luck. I can't believe what just happened.'

'Yeah, of course, that's it, man!'

'That's what?' asked Max.

'The purpose of the hijack. It *needed* to happen to support the poor *campesinos* on the *altiplano*. Out of private misfortune comes public welfare. Okay, getting robbed is unpleasant, but it will bring about good. Our wealth is going to be redistributed more fairly than local taxes collected by the government.'

It took Max a moment to take in what he had just heard, but he still could not believe it.

'What the fuck are you talking about?' He was amazed – they had both come so close to being executed in the middle of nowhere . . .! But then he took a proper look at Sol for the first time. *Of course, he's a fucking hippy!*

Max was done with him, and he left to pick up some of the clothes that had been deemed worthless by the terrorists, along with his day diary. As he no longer had a bag to carry things, he booted away the non-essential guidebook and its 'essential information for every independent traveller'. It would have been helpful had the guide been updated to warn of the danger of night travel on the south coast of Peru since the start of 1991, but Krzysztof, its author, had last visited Peru in 1990.

CHAPTER NINE

Arequipa spreads out on the dry plain beneath Mount Misti. The ancient, snow-capped volcano provided the porous white stone out of which the city was originally built by the Spaniards. The early nineteenth century brought independence, progress and modern building materials to Arequipa, which expanded across the plain in a combination of concrete blocks, hollow clay pot tiles and asphalt. But none of the passengers from Lima seemed to appreciate the transformation from ugly suburb to beautiful city as the bus carried them through the grid of streets towards Ormeño's office just before eleven o'clock in the morning.

It was not only the passengers who had lost money. Ormeño had missed out on a fee from making a breakfast stop, and the four-hour delay meant they had to cancel the eight o'clock service to Lima as there was no bus for the journey. The driver's strict instructions were to proceed to the nearest Ormeño office following any hijack, where a report of the incident would be taken by the police and action taken to apprehend those responsible. There was no way the terrorists would actually be caught after so much time had passed, and everyone was starving, but those were the rules.

Sol had joined Max on the spare seat next to him, and to be honest, Max was pleased to have the company. Their remaining belongings largely consisted of clothes and toiletries that were stuffed into some old shopping bags that one of the passengers had given them. They were the only people on the bus to have lost their bags.

Luckily, Sol hadn't tried out any more of his hippy shit, and Max was more comfortable chatting to him, even though he did not feel particularly sociable. For most of the journey into Arequipa he was lost in his own thoughts anyway and missed the glorious sun that rose slowly behind the *cordillera* and turned the dust beside the highway a deep orange colour. *Why am I always so unlucky?* he thought. *What was the chance of being hijacked by the Sendero Luminoso at the start of my trip? Ormeño and other bus companies run services up and down the coast road every day – why was my bus chosen by the terrorists? I just need some luck for a change . . .*

The other passengers also appeared deep in thought. Some of the *mestizo* Peruvians seemed to be cursing the God that had let them be robbed at gunpoint, whilst others praised the very same God that had delivered them to safety. The woman drunk on *chica* and the other *campesinos* looked like they accepted that this was just the life they lived; sometimes good things happen, other times bad things happen. Maybe having fewer possessions and worries in the world gave them the serenity some of their fellow Peruvians lacked? At least nobody on the bus had to listen anymore to a Colombian singing about his heart bursting and his head spinning when his *morena* blew a kiss; luckily, the driver had decided that belting out salsa music was not appropriate in the circumstances, even though he had been tempted. It seemed obvious to Max that this was not his first hijacking, for he looked totally relaxed about the whole thing.

When the passengers finally arrived at the depot on San Juan de Dios, a couple of police officers were waiting, and before long Max and Sol both had statements for their insurance companies and their American Express travellers cheques had been cancelled. Max was relieved that he had recovered his day diary with the cheque numbers written inside, otherwise he would have had to call his parents and they would have worried. Best that they did not know.

'Let's get some breakfast, dude,' Sol said as they walked into the street. Max had decided not to hang out with him any longer than necessary, but at that moment the prospect of breakfast was too good to turn down.

'Have you got any soles?' Max asked. 'I've only got forty dollars in cash. I'll pay you back when I get to a bank.'

'Forget all that. It's my treat. We're alive and the sun's shining. Breakfast is a small price to pay. Look around,' Sol said, waving a hand at some tatty buildings. 'Arequipa's a great city and we've got everything ahead of us, which is more than could be said for those poor Israelis killed by the Sendero Luminoso in Piura last week. They weren't so lucky.'

Max shook his head and followed Sol down the road with shopping bags in either hand. A few blocks along San Juan de Dios, they found a small café and went in and sat down by the window. Opposite them, men in dark green uniforms with red badges stood chatting beneath a Peruvian flag that hung limply from the wall. This must have been where the police officers were based, but it looked more like a military compound than a police station. A large water cannon was outside, next to which a menacing-looking dark green bus with grills over its windows was parked. Max began to lighten up and wondered if the police here made friendly school visits like they did in England. A bunch of officers turning up in those threatening vehicles would scare the life out of the kids. But maybe that was the point?

'So, Sol. It is Sol, isn't it?' asked Max.

'Yeah, short for Solspang, not Solomon. But you can call me Sol. Everyone does, even my folks, and they were the ones who crafted my unique name in the first place.'

Max sighed. The Westerner had a personalised name, just like a personalised number plate.

'You're going to have to explain that one to me. Has it got something to do with a spring, or the sun, or something like that?'

'Yeah – not a bad guess. I was conceived in a VW Combi on the Marin Headlands. After my birth passage my folks took me back up there, to a quiet spot overlooking the Golden Gate Bridge. It was an early spring morning, sometime in April of sixty-seven. From where they stood, they looked down over the mist that covered everything other than the red supports of the bridge, and, well, the sun was just hitting their rivets and girders. And that was how my parents hit on the name . . . "sol" for sun, and "spang" is an old word for, er, "right in the middle of it". I guess that morning I was the centre of their lives, and the name sort of followed.'

Max's name meant nothing as far as he knew, and he was relieved that his far more conservative parents had not shared any details of his conception.

'Yeah, man,' Sol continued, 'it was pretty cool. My folks actually put some thought into the crafting. Uncle Frank sat in the same spot five months later at midnight and came up with the name Moon Unit for his daughter. He liked the idea that a baby makes a family unit, and well, I guess the moon was bouncing off the bridge when he looked at it. But Moon Unit! It would've been a real downer growing up as Moon Unit. I mean, that's what we used to call boneheads where I grew up.'

'You really are a genuine hippy, aren't you?' Max said, laughing, and then decided to get something off his chest that had been bothering him.

'When we were robbed, that shit about everything being for the best . . . You don't really believe that? You were in shock, right?'

At that moment the *niña* arrived with a tray of toast, jam, scrambled eggs and coffee, and they both tucked in. Sol looked up from the feast in front of him with a piece of toast in his hand.

'This is great, man. Best breakfast I've had in South America.' He started to spread some more jam out on one of the slices and continued, 'I'm not here to try and convince you of anything. I'm just travelling on the road I'm on and trying to spread some kindness on the way. That's my dharma.'

By now the shock of the previous night was starting to fade, and a feeling of well-being was spreading through Max. Spurred on by the delicious toast, scrambled eggs and Colombian coffee, he asked, 'Your what? I've got no idea what you're on about.'

'Dharma, man. It just means the right way of living, you know, if you want a cosmic balance. Sort of a Buddhist thing, but not really. It's open to everyone.'

'So you're a Buddhist?'

'No, I'm a Humanarian.'

'What the hell is a Humanarian?'

'Someone who is into human well-being.'

'A Humanarian? That's priceless, mate. I've got to use that one when I get home! You know what?' he said, taking an exaggerated sip of coffee. 'I'm into coffee. I guess that makes me a Cafetièrian?' Max burst out laughing, having tickled himself no end, but he could tell that Sol did not find it very funny.

For the first time, Sol looked irritated by the British traveller.

'Listen, when your parents made you say prayers at night as a kid, did it make a difference to you? Did you feel anything?' Max shrugged and continued eating his eggs. 'Well, we sat crossed-legged as a family, held hands and would repeat Uncle Frank's mantra at night, and we're all grounded, man, none of us are bobbing around on life's ocean without a mast,' Sol said firmly.

Max could tell that Sol was annoyed by his remark and wondered if he saw him bobbing, lost at sea.

'Just ignore me. I'm not normally like this. I think having a gun shoved in my face has something to do with it,' Max apologised. 'I could probably do with some of your optimism right now, if I'm being honest. Is it Uncle Frank's mantra that has given you such an optimistic outlook on life? If it's not private, can you repeat it for me?' he asked, a little abashed.

'It's not private. Millions know it. Uncle Frank put it on an album he sold back in the day. He was in a band with a bunch of guys called the Mothers of Invention who created a mix of music and poetry,' Sol replied, putting down his coffee and looking Max in the eye. 'If you want the secret of optimism, you've got to start by realising that you are the luckiest person on the planet. At first, you'll struggle with the cause and effect of what hits you, but soon you'll realise that everything has a purpose. So, what we used to do is repeat the mantra for ten minutes every night before we embarked on our sleep journey.'

Sol closed his eyes, as if drawing out the words from deep within, and recited:

We will find a place where anyone who is lonely
can jump and spin and dance in love;
We will find a place where our spirits will rise
and crush all wickedness from far above.

Sol opened his eyes, beaming a little. Max looked down awkwardly and just picked up his knife to cut a piece of toast. He did not quite know what to make of it.

After breakfast they made cash withdrawals at Banco de Crédito, just off the majestic Plaza de Armas. Luckily, they both had slightly sweaty but secure 'boxer bags' containing a credit card and their passports; otherwise they would have been stuck waiting for new travellers cheques to arrive. The bank was also an agent for American Express, so their replacement cheques were ordered for the following day, and they left to find a hostel to drop off their shopping bags.

Sol had been recommended Hostal Nuñez on Jerusalén but wanted to stop off at the Central Post Office on their way. The large concrete-framed building on Calle Moral had been built twenty years earlier, and it looked a bit like a Lego construction with exposed beams hanging over the pavement in which pigeons roosted. Inside, it was like any other post office, and the Lista de Correos had five new letters waiting for Sol, which he added to the others that he had read at least a dozen times. Max had not been away long enough for people to write, but he had given the Central Post Office as a contact point and hoped to receive some letters when he returned from the source of the Amazon.

The next few days they wandered around the local sights and tried to find some new luggage. The only packs on sale were cheap green polyester bags attached to silver L-frames, but the hostel owner told them of a large market in Puno where trekkers leaving Peru frequently sold packs to raise cash before heading into Bolivia, and Max and Sol decided to head up there. In fact, despite the unfortunate circumstances in which they had met, they were beginning to enjoy each other's company.

The road up to Puno was in poor condition, so they bought a Pullman-class seat on the nine o'clock evening train and arrived in

Puno on the edge of Lake Titicaca the following morning. From there, they had decided to visit the famous Uros floating islands before Max headed off to Mount Misti and Sol went into Bolivia. Both of them hoped to pick up a decent pack in the market, but for the time being they each had to make do with large barrel bags, which were for now, at least, a huge improvement on the shopping bags.

CHAPTER TEN

Federico found the rusty corrugated sheet at the side of the road. It had been thrown away, along with some broken concrete and floor tiles from a building site. With his bolt cutters he deftly cut out a section of the metal sheet and began to shape it into a jagged, long, thin triangle with a sharp point at one end and a small rectangular handle at the other. Tightening it in a vice, he straightened out most of the corrugation and finished off the remaining kinks with a lump hammer on a wooden plank. He had borrowed a brace drill, which he used to make two equal-spaced holes in the small rectangle and four pilot holes in a block of wood, cut in half on the floor. The handle fitted neatly into the small recess he had chiselled into one of the blocks. All that remained was to drill through the wood, fix two bolts through the metal and then screw the blocks together, which he did in no time. Picking up his creation, Federico stood with the knife pointed to the floor and the handle level with his hip. The next hour he would spend sharpening it.

Out on Lake Titicaca, Max and Sol sat on the edge of a wooden boat with some other travellers. A few of them were wearing red-and-white knitted woollen hats with pointy ends that flopped down the back of their necks. Others, like Max and Sol, just wore ordinary beanie hats. It was early in the morning and a light mist drifted over the surface of the lake, hiding a family of Andean Coots that screeched as they bobbed up and down in the wake of the disappearing boat. Puno was still a further two and a half hours away on the vast expanse of water that made the small boat seem equally insignificant.

Max and Sol had come prepared with alpaca jumpers bought in Puno, but it had still been cold on the island of Taquile, where they had stayed with a local family for the past two nights. The instant Nescafé at breakfast had gone some way to warming them up, but they would have to wait for the mid-morning sun to arrive before they were comfortable.

'Man, this is where it's at. I wish I'd bought a knitted hat now. They're sort of cool. I mean, they're practical as well as cool. Wow, this is the coldest I've been in Peru,' said Sol, and Max saw a shiver run through his body. But even that brought a smile to his face, as though he found pleasure in discomfort. Max had grown to like the tall American with his matted brown hair and permanent smile. He had never met anyone who took such pleasure in all kinds of sensations, and Max looked at him somewhat curiously.

'Sol, mate, how is it you enjoy every experience, good or bad? You could be tied to the back of the boat and dragged all the way back to Puno through the freezing water and you'd still come out smiling.'

Sol laughed. 'I just think if we don't meet with something agreeable, at least we can enjoy something new,' he replied. 'When was the last time you were cruising over the highest lake in the world waiting for the sun to warm you up? I mean, man, this is *real*. Being in a comfy, warm boat and snoozing through the experience is no experience at all.'

Max took his point, and even though he was bitterly cold, he was *sort* of enjoying the journey back.

The market in Puno would be where they would find the vendors with camping gear, beyond the agricultural machinery, fertiliser and farming tool stalls. They had been told to look out for a woman selling nothing but bright plastic buckets, and they would find the camping stalls set out right next to her. This was the day when they would get new backpacks and go their separate ways. But he was starting to realise that he would miss Sol, with his endless optimism and his unusual talent for finding the best in any situation. Even though his take on the hijacking was insane, he could see there was actually some merit to his other observations.

Watching the lake slip under the prow of the boat, Max thought, *Perhaps there was a purpose to what happened to me at the firm. As Sol says, everything has its purpose, and maybe something bad creates something good elsewhere? Mind you, the only good that came from having my contract doctored was to help Roe appear efficient. Oh, and of course it allowed Ian to bully me, so that was good for him. He called me a liar and a troublemaker and I didn't even challenge him. Why did I let such an obnoxious person push me around like that? And it's not as if he could have sacked me. I'd already been sacked! Shit, no wonder the firm got rid of you.*

Unbeknownst to Max, Sol had his eye on him and was watching his expression. Max was far off, unaware of the scowls that flashed across his face. During his time with Max, he had noticed how he would often fade away a little, and he could tell that he was turning something over and over in his mind. If only Max could rid himself of whatever it was that was torturing him. If only he could see it from a new perspective. He would then realise that it paled in significance to the world around him and that it did not matter at all.

When they visited the Uros Islands on their way to Taquile, both of them ended up accidentally stepping off the dry reed path into the water, which soaked their feet. For Sol it was funny, for Max it was irritating. Sol laughed at it again when they were eating that evening but realised that, for some bizarre reason, Max had taken his misstep as a sign of weakness.

'I mean, you got your feet wet on an island made of reeds floating on the lake. What do you expect?' Sol found it hard to understand. He knew people back home who seemed to take great pleasure by dwelling in displeasure, which also puzzled him.

The boat would take just over three hours to reach Puno. It gave them plenty of time to decide how best to get warm, which, despite the beauty of the lake around them, was all they could really think about. The walk up to their hostel on Avenida La Torre, where they had left most of their things, was quite a distance from the port, and the showers there were only lukewarm. So Sol came up with the idea of having a hot, luxurious shower at the public baths in the city centre, and this plan became their sole focus for the remainder of the journey.

It turned out that the showers at the public baths were not that luxurious; rather, they were a little grimy. But they were most definitely hot, so hot that they teetered on the point of scolding. Max luxuriated under the spray, eyes closed, and did not really want to ever leave. Half an hour later they both emerged refreshed and ready for the central market. But first they found a reasonable looking *chifa*, or Chinese restaurant, on a street named Jirón Fermin Arbulu, and went in for a cheap buffet lunch.

Sitting on a shiny black lacquered chair, with a brilliant red cushion beneath him and a swirly dragon behind, Max tucked into a plate of lemon chicken, hoisin duck and rice. He had left his storm cloud bobbing up and down on the boat on Lake Titicaca and was feeling pretty good. Spreading the hoisin sauce over the chicken and rice that had only cost him a single sol, he chuckled.

'I've just realised the Peruvians named their national currency after you. How *did* your folks manage that? Their word craft must be the real deal.'

Sol shook his head. 'What's that phrase you Brits come out with . . . something like "don't take the piss",' he said, laughing.

Max was reminded that the outdated Lively Places guide still being sold in WH Smith no longer even listed the correct currency for Peru. When Krzysztof and his pals last visited the country in 1990, they spent inti at a rate of sixty-two thousand to the dollar. With a new currency now in circulation, their section on 'Money' was even less relevant than the other 'Essential Information' that was currently blowing around on dried-up pages somewhere near the coast road.

They spent the next hour or so chatting like the good friends they had become, before leaving for the huge central market a few blocks up from the *chifa*. On their way, they passed three elderly *campesino* women sitting on the pavement, covered in layers of skirt and wearing a selection of blue and pink patterned aprons. They were selling onions and potatoes from a low metal cart and toilet rolls from a huge clear plastic bag. Either they had been barred from selling in the market or they did not want to pay a stall fee. They didn't look like they partied much to Max, so he concluded they were saving on fees, rather than having disgraced themselves on *chicha*.

Passing under the large canvas sign welcoming them to the Central Market of Puno, they were met by an array of vivid colour, by short fat ladies wearing bustling red and black mushroom skirts, straw hats, pleated jet-black hair, by little people, by laughter, shouting, the smell of mud, the sight of raw meat, and mounds and mounds of potatoes that spilled over the floor. The produce soon gave way to wool jumpers, hats, jeans, jackets, and finally, the stall of plastic buckets that Max and Sol had been seeking. And there it was, right alongside it, a single but crowded stall. Around a dozen medium and large packs hung from a metal frame over the stand, with sleeping bags, hiking boots, stoves, head lamps, gloves, waterproof jackets and aluminium plates laid out down below. Max spotted a large red North Face pack that looked pretty similar to the one he had lost and asked the owner to bring it down so he could take a look.

As the red pack swung towards him on a wooden pole, he saw a distinctive patch on one of its side pockets. Grabbing it, he pulled the patch closer to him.

'That's my Manchester Hacienda patch! This doesn't just *look* like my pack, this *is* my pack,' he said, quickly taking it off the pole. Inside he found the label with his name spelled out in capital letters, and outside he found another label with '150 soles' written on it.

He looked the vendor in the eye. 'This is my pack.'

'Hundred and fifty soles,' the vendor replied.

No, he didn't want to buy it. He wanted it back. 'No, this is my pack.'

'Yes, your pack, for hundred and fifty soles.'

'You don't understand. This was stolen from me last week, at gunpoint. It *belongs* to me. Look,' Max said, turning the inside of the pack towards the vendor. 'Max Hansell. *I'm* Max Hansell.'

'Where you from?'

'England.'

'Must be very common name in England. That was the name of the gringo that sold it to me.'

'Listen, there's only one Max Hansell in Peru and probably the whole of South America right now. And you want a hundred and fifty soles for my pack? I paid less for it new.'

Either the Sendero Luminoso had sold the pack to the stall owner or he was associated with them. Sol stepped in.

'Man, this is bad karma,' he said to the stall owner. 'I think you've got a pack that was stolen from this dude. Max, show him your passport.' Max dug it out of his pocket and showed it to the man as though he were airport security. He glanced at it for a second and then back at Max.

'So what?'

'It says it right here,' said Max, pointing at the name. 'Maximilian Hansell. See?' He then held the passport up to his head and pointed at the photo.

'You don't look the same,' said the man. 'Fake passport?'

Granted, the photo was by that point quite out of date, and it was no longer the best likeness.

Then the man just lost patience and picked up the pack from the table. But Max grabbed it, and what followed was a short battle of wills, with each one pulling at it from either side before the man eventually won, snatching it away and quickly swinging it up on his pole, where it was hung out of reach with all of the other packs.

'Make him an offer,' said Sol, his voice lowered.

'What?' said Max, turning his head away a little from the stall owner. 'I'm not paying him.'

'You want your pack back, you're going to have to pay for it. There's no way you're getting that pack without stealing it, and you know that's not going to work. Make him an offer.'

Max was infuriated. He knew that he needed that pack if he wanted to continue his journey. He had looked everywhere for the perfect pack, had found it, but now it was hanging out of reach. He turned back to the stall owner and could not believe he was about to haggle for his own property.

'Look, help me, *señor*,' he said, taking a different tack. 'I was robbed by the Sendero Luminoso. They stole my money and my backpack. Somehow, you've ended up with it through no fault of your own,' he continued, though not at all convinced. 'But I'm also guessing that you did not pay one hundred and fifty soles for it. I'm going to make you an offer right now. I'll give you seventy-five soles, no questions asked.'

He did not look impressed. 'Seventy-five? One hundred and fifty.'

'No, one hundred and fifty is more than I paid for it new. How about eighty?'

The vendor looked like he was getting tired. 'One hundred and fifty,' he said again.

'Come on, help me out. I was robbed. Make me an offer.'

'Okay, I'll make you offer. This pack and a sleeping bag, one hundred and sixty soles,' he said, nodding at a rolled bag in a blue cover and slapping his hands as if the deal was done.

Max could not believe that he was counting out one hundred and sixty soles and passing them to the vendor, who laughed a little when he took the pack down, but it felt good to be reunited with his old pack again. He then watched Sol try out some others and hand over yet another one hundred and fifty. Max still needed a pair of hiking boots, but there was no way he was going to give that man any more money, and he suggested that they leave the market.

Sol put an arm around his shoulder.

'For sure – let's go celebrate.'

'Celebrate?' asked Max.

'Of course. That guy was a crook, but you've got your old pack back and I've got a new lucky pack. This is the beginning of our next journey. Let's head back to the hostel and grab a beer.'

'You go ahead. I need to get some boots and maybe a camera, if I can find one,' Max replied. 'Do me a favour, take my daypack, will you? I don't want to be wandering around Puno with valuables once it gets dark. I'm short on soles, but will use my credit card if I find anything decent.' He removed the card from his money belt and shoved it into his boxer bag.

'Okay, how about we meet at the *chifa* at seven for dinner?'

'Sorted,' replied Max, and the pair of them walked off, Sol up to Hostal Don Miguel on Avenida La Torre and Max down into the centre of Puno. He was surprised to find a spring in his step.

Max cast an eye up at the storm that was now rolling over the city. Out of nowhere he watched a bolt of lightning light up a dismal hill of bare brick buildings before plunging them back into darkness and delivering a peal of thunder that exploded over the streets below. The torrential rain that followed poured from the edges of flat roofs, out of broken gutters, over blue plastic sheets covering shop stalls and down cobbled streets that glistened in a torrent of water and mud. And yet Puno was still alive with people scrambling for shelter, frantically waving for taxis or being picked up, like the woman he saw lifted into the cage of her husband's three-wheeled delivery bike before being whisked down the street covered in a plastic sheet.

When the rain finally eased, Max took a map from his pocket and checked the route back to the hostel. Finding a new pack would have to do. It was too much hassle shopping for boots in the rain, and he was going to join Sol for that beer after all.

Federico watched him emerge from beneath the shelter of a dripping canopy and walk casually along Calle Pardo. Not only had he been carefully followed for over an hour, but he had made it easy by being completely unaware of who was around him. He felt safe in the throng of people, but Federico knew that he would eventually tire of the shops and leave the crowds to find another outlet for his leisure. He had waited patiently with his two partners, watching the lone gringo, rich and exposed: no match for the three men now tracking him along Calle Pardo.

Once Max reached a stretch of Avenida La Torre that was devoid of shops and empty of people, the men quickened their step and closed in on him. The first man locked an arm around his neck and pulled him roughly into a small passageway where the rain once more pelted down onto the jagged edge of a crudely made knife held by his face. Another man stood in front and demanded money. Max froze. Time seemed to stop and his body seized up. He could hear the traffic on Avenida La Torre, but it sounded muffled and somewhat distant. The man in front frantically waved his arms and repeated his demand for *plata*, and only then did Max start to focus. *Plata? Plata? Plate . . .? Why would he want a plate? Ah, no, plata! Money! Yes, of course, money. Money or my life.*

The arm around his throat relaxed and he gasped for air, yet Federico still held the knife tight to his face where it could stab his eye with the slightest movement.

'*Sí, sí, plata.*' Max's voice trembled as he pulled out his pockets, mindful of the vicious blade. Shaking, he handed over all his money and then pulled up his shirt to show that he did not have a money belt.

The man behind him checked his back pockets, pulled off the backpack and then threw it to the man in front, who cursed loudly when he found nothing inside but a sleeping bag. He booted the backpack away in disgust, and Max watched it sail across the passageway as the three of them slipped off silently into the night, along with their terrifying blade. Sobbing, he crumpled to the ground with the rain pouring down his face and over his legs, which were splayed out, shaking, unable to lift his sodden frame from the mud and rubbish in which it lay.

CHAPTER ELEVEN

Sol and Esther walked into the hostel courtyard with a cup in each hand. The mass of coca leaves swirling in steaming green water was a cure for the altitude sickness from which she was suffering. But it was also neat to be drinking the bitter and authentically local drink in the middle of La Paz, even if feeling fine.

Esther handed a cup to Moshe, who smiled a thank you. Max was too busy staring at a cat asleep in the courtyard to notice, so Sol just left it on the table for him. Outside, the traffic hummed up and down Calle Socabaya, shopkeepers shouted at passing trade, and the city buzzed, alive and vibrant just beyond the colonial façade of the hostel.

'Yeah, get a load of this coca leaf tea, Esther. You'll start feeling better before long. Neither of us suffered when we got to the *altiplano*, did we, man?' Sol asked Max, but with no reply.

He clicked his fingers at him. 'Dude, come back to me. I was saying you missed out on altitude sickness up on Lake Titicaca.'

'Huh?' Max mumbled. 'That was just something that went my way, I guess.'

Moshe took a sip of his tea and thought a bit of conversation might cheer Max up.

'What's the best thing you did in Peru?' he asked him. 'We're heading south, down to Chile and Argentina, but we'd like to make it to Peru at some point.'

'Leave it,' said Max.

'What?' he asked.

'The best thing I did in Peru was to leave it.'

Max went back to staring at the cat, which was now wide awake, and its sharp eyes were tracking a scabby pigeon pecking its way across the courtyard. Sol raised his eyebrows at the Israelis opposite him. Max had been in a deep depression for a few days, and it was only by waving a bus ticket to La Paz that Sol had managed to extract him from his room.

'You know what?' he muttered. 'That pigeon and cat are a thousand times less miserable than me.' Only Sol really heard him; the Israeli couple did not quite catch what he had said, despite their English being near perfect. Sol looked over at the pigeon, which seemed unaware of the threat it faced, and took a sip of his tea.

Esther thought she would have a go at cheering up this weird English guy.

'I love some of the British music we get in Tel Aviv, especially Robert Palmer and Dire Straits. You're so lucky having such good music in your country.' Actually, Max thought Robert Palmer sang turgid, boring, unimaginative songs written for people who tapped their feet to supermarket music, but he chose not to share his opinion with the friendly woman opposite.

'Well, yeah, Mark Knopfler can play the guitar,' said Max, 'but that awful headband he wears sort of consigns him to the seventies. It's a bit like watching John McEnroe rocking out with his tennis racket. Well, "Sultans of Swing" *is* a bit of a racket, come to think of it.'

Esther just smiled. Maybe music was not his thing. 'I think you need cheering up. You seem sad about something.'

'Yes. Because I lived,' he said, not looking any of them in the eye.

'Sorry, I don't understand,' she replied.

'I'm bitter because I've lived,' Max said, turning back towards the cat. Esther and Moshe finished their tea and left Max and Sol to themselves.

For the rest of the day Sol looked after Max. He knew that the mugging in Puno had hit him hard. What he did not know was that no matter how hard he tried, the mean-spirited way he had been treated in London ran deep, and it would take more than Sol's encouragement to expunge his feeling of failure.

Sol had enjoyed the bus trip across the *altiplano*, with its adobe brick houses, coarse tussock grass and backdrop of snow-capped mountains. He kept looking out for La Paz, which he expected to see in the distance anytime soon, but the flat, barren *altiplano* continued endlessly, and he had just resigned himself to a late arrival in Bolivia's capital when suddenly the bus dropped into an enormous chasm and there was La Paz below him. 'Bang, man, awesome!' Next to him, he knew that Max had not noticed much since leaving Puno.

For the next few days, Max stayed in the hostel drinking tea and reading books, sometimes in the courtyard, other times in bed. He had lost his copy of Gabriel García Márquez's *The General in His Labyrinth*, but the hostel had a battered paperback of *One Hundred Years of Solitude*, so he set himself the task of finishing the novel with its ghostly apparitions and confusing jumble of names. Besides, the life described in it reminded him a bit of Ireland, where the transcendent also mixed with the mundane in a casual acceptance of the supernatural, and it felt strangely familiar to him. His mother firmly believed in fairy rings on which no building should be built, and indeed none *were* ever built lest they fall down. 'Shake Hands William' lived in a disused well, down which he had pulled one of the village children in 1937, and the Virgin Mary had appeared as a visitation at Knock, only fourteen miles away. The supernatural was most definitely woven into everyday life in Toocanagh, much like the village of Macondo in *One Hundred Years of Solitude*.

It got him thinking about the account of his great-uncle, who had emigrated to America on the instructions of a celestial figure perched in a yew tree. It was straight out of *One Hundred Years of Solitude*, but it was accepted as a fact in the same way as the apparition of Our Lady of Knock was thirty-six years earlier. Max was less convinced by the supernatural than his mother, but it felt very real when visiting Toocanagh, despite seeming ridiculous in England. The ghost of his grandfather had once stood over his brother in the old family home and woken him gently; in a way Max was a little jealous, and he hoped for a somewhat similar experience on the continent that was renowned for its tales of the supernatural.

Within a few days he had recovered enough to join Sol, Esther and Moshe one morning for a coffee on Avenida Perez Velasco. The coffee was delicious, yet the real attraction lay in the large avenue in front, swarming with small white buses that were identical but for the red, dark green or blue stripes that ran down their sides. Each new arrival attracted a fresh surge of bulbous skirts, patterned aprons and light brown bowler hats or old ski jackets and jeans pushing to get on as people scrambled to get off. Yet the mayhem worked, and the mass of people that ebbed and flowed across Avenida Perez Velasco seemed to be safely delivered and collected from the street.

Sol stirred his coffee and turned to Max.

'Dude, you should join us. The Yungas is where it's at. It's warm, green, friendly, and you could go on from there into the lowlands and the Amazon.'

Sol, Esther and Moshe had visited the various markets at Plaza San Francisco, on Sagarnaga and along Santa Cruz de la Sierra. Despite being in the capital, there was now little else to do other than go to one of the numerous cinemas. For that reason, along with Esther's altitude sickness, they had decided to leave La Paz and head down to the Yungas.

Max did not like being reminded that he had failed to get to the source of the Amazon, and his shoulders sagged slightly.

'Yeah, come with us, Max. We're just going to chill by a pool in the sun. That's all I feel up to anyway,' Esther added. Sol had told her about Max's run of bad luck, and he could tell that she felt sorry for him.

'Maybe,' he said. 'That could be good. I'm sorry if I haven't been the best company. Bad luck seems to be following me around at the moment.'

She nodded sympathetically.

Max knew that, ultimately, he had not been seriously hurt and it could have been so much worse. And yet he blamed himself for being mugged. It was his fault for going off on his own, for not being more aware of his surroundings and for having too much faith in people. And he didn't like having to discuss it. He didn't like the questions Esther and Moshe asked and the pity that had become almost permanently embedded in their voices whenever they said anything to him. And, more privately, his failure as a traveller brought back painful memories of his failure back in London, of his redundancy and of his fleeing his country with his pack, his Walkman and his guidebook. He thought that perhaps he had been a coward to flee and a fool to think that none of his problems would follow him halfway around the world.

On the other hand, he knew that he had to sound positive, and with that in mind, and only the slightest pause, he put on a brave face and continued.

'I was aiming to get to the source of the Amazon. Perhaps that wasn't to be? If I came with you, maybe I could get to the end of the river instead? Do any of you know anything about getting down the Amazon? My guidebook was lost. What does your *South American Handbook* say? Is there a section on the Amazon River in it?'

Moshe smiled and handed him their guidebook. Of course, it was far superior to the one Max had lost and contained all the information anyone needed about travelling down the river's tributaries and joining the huge expanse of water to the Atlantic Ocean. For the rest of the day Max pored through its pages, and by the end of it he had come up with a rudimentary plan of how to reach the end of the Amazon.

The following day they boarded a Flota Yungeña minibus to Coroico via 'The Death Road', as it was known. At first, the wide, smooth section of tarmac crossing the *altiplano* convinced them that the dangers of the journey had been massively exaggerated. Nowhere were the legendary precipitous drops or narrow roads to be seen, and they all relaxed. That was until the bus left the tarmac for a gravel road that descended into a deep, bottomless valley. Each stretch of the twisting, unpaved, mainly single-track road they now passed seemed to crumble and send a cascade of gravel plunging into the depths below, past crudely made crosses that marked the point where another vehicle had slipped off. Deep in the valley, the scattered, crumpled minibuses were too small to be spotted, and only the wheels of upturned lorries could be seen. The very same lorries used the road intensively and seemed to approach the minibus head on, squeezing it towards the edge of the road, which lacked even the most basic of barriers, before trundling off up the valley.

And yet they did survive, and Coroico finally came into view after a total journey time of three and a half hours. They quickly secured rooms at Hostal Kory, where Esther not only found the pool she wanted and Moshe found his view of lush green forest, but Max also rediscovered his sense of humour. As for Sol . . . well, Sol wasn't searching for anything. He was perfectly happy in the best of all possible worlds.

Later, they stood at a makeshift counter drinking large bottles of Pilsner in a rundown building that was the principal social venue in Coroico. It was dimly lit and full of men who had come to watch a local beauty contest organised by the *ayuntamiento*, or town hall. They were keenly aware of being watched and assumed it was because they stood out amongst the locals. Gradually, they realised that it was because they had a bottle of Pilsner each, whereas the groups of young men shared a single bottle between them.

At one end of the hall, behind two rickety old wooden doors, basic male and female toilet facilities had been added by the *ayuntamiento*. One of them swung open, and out of nowhere the acrid, biting smell of urine wafted into the hall, followed quickly by six beauty contestants who rushed down a narrow gauntlet of men and climbed onto a low stage wearing just clumpy sandals and skimpy bikinis. Then a man with a booming mike and a shiny gold jacket joined them, and that was the signal for the men to approach the stage and gawp at the poor girls vying to be Miss Coroico 1992. An annual beauty contest was the last thing they had expected, and Max thought it all quite bizarre.

It was almost midnight when they returned to Hostal Kory in good spirits, clutching more beer from the makeshift bar. Pulling up seats on Esther and Moshe's balcony, they looked down over the pool and across to the dark forest that stretched far beyond Coroico into the lowlands below.

'Those crosses on the road were creepy, weren't they?' said Esther, shuddering a little.

'For sure,' added Moshe. 'We came so close to slipping off the road, but that driver didn't seem to care.'

'That would've been a downer,' said Sol. 'Literally.' He laughed to himself.

Warmed by the delicious salteñas he had eaten with the Pilsner beer, Max decided that this was an ideal opportunity to prod his newfound friend about his eternal optimism.

'There you have it, mate, you said it yourself. Disappearing off the edge of a cliff would be a personal disaster entirely independent of cause and effect and would be a situation that no amount of optimism could improve.'

Sol laughed.

'You're talking about the microcosm of an individual, dude. As Uncle Frank puts it, we're on a globe spinning on the axis of greatness; all our actions ultimately have good consequences. You see dead drivers and rusted axles; I see the lives they saved by warning of the dangers ahead.'

'Hey, don't tell me you listen to the Mothers of Invention?' asked Moshe, whose musical tastes were slightly less mainstream than his girlfriend's.

'He's my uncle, man. Well, spiritual uncle. I don't think he's actually a blood relation.'

'Oh, come on,' interrupted Max. 'So, what would he have to say about my mugging? What good would that have brought into the world? You'd probably say I helped pay for the schooling of one of the mugger's kids – that was charitable of me!'

Sol turned back to him and chuckled. 'I'm not really sure. Maybe there's something even bigger going on that took you away from the source of the Amazon. Who can say, but you're on a new journey now, and maybe this is the journey you were always meant to be on. Maybe something awesome's going to happen, and you're going to look back at the mugging and see it as a crossroads in your life.'

He took a swig of beer and gulped it down. 'Uncle Frank would've told you that your troubles in Peru are just the shadows in a beautiful picture. Take a step back and enjoy the picture in front of you, dude. Do you know anyone who's woken up to snow-capped mountains, escaped near death on a Flota Yungeña bus, eaten salteñas, drunk beer surrounded by Bolivians cheering girls in bikinis and enjoyed a beer with friends looking down over the glorious Yungas? I mean, all on the same day, man!'

Sol was right. Today was an experience he would never forget. He was starting to feel stronger in himself. He knew that there were so many positive things to take from today. He just needed to stop and appreciate them.

The next few days were spent relaxing and enjoying the wonderful climate and stunning views across the misty Yungas. Sol had become attached to some local farmers he had met, or rather, they had become attached to him, for he was such a pleasure to be with. Back at the hostel he had explained to them how they were being suppressed by the Bolivian government. In 1988 it became illegal to cultivate coca plants outside so-called 'zones of traditional production', which included most of the Yungas but excluded much of the land their relations farmed in the Chapare, Carrasco, Tiraque and Arani provinces in the Cochabamba region. At least farmers in these provinces were being offered compensation for the eradication of their coca crops; anyone unlucky enough to be outside these provinces received nothing.

Apparently, a young guy called Evo Morales was organising protests against the government's efforts to eradicate coca. He had publicly denounced the War on Drugs as an imperialist violation of his indigenous culture, and Sol was going to head across to the Chapare and help marshal Evo's *cocaleros* into a coherent protest group. His family had years of experience protesting against the federal government, and he knew he could help the local farmers in the fight to protect their livelihood.

Max was sad when the day arrived for Sol to leave, but he was determined not to waste the experience of being with him for almost a month. He was determined to try and follow his approach to life and look for something positive each day, no matter how small it might seem. Esther and Moshe were heading further down into the Yungas, to a small place called Guanay, where they planned on catching a boat to Rurrenabaque in the lowlands, and he had agreed to join them. His plan was to continue on from there to Riberalta and eventually reach the Rondônia region of Brazil, where the Rio Medeira would take him into the Amazon River, just past Manaus.

As they parted, Max knew that they would meet again.

'Sol, I wouldn't be here without you. If I can ever repay you or help in some small way, promise you'll contact me.'

'Appreciated, dude. You just need to take a step back and ditch that monkey on your shoulder. You're going to have an awesome time in Bolivia and achieve great things. Take each small peak as it comes, man. Don't worry about the next one. Just focus on what is in front of you.'

He hugged Max, waved to Esther and Moshe and disappeared into a white bus with blue stripes and a split windscreen with the words 'Flota Yungeña' written in large black letters above. His pack then slid precariously down the roof rack of the bus as it lurched off towards Coripata, where women wearing bowler hats and mushroom skirts waited for it with plastic bags full of coca leaves and the odd bottle of *chica*.

Max awoke the following morning with stomach cramps. Moshe was also suffering, so they both avoided breakfast and sat groaning as Esther enjoyed her toast, fruit and coffee in front of them.

'I feel as rotten as you look, Mosh. Did you eat the same as me last night?'

'Yeah, the *pique macho*. Maybe the meat was off?' he replied, letting out an enormous burp. An invisible cloud of pungent sulphur fumes spread over Esther and Max.

'That's foul, Mosh! What's wrong with you?' Esther said as she sat back from her half-eaten plate of fruit.

He let off another burst, and some people nearby looked over in disgust. It was not long before the owner came across and kicked all three of them out of the restaurant. Outside, Max retched and brought up a yellow liquid, followed by some meat and onions from the previous evening. Moshe managed to keep control of his stomach but dashed back to the hostel and locked himself in one of the toilet cubicles. The next few days both of them became reconciled to the giardia parasites that were lodged in their digestive tracts. They wondered if they'd caught them from something they ate in La Paz, but the *pique macho* served up in Casa Felipe was the villain in their eyes.

Within a few days they were back eating, but only the plainest food possible, and they decided to brave the journey to Guanay. Stocked up with water, dry biscuits and a little bit of sympathy from Esther, they boarded a bus identical to the one Sol had caught. The journey down to Guanay made their trip to Coroico seem like a gentle drive. This one was terrifying, with narrow, broken roads, and it felt like it was never going to end. It was deeply unpleasant, both for the Westerners worrying about upturned lorries and for the local farmers suffering from sulphur gas attacks. Max and Moshe realised they could direct their silent, rotten-egg burps by cupping their hands, which of course gave them immense schoolboy pleasure, especially when the selected victim struggled in a vain attempt to open a sliding window that had not slid open for a good many years.

Eventually, at the end of a challenging seven-hour journey, the bus reached Guanay and the travellers disembarked into the relative freshness of the small town with its tropical climate, bright green foliage and concrete buildings.

CHAPTER TWELVE

Rich sat forward, leant his elbows on the table and stared eagerly at the new slide that now appeared on the projector screen. Not only was he in the heart of the DEA's operation in Bolivia, but he had also been handpicked for a special mission to protect society and cleanse it of cocaine. His duty was to advance the interests of his country by disabling its enemies, no matter what that entailed, and he ran his thumb down the side of his precious DEA badge and smiled.

At the end of the room, Don Ferrarone stood next to a slide with the title 'Operation Moses'. He had just finished describing Law 1008, which banned the use of defoliants and herbicides in Bolivia, having wasted precious minutes discussing Colombia's dependence on coca paste. At least, they were wasted in Rich's opinion, who wanted him to get on to the meat of the presentation.

'Destroying pozo pits is inefficient. It's costly, needs a bunch of luck and the labs are replaced by new ones in a matter of weeks,' Don said in a quick, matter-of-fact style. 'I'm not here to denigrate your efforts, gentlemen, and I know you are compromised by UMOPAR, but even with perfect information, unlimited resources and the full support of the Bolivian anti-narcotics service, the best we could do is stem the tide.'

He then paused for dramatic effect, and Rich felt as though he were almost addressing him personally.

'With the support of the President, we've decided the time has come to drain the stinking ocean once and for all.'

Rich was elated. He was ready to pull the plug, smash those levee walls and vaporise anything in his path, just as long as the cesspool was emptied.

The next slide showed a Petri dish with a colony of mould over a yellow-coloured material. Pointing at the slide, Don continued.

'Operation Moses is an initiative the American public will never hear about, but it'll be *the* game changer in the War on Drugs, of that I have no doubt, not one doubt in my mind. Jim, you know what's coming. Young man,' he said, looking at Rich, 'I'm guessing you need reminding of your Old Testament?' Don nodded, and then continued, 'Moses took the Israelites out of Egypt and broke Pharaoh's chains of slavery. It was Moses that had God on his side, and Pharaoh was no match for God.'

Rich basked in the attention lavished on him by the chief of the DEA.

'Gentlemen, make no mistake, right now *we* are Moses, and it is God who has entrusted us to break the chains of cocaine slavery that have been fastened on our society. But we are not alone, no sir, we have help from God's agent on earth, the United States Army Chemical Corps. These gentlemen are here today and are going to help us deliver our sacred mission.'

Rich was totally committed to whatever Operation Moses entailed. He turned to the Stars and Stripes that was hanging on the wall and felt the urge to salute it, right there and then, but a man lurking near the flag approached the projector screen and the moment passed.

'Gentlemen, our team in Fort Leonard have been working on a solution for you, and I have the privilege this afternoon to take you through what we have up here.' He then waved a pointer at the screen. 'Ascomycota MecgoR is a fungus, not dissimilar to mildew, that attaches harmlessly to vegetation but is attracted to the methylecgonone reductase enzyme in coca paste, where it secretes a mitotic enzyme that is absorbed into any exposed batch within twenty-four hours. The pathogen has been engineered to thrive in the high humidity and high UV conditions found in the Amazon, and will seek and destroy any coca paste in its environment.'

The slide was then swapped. The new one featured the same Petri dish, but now the coca paste was partially broken down, lumpy and covered in a red-tinged fluid. He continued.

'We estimate that within three months, any lab processing coca paste or refining it into cocaine base within the proximity of Ascomycota MecgoR, or AMR for short, will be totally disabled.'

Another colleague now joined him and waved the pointer over a map of the Beni region up on the screen.

'Operation Moses will see AMR first introduced along the Rio Beni, which as you know is one of the principal areas of coca paste production. Our tests in Panama have shown that its spores can disperse for up to ten miles, subject to the prevailing winds. Spraying is not an option in Bolivia, so we'll release the fungi at fixed intervals and rely upon the wind to spread spores and form new colonies. The calculations are being finalised, but with the wind patterns in the Beni, we estimate a concentrated release of the pathogen will be effective up to a five-mile radius. A simple canister with a timer attached to a fixed object at shoulder height will disperse the agent. All indications are that the fungi will be established and releasing sufficient spores within a month or two to be classed as weaponised.'

Another acetate was placed over the one on the overhead projector, and Don stepped in to explain the arrows that now covered the map.

'The prevailing winds in the dry season are south-easterlies that sweep across the region and up into the Yungas. Between Rurrenabaque and a point around a hundred miles to the north, the winds cross perpendicular to the river. Thereafter, they broadly follow the course of the river north. The pattern changes in the wet season and the winds become north-easterlies, carrying rain back upriver, so we have the dry season to act.

'We have selected July as the ideal month to release the agent in an area up to what we've named "Point Mile One Hundred". The prevailing wind will disperse the agent west across the Rio Beni, and then northwards as the area is approached. The *surazos* that intermittently sweep up from the Pole in the dry season are strong southerlies; we'll take advantage of them and make a large deposit of the agent at Point Mile One Hundred. The *surazos* will carry it far into the northern stretches of the river. By the time the north-easterlies arrive in the wet season, plenty of fungi will have grown and their spores will be blown back over the southern stretches of the river.'

Rich raised his hand. 'Sir, I've got to ask, why not spread the agent by adding it to the river? Relying upon wind patterns sounds kind of risky to me, and we all know it passes every pozo pit in the Beni.'

Don turned to the young agent. 'Good point, Rich. An effective dispersal of the pathogen is up there on our risk register. Early tests used a slightly different agent moving through a watercourse, but it proved less effective in attaching to the coca paste enzyme. Equally, we considered a soil-based pathogen, but it would be too slow to establish the sort of coverage we need.'

Even the slightest compliment from Don Ferrarone made Rich glow. At that moment he would have followed this man anywhere and executed his orders without question.

A slide labelled 'Public Relations' then flashed up along with a photograph of Army engineers and heavy machinery.

'Since Operation Blast Furnace we have lost the hearts and minds of the locals. Well, that distrust cuts both ways,' Don continued, turning to the slide. 'This is the compound in Santa Ana del Yacuma where US Army engineers are building a new school. We agreed the goodwill mission with President Paz Zamora directly, and made sure that he didn't seek congressional approval, which is the usual protocol. Using our retainers in National Congress and local deputies, we've stirred up resentment of the troops arriving and spread rumours it's a new US military base being built, not a school. Of course, people love hearing what they fear. It's reached the Beni cartel, who are marshalling local resistance to the project. With their attention diverted, we'll have a small window to operate freely further west. To create more opposition, we're also spreading rumours that the base will receive nuclear waste for future disposal deep in the Beni.'

Rich nodded in admiration. This guy was good and the subterfuge was inspired. He knew about the school project, but he'd never suspected the real reason for such munificence.

The next slide was a photograph of a young boy. All his nose cartilage was missing, and his face made the agents wince.

'Yeah, nasty, isn't it?' Don casually remarked. 'It's a disease called mucocutaneous leishmaniasis that's prevalent in the Beni. Female sandflies spread it by infecting a host with a parasite that destroys the nose cartilage. You're both going to become experts in our programme to eradicate leishmaniasis in the Beni. The AMR canisters will be prominently labelled with the Stars and Stripes and an image of a sandfly. Using our contacts in Rurrenabaque, you'll get the support of the communities downriver, who will welcome the canisters into their community. Moreover, they are going to protect them. I mean, nobody wants their kid infected with the leishmaniasis parasite. If that canister is going to remove the threat, you bet your ass you would want as many of them as you can lay your hands on.'

Finally, he wrapped up.

'Unless you have any questions, please read the pack that Claudia will give you, and good luck, gentlemen.'

Later that night, Rich hungrily consumed the information provided by Claudia and marvelled at the miracle pathogen. The mould, or fungal mycelia, had been engineered to live on the underside of vegetation and reproduce three times as fast as other fungi. The reproductive structure was specifically designed to create an explosive dispersal of sporangiospores into the air, capable of travelling long distances. These so-called propagules, or infectious units, transmitted the fungi to its host, the methylecgonone reductase, or MecgoR enzyme, in the coca paste. It was pure mastery.

There was a medium-to-high risk that the spores would damage the respiratory systems of the young and physically vulnerable, and that contact with the fungus would cause skin inflammation and scarring. Human habitation in an infected area was not recommended, and its effect on the ecosystem was uncertain but likely to be significant. Rich agreed it was an acceptable level of collateral damage in the War on Drugs, and he was proud to be involved in such a bold and incisive campaign.

He was reminded of one of his boyhood heroes who had achieved great things by not flinching at the consequences of his actions. Rich particularly liked his famous retort when criticised about the behaviour of his secret police, and it came to mind in that moment. He mumbled, 'You can't make an omelette without breaking eggs,' and knew that it was still perfectly apt, even though it was back in 1934 that Göring had said it.

CHAPTER THIRTEEN

The Rio Mapiri is neither a grand river nor a well-known river, but it tumbles down from the Yungas and flows fast around Guanay on its way to the lowlands below. It bobs up and down as it speeds around sharp bends, and swirls and jumps when it passes the submerged hulks of trees below its surface.

Not far from the river, Santiago got out of bed and pulled on a pair of bright red cotton Wolsey Y-fronts. His wife was preparing him coffee and cooking breakfast, and he could hear her busily bashing utensils in the kitchen whilst his cockerel crowed loudly in their yard. He had slept well; he always did. Stretching and then yawning loudly, he dragged on a pair of black Adidas shorts, stepped into some rubber sandals and went through to see his daughters in the main room. They were still asleep, so he tiptoed quietly past and went into the kitchen. Picking up the fried plantain mashed with salted llama, he walked out into the cool morning and stood there admiring his fine cockerel. It had fought well for him these past two years and supplemented the family income, which fluctuated in line with his success, or lack of it, in the gold fields.

He had brought his family down to Guanay from the *altiplano* around the same time as his brother had moved to the Chapare, but he was yet to make any serious money and his family's welfare remained precarious. His brother had had a good life farming coca leaves until UMOPAR and the gringos made it more difficult to make a living, but at least he had managed to buy a small house with a plot of land during the good years, so his family's future was secure.

Finishing off breakfast, Santiago went inside and drank his coffee. His wife was getting their two small daughters up and dressed in the main room, so he went through to the bedroom and collected his things. His tools were locked in a heavy steel box at the mine, but he would also need the large black rubber balloon that was sitting in one corner of the room. Pulling on an AC Milan shirt, he pecked his wife on the cheek, roughed up the recently brushed thick dark hair of his daughters and walked out of the house with a small polyester bag on his back.

When he reached the edge of Guanay, he clambered over a rudimentary stone wall that had been built to protect the town from flooding and found a quiet spot, away from the dogs that were digging and scratching amongst the rubbish. Pulling down his shorts, his thumb ripped through the thin material of his Y-fronts and left a gaping hole in the back.

'*Puta malparida!*' he shouted, and squatted down deeply, grunted loudly and released a jet of detritus that exploded on the ground, narrowly missing his leg but hitting the side of his sandal.

Lighting up a cigarette, he perched there for several minutes, and muttered, '*Chucha madre*' when he saw that the hole was large enough for four fingers to pass through. And yet rather than being thrown away, the Y-fronts would have to be mended to save on money. It was only then, with his fingers poking through them, that he realised this was exactly the sign he had been waiting for. It was the last straw in a long line of challenges, and the time had finally come to work for the cartel, make some decent money and put gold mining behind him. He knew that they were converting a disused mine further downstream to process cocaine base; it was only last week that he had been approached to fill his balloon with packets of paste and deliver them to the lab. He should have taken up the offer, but he was going to put that right, and what's more, he would ask for work in the laboratory, where he would earn double what he earned in the mine.

Santiago tossed his cigarette away along with some soiled tissue paper. The dogs would clean up the mess once he left, but the tissue paper would hang around for several weeks, for the river was still relatively low and it did not come up to the furthest reaches of the bank yet. Pulling up his shorts, he walked over to the river with a purpose in his stride and confidence in his decision. Then the AC Milan shirt was ripped off, the shorts hitched down again and both of them stuffed into the small polyester bag along with the rubber sandals, one of which he had taken care to rinse first.

Standing there in his ripped Y-fronts, facing the river, Santiago held the balloon tight against his hip and chuckled about what it was that had finally made him see the light. Ahead of him, a fine mist rose from the forest and small swallows darted around chasing insects that flitted through the dense vegetation. He realised there and then to follow his instinct and seize the opportunity before it went, much like the swallows chasing the insects. With that in mind and pleased with his decision, he gripped the balloon and threw himself into the swirling river, clinging on tightly to its rubbery surface as it dragged him around the corner. It was not long before the muddy banks of the Mapiri were racing past, Guanay was far behind and he was little more than a red dot bobbing down the river that cut through the vast forest of the Yungas.

Twenty minutes later he reached the rusting hulk of a discarded gold-panning conveyor that was a marker for his journey, but something felt out of place and strangely different that morning. Looking over his shoulder, he saw a thick mist approach, swirling as if blown by a wind even though the morning was still. It billowed towards him and then suddenly he was in it, and he could barely see his hand in front of his face. But he could clearly make out the distinctive creak and rattle of two oars being pulled through rowlocks and the sound of water lapping against the bow of a boat. The mist passed quickly over him, and as it continued downriver he spotted the back of a rowing boat with the words 'Police Boat' painted on it in bright white letters. Beneath them, 'West India Dock' was written in smaller letters, and someone, or something, was sitting in the boat wearing a deep blue tunic. But he only caught a glimpse of it before the mist swirled again, drifted round a bend and then simply vanished, for the boat was nowhere to be seen when Santiago turned the corner.

He was still shaking his head when the familiar sound of another boat could be heard, and he looked round, this time to see a large wooden craft approach. It was full of gringos that were laughing and joking, and he relaxed. He knew that all the tourists passing through his country had tight agendas, trying to pack in as many places as possible on their short trips, and he often saw boats like this one racing to deliver them to their next destination. It had been explained to him that they were always 'looking forward to something', but he knew that in their rush forward they inevitably missed the moments passing in front of them. Despite the fact that the gringos were now pointing at him, he paid them no attention. He had long since stopped caring what others thought of him, and he got back to puzzling over what he had just seen. He knew it was real – *And yet a rowing boat going that fast and then just disappearing?* There could be no explanation other than it was yet another sign that his life was about to change, but then again, it had been a police boat, so maybe it was a warning *not* to go down the path he had just chosen?

A little less convinced now of what he should do, Santiago hacked deeply and spat over his shoulder before using his legs as a rudimentary rudder to manoeuvre around a large log trapped in the branches of a submerged tree. He would have to give the subject some more thought; the message from the ripped Y-fronts had seemed perfectly clear, but the ghostly apparition had thrown him.

It was Max who was sitting in that boat, directly behind Esther and Moshe. All three of them thought it hilarious that a man was clinging to a balloon in the middle of nowhere, without a care in the world. But something about him fascinated Max, and he continued to stare long after the others had turned back. Maybe it was his casual demeanour in the middle of a swirling river, or perhaps it was his sense of composure that resonated with Max? He could not say for sure, but he was dimly aware of a connection with his experience at the source of the Thames and the tranquillity that came from accepting circumstances as they are, rather than as he would wish them to be. But after a short while, the man was far behind and Max turned back to watch the spray rise and fall as they crashed through the Rio Mapiri, flying past men panning water and discarded mining equipment and on towards a group of flame-coloured trees that almost seemed on fire in the distant black forest.

It was only several years later that Max realised this was the morning when he finally put his troubles behind him. He could not put his finger on what had made his chest hum and swell with something good that day, but something *had* changed, and he relished life like never before. Perhaps it was following Sol's advice; but then, the serenity of the man on the rubber balloon had affected him deeply. Maybe it was no more than a natural healing process; but then, it had come on so suddenly. He did not know about the ghostly rowing boat, otherwise he might have thought that the indiscernible figure in it was a guardian angel, come to give him peace of mind.

Whatever it was, he accepted that he could not add a single hour to his life by worrying, any more than he could change the colour of the flame-coloured trees racing towards him. And with that in mind, he sat back, determined to finally embrace, rather than fret about, the life ahead of him.

CHAPTER FOURTEEN

The hills looking down on Rurrenabaque seem curiously out of place, but they mark the point at which the copper-brown Rio Beni splits in two. Slipping past the hills, part of the river turns left towards San Buenaventura whilst the rest of it drifts through Rurrenabaque, sloshing over wooden boats, past small beaches and sand spits before becoming whole again further downriver. Esther, Moshe and Max were sitting in a wooden building overlooking the river, which doubled as a restaurant, store and general office for business on the waterfront.

'Did you hear what those other Westerners were saying?' asked Esther, pointing to a couple two tables away.

'Yeah, they've been waiting two weeks for a cargo boat down to Riberalta,' said Max.

Moshe got up and went over to them. Esther and Max watched as they exchanged words, and when Moshe returned, he looked concerned.

'They said there are no cargo boats in the dry season and there haven't been any boats downriver for the past two weeks. A new road was built a couple of years ago that takes all cargo north until the rain arrives.'

'Is there no other way for us to get there?' Max asked, but Moshe shook his head.

'That couple have got a TAM flight out tomorrow – there's an air strip only forty-five minutes away, in Reyes. It looks like we're stuck and we aren't going to get to Riberalta after all,' he said.

'And there's no other way?' Max sighed. 'Are you two going to catch a flight back up to the *altiplano* then?' he asked, disappointed that he might end up travelling on his own again.

'I don't know,' replied Moshe. 'But it sounds like it.'

Esther could see both Moshe and Max were disappointed, and she decided to lighten things up.

'Come on, let's have a beer to celebrate arriving in Rurrenabaque, my treat.' Taking a ten-boliviano note from her wallet, she got up and walked to the counter at the back of the shop, where she spent the next few minutes trying to grab the attention of a man snoozing in the corner.

Nowhere else had Max experienced the magic that he felt in that small town, cut off by atrocious roads that turned into a stream of mud at the slightest hint of rain and where the boat traffic was now sporadic on the river that had once thrived. Yet the pace of life in Rurrenabaque mirrored that of its meandering river, its streets were full of colonial buildings that bathed in glorious sunsets and its inhabitants were content and smiling. Earlier, he had eaten breakfast in the courtyard of the hostel, next to a large dragon fruit tree from which red ovenbirds had jumped and pounced on the slightest crumb falling from the table. Across from the restaurant a man ferried people to and fro, presumably from the neighbouring settlement of San Buenaventura, and children splashed and played on the sand spits nearby. In fact, Max was in no hurry to leave Rurrenabaque, for it had to be one of the best towns in South America.

Esther returned with the beer.

'Guess what?' she asked, handing out the bottles. 'I got chatting to the guy at the counter. It's true that there are no cargo boats downriver at the moment, but there are still boats heading down. Anyway, he was really friendly, guessed we were Israeli, asked about our national service – you know, the usual stuff – and said he knows someone who's going downriver in a few days. It sounded like he might take us. Maybe he could drop you off somewhere, Max, before coming back here? What do you think?'

'That could work,' said Max, already excited.

'How's it been left?' asked Moshe.

'I told him we're all staying at Hostal Porteño. The boatman will come round to see us. If we're not there, he'll leave a message in reception.'

Whilst the three of them raised their bottles and waited to see how the next part of their journey would unfold, a lanky man picked out two small cases that were slowly moving around the conveyor belt at Trinidad airport. With one in each hand, he disappeared into an office at the back of the security area and locked the door. Turning on an electric fan, he took out a small pouch from a drawer, unrolled it on his desk and selected two tools from the Hook and Pick set whilst the fan clanked louder and louder, gathering momentum and blowing warm air around the room. The lock on the first case opened more easily than the second, but within a couple of minutes both were unlocked and their security tags removed.

Picking up one of the Glock 17 pistols, he put it on a towel and detached the rail, barrel and spring. The firing pin, spacer and firing pin spring were then taken off the gun and replaced with smaller ones before the mechanism was reassembled. The second gun was identically modified, and both of them were returned to their spaces in the foam padding, next to the neatly packed ammunition, magazines and lubricating oil.

Then he locked the cases, fitted new security tags and carried them back to the conveyor belt to rejoin the other luggage being loaded onto the flight for Reyes. In the cabin above, Jim Wernham and Rich McDonnell paid little attention to the pre-flight safety announcement. This was the day that Operation Moses was about to be initiated and they had more important things on their mind. Neither of the agents spoke and Jim was quiet and pensive, not least as he was worried about carrying out an operation for the first time without a functioning firearm.

Back in Rurrenabaque, Martín sipped his Double Cola in the shade of the dragon fruit tree, near the spot where Esther, Moshe and Max had sat earlier. It was midday and the temperature was now approaching thirty degrees, but the air in the courtyard was cooled by a stream of water that ran around it in a wide stone trough, making it comfortable to sit there. Around him, thick whitewashed walls and a large shady veranda hid a small row of rooms that would have been invisible to the eye were it not for their bright yellow doors and blue-painted shutters. The courtyard made a pleasant change to pozo pits, and for this reason alone he was perfectly happy to remain there all afternoon if necessary.

It wasn't long, however, before the gringos strolled into the courtyard, and he stood up to greet them.

'You the people looking to get downriver?' he asked directly, shaking their hands before introducing himself.

'That was quick!' said Esther, laughing. 'Yes, we're looking for a boat down to Riberalta, and the guy at the store said you might be able to help. I'm Esther, and this is Moshe and Max.'

'Ah,' he said, ignoring Max and looking at Esther and Moshe. 'I'm going downriver but not to Riberalta. Why you so eager to get to Riberalta? Rurre is a much nicer place. What's in Riberalta for you?'

'I'm trying to get there,' Max interjected. He did not want his plan to be disrupted, and he did not like being cut out of the conversation.

'Irish?' Martín asked, turning to Max and looking him up and down.

'What?'

'Pale skin. I can tell you are Irish. Lots of Irish come to South America.'

Max was lost for words, and Martín turned once more to Esther.

'Israeli, right?'

'Yes,' she said.

'How long you been in Army?' he asked with a grin.

'What?' Now it was Moshe's turn to be annoyed by the pushy Bolivian. 'Listen, *manyak*, there's more to Israel than the IDF,' he replied, both irritated by the tired reference to national conscription and surprised by how quickly it had come up. 'We've got a beautiful country and an ancient culture, it's just unfortunate that we need the IDF to defend it right now,' he snapped, making Esther realise that she needed to calm things down.

'To answer your question, I served two years in the IDF and my boyfriend three years,' she replied, before changing the subject back to finding a boat. 'Max needs to get to Riberalta,' she said, looking at him with a smile, 'and we would like to join him on his journey before flying back to the *altiplano*.'

'Ah, sight-seeing,' said Martín. 'You want to experience the beauty of the Beni but not go anywhere specific. Okay, I've got deliveries seven hours downriver and will be away two, maybe three days.' Pausing for thought, he nodded and said firmly, 'Okay, I take you two. Boat then full.' Turning to Max, he said, 'You have to find other way.'

Max was furious with the over-confident, over-bearing Bolivian who had assumed that he was Irish without asking, who was largely ignoring him and who was now trying to split them up.

'You can go fu—'

Esther grabbed his arm.

'That's a real shame,' she said quickly. 'But the three of us are travelling together, so we'll have to find another way. Do you know anyone else we might approach?'

'No, no,' said Martín, laughing and changing tack. 'Come on, come on. Sit down, sit down.' Shouting to the *niña*, he ordered three bottles of Double Cola and waved at chairs next to him. 'I deliver materials to labs owned by the Universidad Católica in Cochabamba. They check on ecology in the Beni. All materials I deliver are expensive and difficult to buy, and lots of thieves round here,' he said, now laughing and waving his arm above his head. 'Lots of *bandidos*, bad men, need guns to stop them!'

Max stared at the man, who was obviously interested only in his Israeli friends because of their Army experience. He was trying hard to think up a sarcastic comment about British national service, or something disparaging about the Bolivian Army, when Moshe spoke up.

'Listen, *manyak*, I don't know what you are thinking. But let's be clear, we are *tourists*, not armed guards. Do you think we came all this way just to be shot at?'

Martín took a slug of his drink and smiled. Max could see that he was thinking hard, and when he got up with a small theatrical bow and dropped a five-boliviano note on the table for the drinks, he knew that he was not in the least deterred.

'Of course, of course. I am sorry. You been shot too much by the PLO and you need a rest. Nerves now shot,' he said without a trace of irony, as if he were truly sorry for the poor Israeli soldier recovering from the experience of three years in the Army. 'But I thought it'd be an adventure for you and perfectly safe. I mean, who isn't safe with an Uzi?' he continued, as though sad that they would be missing out on a great experience.

Max noticed that Esther was looking intently at Moshe and was about to whisper something. But before she could, Moshe grabbed the arm of the man pretending to leave the table and stopped him.

'Wait. Hold on. Let's just talk a bit. You haven't told us what the deal is yet,' he said, ignoring the shake of Esther's head and Max's laugh. 'Let's hear what you have to say before *you* decide that we aren't interested in it.'

Martín sat down once more, and Max noticed the slightest hint of amusement in his face.

'Okay, okay, I see you are good friends,' he said, facing Esther. 'I take the Irishman as well, but he'll have to sit on my materials, which is not so comfortable.' Turning back to Moshe, he continued, 'I give you Uzis for show and you know how to hold them. No *bandido* coming anywhere near Israeli soldiers holding two Uzis!' Then finally, turning to Max, he said with a flourish of his hand, 'Easy to catch a pickup to Riberalta further downriver. I find one for you, no problem.'

Max could contain himself no longer. 'Mate, I'm English, not Irish. There's a big fucking difference between—' But Martín cut him off.

'English, Irish, same thing. We have deal?' he said, facing Esther and Moshe.

Both of them looked interested. Despite the clear danger, Max decided to trust their judgement.

After a long pause and some conferring, Esther looked at Max and then turned to Martín and accepted his offer. A price of ninety dollars was agreed and a departure date fixed for Tuesday 7th July, by which time all of the laboratory materials would have arrived in Rurrenabaque. Martín then left them to enjoy their Double Cola in the old colonial courtyard, observed by a row of beady eyes that blinked and twitched in the dragon fruit tree for any crumbs that might fall from their table.

It was around the same time that Jim and Rich began their descent towards a long strip of dried grass bounded by huge, tall trees. Rich watched as a row of them surged up to the plane, and he trusted the pilot to miss them, but instead there was a sudden crash, the plane twisted violently and it plunged down towards the landing strip.

'Fuck me!' Rich shouted, grabbing the seat in front, making its occupant lurch back violently.

They hit the landing strip heavily and side on, but the landing gear was intact and the pilots managed to prevent the plane from hurtling off the runway. A minute later, a voice crackled over the intercom, perfectly calm and with no reference to their near miss.

'Welcome to Reyes, *señores* and *señoras*.'

'Motherfucker!' Rich muttered as he released the back of the seat and the passenger in front sprang forward.

The morning had not started well, and it certainly had not got any better. Jim had taken him to one side just before they were about to board, and he had the fucking cheek to question his loyalty. *Well, maybe not loyalty, but certainly commitment*, he reflected as he looked out of the window at the small single-storey building that was Reyes Airport. Something about 'not being locked in' and 'being able to step down without losing face' if he wanted. He wondered if perhaps Jim wanted the glory all for himself. But he was glad he'd told him in no uncertain terms that this was his destiny, and that 'Rich McDonnell never chokes at the altar of opportunity'.

Jim had just shrugged his shoulders as if nothing had happened, and they boarded the plane in silence. But it *had* affected him, and during the flight he had begun to worry that Jim was more anxious than he was letting on. He knew that it was no way to behave, projecting his fear onto a partner, and it made him cross, but he was prepared and nothing could go wrong ... could it? Deep down, he was pleased that it had been too noisy in the turboprop to hold a proper conversation. He would have hated Jim to pick up on his nervousness.

Below them, the luggage was now being unloaded, the propellers were gradually slowing and a sparkling aluminium ladder was being wheeled up. Once down, they picked up their bags from a pile of luggage on the grass, handed over their tickets for the cases containing the Glocks and then sauntered over to the airport building, where a large pickup was waiting for them next to the perimeter fence.

Two men sat inside with the engine running and the air conditioning on high. Behind them, four metal cases were covered in tarpaulin and pushed up against the tailgate. Later that afternoon they would take the agents and the AMR canisters across a network of dirt roads and up to a pre-stage forty miles north of Rurrenabaque. The following day, a boat would take them all downriver to Point Mile One Hundred, where the village elders would select the best location for the first of the canisters to be deployed.

Rich turned around and watched the small airport disappear in a cloud of red dust. Watching it fall over the tarpaulin covering the AMR canisters, he knew nothing could stop him and that, with both God and history on his side, he would prevail. For not only was Don's invocation of Old Testament retribution inspired, but launching the mission on American Independence Day was, for a patriot like Rich, a stroke of genius.

CHAPTER FIFTEEN

The sun was up, but thick clouds made the river look still and muddy and the rainforest lifeless and grey. It was only the aluminium hull of the boat that stood out, creeping along with a small wake that hardly reached the riverbank. Up above, a man was hiding in the trees with a set of binoculars; watching the boat pass, he quickly swapped them for a radio and barked something into it, before pulling a canoe out from under a tree and paddling off in the opposite direction.

The boat continued on around a sweeping curve, with four men sitting between some steel cases and a large box of supplies hidden under tarpaulin. A fifth man stood at the back, steering the boat around sandbanks and tree trunks that lay just below the surface. Only the noise of the engine broke the stillness of the forest as they wound their way through it, past steep riverbanks and dense foliage and towards a tight corner where two soldiers lay perfectly still beneath camouflage netting that covered SVD-63 Dragunov sniper rifles.

Rich leant over and thrust his hand into the cool water that brushed past in small, undulating waves. Banking slightly through a corner, his sleeve dipped into the river, and he pulled it out quickly and put his feet back on one of the steel cases. It contained AMR canisters and got him thinking about the village downriver. He prayed they would not receive a hero's welcome, for the canisters were no promise of charitable help, rather one of misery and hardship. Only then did he have a pang of guilt that made him wonder if perhaps he could warn of the impending danger without disclosing the true nature of the canisters. *But then, villages and even whole towns have relocated over history, and this will be no different,* he reflected, *other than that it won't be a random plague or natural disaster this time.* Putting his feet down when another corner approached, he leant over once more, determined not to make his sleeve any wetter by flicking the tips of his fingers across the water this time rather than dragging his hand.

And then, as if in slow motion, there was a loud crack, part of a man's head blew off, the boat lurched to one side and Rich almost fell overboard. Another shot rang out, sending bits of blood, bone and hair splattering over his face, and then a third one ripped through the temple of the driver. The scream of the engine made Rich twist round, and he watched in horror as the driver slumped over the tiller, levering the motor out of the water for a brief second before he slipped to the floor and it plunged back into the river. But the impact of its propeller made the engine stall, and the boat now drifted slowly towards the riverbank from where the shots had come.

Rich and Jim fell to the hard metal floor, waiting to see if the hidden gunmen would pick them out. Rich wiped the blood from his face, removed his Glock and gripped it tightly, expecting another shot to ring out. But nothing happened. All was quiet. Jim crawled to the back of the boat through blood that oozed from the driver's broken skull and, crouching, pulled the starter, but it failed to turn. He tried to spot anyone in the dense foliage, but everything looked peaceful, so this time he stood up and pulled hard on the starter, and the engine roared into life. Keeping a tight grip on the tiller, he directed the boat back into the middle of the river whilst Rich crouched low, the barrel of his Glock aimed squarely at the riverbank.

Suddenly, out of the blue, a much larger wooden boat appeared, heading straight towards them with its raised hull smashing through the river. Rich jumped to his feet and squeezed hard on the trigger of his Glock, but it jammed and the prow of the boat crashed into the lighter vessel, throwing him back down into a pool of blood and bone fragments. His head cracked against the gunwale, but he managed to scramble quickly to his feet, stunned but wired by the adrenaline that surged through this body. Throwing his Glock to one side, he grabbed a heavy pole and swung it at a man who now lunged at him, narrowly missing his head but shattering his collarbone and sending him flying. Another three men swarmed towards him, and he stood firm, hoping that Jim would help, but glancing over, he saw that his blood-splattered face was just staring straight ahead, probably in shock. Braced for an attack, Rich knew that he could beat the men in one-on-one combat, and he gripped the heavy pole, ready to break their knee and elbow joints. Instead, one of the men simply pointed a pistol at his chest, and Rich dropped the pole back onto the floor.

One of them slapped him hard across the cheek with a crack that resounded around the forest, followed by a well-delivered punch to his solar plexus that left him unable to breathe and gasping for air. A hood was pulled over his head, his hands zip-tied, and he was pushed down onto the bench, where he listened to the sound of objects hitting the water. He did not know, but it was easy to imagine that it was the bodies of the dead men that would be devoured later by caiman, along with radio sets that would sink into the muddy riverbed without a trace.

Then the motor started up and the boat pulled off. Rich could tell that they were going downriver, but he could not see anything through the hood and he had no idea whether Jim was with him or not. The adrenaline was beginning to wear off, and he was aware of a dull ache spreading across his kidneys and a sharper pain at the back of his head. Sweat dripped into his eyes and stung, but the hood was too coarse to be able to clear them properly. He felt out of his depth and was worried for his safety and that of his partner.

In the other boat, Jim also sat in a hood with zip-tied hands, shaking slightly. His instructions had been to direct the boat to a settlement marked with a large yellow flag on the riverbank, which was a staging post for the operation. But that was about two hours downriver. He knew that the cartel's plan had been to ambush them only once they had reached it, then seize the pathogen canisters and leave them tied up but unharmed. The evidence would prove beyond doubt that Law 1008 was being totally disregarded by the DEA, and the government would be under pressure to revoke their permission to operate in Bolivia. There had clearly been a drastic change of plan. Either that, or something had gone horribly wrong.

Rich was not sure for how long they had been travelling before the engines were cut and both boats drifted to a stop. There was a sudden jolt, and he knew that they must have hit the bank, for he was now pulled up and moved to the edge of the boat. His eyes had adjusted to the hood and he could see through it slightly, but not enough to realise that there was a sharp drop between the edge of the bank and the boat. With a push, he fell onto the bank and heard laughter around him as he was lifted up again, gripped tightly and led up a slippery path and across what must have been cleared scrubland. He heard another thud a few yards behind, followed by more laughter, and assumed that it must have been Jim hitting the bank.

His senses raced, and he was trying to make out the sounds around him when his hands were pushed onto a rough wooden post and he tripped on a stair. Gripping a handrail, he climbed one, two, three, four, five, six . . . seven steps up onto a wooden platform that creaked loudly. As far as he could tell, there were now only two men with him, and he heard them greet someone before he bumped into a doorway and was pushed into what he knew was a dark room, as the light shining through his hood suddenly cut out. One of the men led him across a smooth timber floor, he was shoved onto a chair and his hood was ripped off.

Rich shook his head, blinked for a moment and then looked around. He was in the middle of a large hall, lit by a rectangular skylight that stretched the length of the building, with more light streaming in through the door he had just come through, but the hall itself was dark, cavernous and cool. He watched Jim arrive, trip on the threshold and then sprawl on the floor, before being dragged along by two men and dumped onto the chair next to him.

Rich watched closely as Jim's hood was removed, and he was alarmed to see terror in his eyes. He was starting to whisper some encouragement when a hand slapped the back of his head and pushed it forward.

Facing him, a large table stood with several bottles of water neatly arranged on it. It had three chairs and was set up as though for an interview, or some sort of tribunal. Behind it, six men stood perfectly still as if waiting for someone, or something, to happen. He recognised three of them from the boat and two others as the men who had manhandled Jim, but the last one was unfamiliar. He began to wonder just how many men were behind him when he was distracted by the sound of laughter and chatter coming from the door, and he was roughly pulled up.

Two men appeared, and one of them shouted, 'No, no. Untie them. And give them some water, Pepe.' Rich noticed that he was wearing a brash Hawaiian shirt and tight-fitting cream shorts. Once their hands were untied, a bottle of water was thrown to each of them, but it was clear that they were expected to remain standing.

'Gentlemen, I am sorry we have kept you waiting, but I had first to show Mauricio my potted plants,' the man in the Hawaiian shirt said, gesturing with a pair of secateurs to the man beside him. Mauricio gave a small bow.

Rich watched the men closely as they took a seat either side of a chair that now appeared ominously empty. Jim tried to speak, but Mauricio put a hand up and stopped him.

'Please, drink your water.'

Jim turned to give Rich a reassuring smile, but it was no more than a nervous stare. When Rich looked down at some water he had spilled, he saw the dried blood on his trousers and needed no further reminder of the danger they were in.

Suddenly, the men at the table stood up and those behind them lined up and faced the doorway, where an enormously fat man stood in ill-fitting shorts and sandals, filling the portal entirely with his colossal frame. He was wearing a straw hat with a large brim that gave his silhouette the appearance of an obscene, wobbling table lamp. Taking off the hat, he passed it to a man at the doorway and made his way to the table, his legs rubbing together and his chest panting as he passed in front of the agents, ignoring them. He was too large to fit between the arms of the chair, so he crossly summoned for a stool. Once it had been placed behind him, he slowly lowered his frame onto it, rested his hands on the table and let out a sigh. Only then did he look at the DEA agents. Mopping his brow with a large, stained handkerchief, he took a deep breath and mumbled in a thick Colombian accent, '*Puta* gringos.'

Hacking, he spat on the floor, took a gulp of water and then crossed his arms. 'Today, the fourth of July, we sit in judgement on the actions of the American soldiers operating under the directions of the Drug Enforcement Administration. The decision of the tribunal is final and will be reached with a simple majority. Gentlemen, you're both charged with subjugating the Bolivian nation and imprisoning it in poverty.'

Pointing at Jim, he continued, '*You* are separately accused of accepting bribes and feeding off the lives of the poor.' Addressing Rich, he said, '*You* are separately accused of seeking to destroy the lives of innocent people by poisoning their communities. You're both still alive, as in our beneficence we've granted you the right to defend your actions, should you so choose. The tribunal recognises you as soldiers in your so-called "War on Drugs". It has the power to free you or execute you, depending on the persuasiveness of your arguments.'

As none of Jim's DEA training had come close to a situation like this, he fell back instinctively on experience gained as a police officer.

'*Señor*,' he said, as confidently as he could, 'we understand why you are upset by the DEA's incursion into Bolivia, but we're really just foot soldiers following orders given by politicians in Washington. We have no wish to harm your people or your beautiful country. In fact, I hope the tribunal takes into account the assistance that I have given the cartel over several years, a service which I would be proud to continue should you gentlemen so wish.'

Whilst he spoke, Rich's head was spinning, trying to find a credible defence for his charge. He did not pick up on Jim's admission.

Mauricio answered Jim.

'No, the foot soldiers in your war are UMOPAR. They're the ones following orders, given by the DEA. You've come to this country to enrich yourself, which you've done very well. You are a hypocrite. You make money from the trade you pretend to despise.'

'No, *señor*. You misjudge my actions. I have provided information that's undermined the effectiveness of our operations here and weakened the resolve of the administration. By revealing the details of Operation Moses, I have given you the opportunity to remove the DEA from Bolivia for good. I hope the tribunal can see this.'

There was a short silence, and Rich suddenly realised what was being alleged, but before he could say anything, the man with the secateurs stood up and shouted at Jim, 'No, no, *señor*. Your Paraguayan bank account has half a million dollars in it. Do not pretend you act with altruistic motives. No, no, *señor*, that will not do!' he said, now red in the face and pointing the secateurs accusingly at Jim.

Jim was silenced by the sight of them. Rich seized the moment, and the words almost burst out of him.

'You've got to be fucking stupid to think he's on the take. Anyone hustling for money works out of Bogotá or back in the US, not some shithole like Bolivia!'

Turning to Rich, the secateurs waved dismissively.

'Oh yes, young man. Your heart has been so indoctrinated with fake nationalism and pseudo-patriotism that you cannot see what is in front of you. Your colleague is corrupt. We've preyed on his weakness in exchange for money and *basuco*. He is as much in the pay of the cartel as the UMOPAR officers for whom you have such little regard.' When Rich looked over at Jim, he realised that he was not looking him in the eye. 'What is it that drives young men from the richest country in the world to the poorest nation on the continent, determined to impoverish it further? Does a humane heart beat behind the shield of truth and righteousness that the administration hoists on you? Are you unwittingly exposed to some malign force that justifies releasing chemical weapons on poor innocent people, or are you just inherently evil, *señor*?'

The secateurs and passion for potted plants belied a keen mind that also interrogated suspects in court, and his interpretation of the mission left Rich speechless. The Colombian rolled his belly onto the table and leant forward.

'What is your defence to these charges? Think well, young man, your life depends on it.'

Rich stood facing the men with a hatred and loathing for everything they represented. Everyone watched him glaring, and then he spat at the Colombian, just missing him. One of the men behind the table swore and rushed over to Rich, but the Colombian raised his hand to stop him.

'No, let the gringo speak.'

And Rich began, calmly but with venom.

'My defence is simple. You trade in misery. The drug trade is evil. You destroy lives indiscriminately. The work we do is in the defence of the values held dear by our society. You sit there pretending to exercise some sort of authority. But I don't recognise any authority that takes its power from extortion, murder and suffering.'

Rich then pointed at each one of them before continuing, 'You think you can hide, but you forget that the greatest nation on the face of the earth is after you, one person at a time. Our President has reminded us that we're citizens with obligations to each other, to our country and history. For too long our culture has said, "If it feels good, do it," but we're embracing a new ethic now, a new creed that marks the end of you. Where I go, more will follow. Tell your bosses we're going to bury you underground and piss on your graves, but not before we've ground your *cojones* in a mincer that—'

The echoes of his tirade were still resonating through the hall when the Colombian stopped him and laughed loudly.

'And trust me, those invaders will be slaughtered without mercy. You think you will prevail, but your promise of poverty is no match for the welfare we support. You will never succeed. Mark my words, before the decade is finished, your masters will have moved on and created another "war" on something else for low intellects like you to follow in blind obedience.'

And Rich was pushed roughly down onto his chair, leaving only Jim standing. Turning to him, the Colombian asked, '*Señor*, do I need to remind you of the charges laid before you?'

Jim looked down at Rich and saw the fire in his eyes. He wished he still believed in a noble cause, but that had gone years earlier and his creed was now one of self-preservation.

'*Señor*, I simply make my case that I am acting, and have always acted, in the best interests of the cartel. I carried out my mission as instructed, and I safely delivered the pathogen canisters to you. I accept that the payment received for my services is not insubstantial, but it has delivered far more value to your production chain. If there is some way in which I have offended the cartel, please tell me. If not, then I respectfully ask you release me and allow me to continue my work protecting your interests in Bolivia.'

It was Mauricio who now spoke. 'What you say has some truth, but your work relates to the previous organisation. The new cartel does not recognise informants in the DEA.'

Jim had been unlucky.

The cartel had been transformed by Decree no. 22881, the so-called *Decreto de Arrepentimiento*, or 'Decree of Repentance', that was passed by the Bolivian government on 29th July 1991. It gave the traffickers one hundred and twenty days to surrender in return for a guarantee they would be immune from extradition to the United States. By December 1991, seven major figures in the Beni cartel had surrendered and the Colombians began moving in to fill the void left by the imprisoned Bolivians. The Beni cartel had fought to protect their territory but were ineffective in directing operations from prison. The result was a transition throughout May and June to a Colombian-dominated organisation.

Jim was now sitting on the wrong side of history.

Standing up again, the man in the Hawaiian shirt took over as if he had been simply tolerating this charade of a trial, and he shouted, 'You are no more than a leech on the ankle of the *campesinos*. You suck their blood until you bloat and fall off for a smoke of *basuco*. As you disappear into a haze of relaxation and music, the poor families in the Yungas and the Chapare worry about their sick children and the poverty that grinds their lives and imprisons them.'

He then began to pace the room as though playing to an imaginary jury. 'You may be amused that we followed their ridiculous penchant for naming operations. Today you witnessed Operation Rob the Rich unleashed on the administration. You won't fail to notice it's a play on the name of one of the DEA agents sat in front of the tribunal, but it strikes at the essence of the cartel.'

Then turning to the agents, he continued, 'We are just simple businessmen trading with your great nation. You have unquenchable demand for cocaine, and we are simply supplying the demand that you cannot supply, or are not willing to supply. Our interest is in taking a small part of the immense wealth from your country and redistributing it to our poor nation. Bolivia would not exist without coca. Operation Rob the Rich has protected our nation, and whilst we see it more as trading with the rich and not robbing it, the fact remains that we *will* have some of the riches from "the greatest nation on the face of the earth", as you put it.'

Facing the other members of the tribunal, he opened both arms and declared, '*Señores*, we have in front of us two men, one of whom has sucked the blood from our country whilst the other squeezes the life out of its emaciated body. I petition for a sentence appropriate to the actions that these two men have taken, freely and without compassion.'

CHAPTER SIXTEEN

Rich awoke with a start and found that he was tied to a post with his hands behind his back. It took a brief second to remember where he was and what had happened, before an overwhelming sense of dread hit him. He knew that he had been condemned by a unanimous decision, but the tribunal and its members had been a sham and he was glad that he had not indulged them, unlike his partner. Rich looked across at the figure next to him, slumped, presumably asleep.

His forehead then began to itch like mad and he shuddered, remembering the mosquitoes feeding all night whilst his hands were tied behind his back. He knew instinctively that he had to free himself from the post, for escape was now his only option. Pulling hard, he tested its strength. It was thick and supported a truss, but it was fixed to a plate on the floor that might be loosened with some effort. He stood up, placed his heels at the bottom of the post, crouched down and then pushed with all his might. Nothing moved. Sitting back down, he rocked and pulled, straining his body for just the slightest sign of movement. There was none.

He sat back, anxious and frustrated, his eyes darting around the hall, which was plunged in complete darkness but for some light creeping in from the dawn that was breaking. Straining, he could make out a row of large objects strung up opposite, presumably hammocks, but he could not see the table and chairs as it was too dark. Eventually, the sun burst through the roof light, and the gloom in the hall lifted to reveal that the table and chairs were gone and the large objects were indeed hammocks, covered in mosquito nets. The men inside them began to twist and yawn, and it seemed Jim was also awake, but Rich ignored him.

After a short while, the men fell from their hammocks, grumbling, and one of them opened the door. Light poured in, and shortly afterwards, a man appeared holding a large knife. He paused before walking slowly over to Rich, who coiled up ready to lash out with his feet, but the man simply walked behind and cut his cable ties. Rich grabbed his burning wrists and felt instant relief now that he could move his aching arms. The man then knelt down by Jim and freed him. A mug of coffee, some bananas and a large bottle of water were placed before each of them, and they were encouraged to eat. Rich grabbed the water and gulped it down before pouring some over his wrists. Then he ripped open one of the bananas and stuffed it into his mouth. He looked over at Jim, and even though his hands were freed, he barely moved. He did not touch the food or drink.

Rich kept a close eye on the man with the knife and tried to figure out why he looked so remarkably relaxed, as if this was perfectly normal. It made him relax a little, and he drank his coffee with the growing sense that things perhaps were not as bad as they seemed, *For this was not how you treated people about to be executed.*

But then another man came into the hall with a white plastic bag, and the atmosphere changed.

'Change into these,' he barked, throwing a pair of yellow polyester Mickey Mouse boxers and a matching Minnie Mouse vest to Rich. A pair of blue leggings with red trunks were flung at Jim. Reaching into the plastic bag, he pulled out a blue top and red cape. The blue top had a large red 'S' on a yellow background and a yellow belt at its base. Rich immediately went back to thinking about escape.

He knew he would need the help of the scumbag beside him, and he angrily shouted 'Eat!' at him.

With his hands free and the guards chatting by the door, he realised that this might be his only chance. Pulling on the yellow boxers, he looked carefully around the room and spotted a small trapdoor that must have opened out under the building, for he recalled climbing up a number of stairs to reach the hall. The trap-door had a simple brass ring on it and there was no lock. Rich knew the guards needed to remain distracted if he were to avoid capture once outside, and Jim would have to sacrifice himself. So, turning to his partner, he whispered, 'You make a rush for the door. I'll try find another way.' But Jim was not listening and just stared at his Superman outfit.

Rich knew that he had to act quickly and, moreover, that Jim was of no use. The four guards still had their backs turned, so he pulled on the Minnie Mouse vest, rolled away from the post and crawled on his belly towards the trapdoor. He reached it in no time and gently pulled the brass ring, yet despite lifting it with only the slightest sound, one of the guards spotted him. The void below seemed surprisingly dark, but there was no time to lose, and Rich jumped down the hatch and fell heavily on some metal objects that rolled and sent him sprawling across the floor. He lay there stunned for a moment before realising that he was on concrete, not grass, and he was surrounded by walls of rough-cut planks, not an open clearing. His heart raced and he looked frantically at the food tins still rolling across the floor, when a door flew open, light streamed in and something hard smashed him on the head.

Jim looked down at the young agent, trussed up and groaning on the floor of the boat. Some blood from his head had dripped over his yellow vest and the spray was making it spread out in a pink-edged stain. Jim's hands were once more tied even though he had made no attempt to escape. He was infuriated by Rich. He was just so gung-ho, and it was making their situation worse, not better. Despite being convicted by the tribunal, Jim had hoped for a punishment no worse than ritual humiliation in the ridiculous outfits, but that option might be off the table now that Rich had tried to escape. He kicked him hard, and he groaned some more.

They flew down the Rio Beni for the next fifteen minutes in the hands of an experienced driver, powering out of corners and taking the sandbank chicanes at speed, which made Jim's Superman cape flap and wave behind him, much to the delight of the men following in another boat. When a tight bend approached, the boats slowed down, almost stopping. Jim looked around and saw the tell-tale sign of a makeshift runway that had been cleared on a large spit of land next to the bend, but then the boat swung up a tributary and his head was pushed down as they passed under a large, overhanging tree. They passed an odd-looking bamboo cage partially submerged in the water and continued for a few minutes before a pozo pit came into view.

The agents were taken out of the boat and up to the camp, which looked like it had not been in use for a while. Their hands were then untied, and they were pushed onto a wooden platform before their captors turned around and wandered back to the riverbank for a smoke. Neither of the agents spoke. The cold spray had revived Rich, and he had been able to walk up to the laboratory unassisted, an improvement on his bloody condition immediately after his escape attempt, but he was sullen and withdrawn.

A few minutes passed before the sound of another boat reached the camp, and the men at the riverbank waved as it approached. Jim saw it pass, turn around and then gently bump alongside the riverbank and come to a stop. A small, bony man wearing a white vest sat there smiling, and gestured for the men to help with some bamboo poles and ratchet straps. Jim could just make out, hanging off the side of the boat and almost completely submerged in water, what looked like a metal cage. It seemed to have a large steel pin sticking out of one corner, but he lost sight of it when the men started unloading the boat.

Two men then grabbed Rich and led him over to the riverbank, where his hands were retied and raised over his head before they slid a bamboo pole between his arms and his back. Another man removed his shoes whilst a fourth man peed into a small black sack and pulled it over his head. Once he had been tightened to the pole with a ratchet strap, he was pushed to the ground and the men took turns rolling him around the camp in his Mickey Mouse shorts and Minnie Mouse vest.

Laughing, they eventually lifted him onto a short bamboo frame that sagged but held him securely. Jim heard Rich curse loudly as his hood was removed and drops of sweat and urine dripped down his nose onto the dirt. He looked dazed, disorientated and so furious that he did not realise that he had been hung on a roasting spit. But Jim realised, and it was only then that he knew he was not going to be simply humiliated in the Superman outfit after all. The tribunal were in deadly earnest, and the ridiculous costumes were just evidence of their psychopathic intentions.

'You motherfuckers!' Jim shouted. 'Don't think the DEA will let you get away with this. Kill us and you'll be hunted like the dogs you are. Release us before you regret it.'

But all this did was catch the attention of the man with bony shoulders, who walked over and placed a gentle hand on his head. Smoothing out Jim's red cape, which had become bundled, he smiled.

'*Tranquilo, hermano*, I have something here that will calm you.'

He took out a small box from his pocket, removed its lid and tipped it towards him. There were two large *basuco* smokes inside, one of which he now lit. Jim would have loved to have thrown it in the face of the smiling man, but the urge for some *basuco* was too great and he grabbed it from him.

He took a long, deep drag of the magical drug and grimaced slightly as Rich cursed and swore on the spit. He regretted getting the young agent involved, but it was his own stupid fault. He had given him the chance to step away, and his behaviour had made it so much worse for him. Once the *basuco* was half finished, he was picked up gently from behind and led to the boat, where the bony man waited with three of his men. The smoke felt incredibly strong, and Jim realised it must have been hallucinogenic, for small patterns now appeared on his hands and the boat had a slight shimmer around it.

Getting in, he knew that he was being released and Rich was to be sacrificed. He felt bad for the young agent, but if he were to continue working for the cartel, Rich would have to die, otherwise his cover was blown and he would be spending many, many years in a US penitentiary. Then the boat glided out into the river, Jim took another deep drag and simply turned away from his trussed-up partner towards the freedom his loyalty had secured.

Soon they reached the bamboo cage that they had passed on the way in. The boat nosed up to it and one of the men fixed a large tape player with silver speakers to its top. Jim marvelled at the sun that hit the speakers and burst into a million tiny sparkling dots and was mesmerised by the music that now surrounded him in quadrophonic sound.

Everyone in the boat smiled, including Jim, who was thoroughly enjoying himself as he smoked his second *basuco*. He felt strange, sitting in a Superman outfit surrounded by smiling Bolivians, but at the same time, oddly calm. Half an hour later, two of the men grabbed him and removed his blue leggings and red trunks. Not that he put up much of a fight. Instead, he grinned at his captors as they checked the knot on his cape and laughed as they pushed him into the water and he emerged with it floating on the surface. The men jumped straight in after him and guided him into the half-submerged wooden cage. It was cool and refreshing in the water, and to Jim it seemed like the right place to be, in a cage with his arms being lifted over his head and his hands handcuffed to the bamboo above.

Somehow, by closing the door, a sitar started up in the tree opposite. Jim marvelled as its sound resonated around the forest, added to by a tambourine and a melodic bass, and then joined by some deep vocals that he recognised instantly from his record collection.

This is the end,
beautiful friend.
This is the end,
my only friend the end.

He swayed gently to the sound of the organ reverberating on his ribs and to the music that echoed around the forest with its mournful and haunting lyrics.

Of our elaborate plans, the end.
Of everything that stands, the end.
I'll never look into your eyes again.

A snare drum and cymbals were layered over the track, and he nodded to the song that he found sad but also strangely peaceful. He did not notice a man lean over the side of the boat and thrust a rod into the smaller metal cage that was hanging off it. It was shaken viciously, but Jim did not see the water in the cage boil and seethe, for his mind was now back in Vietnam, surrounded by jungle, water and bamboo.

Can you picture what will be
so limitless and free?
Desperately in need
of some stranger's hand.
In a desperate land.

Lifting the rod out, the man now drummed it against the metal cage to the beat of the music, making Jim turn towards him. He could see the top of the cage hanging off the side of the boat, and something was making it shake violently, much to the delight of the men, but he could not make out what it was that was trapped inside. One of the men waved across to Jim. He tried to wave back, but of course his hands were tied to the bamboo cage. With a flourish, the drumming came to an abrupt end, and Jim watched the man slowly pull out the steel pin that held the side of the cage shut. It burst open the second it was removed, a swirling, shaking mass of water shot out, and Jim looked in horror at the seething wave that now made a beeline for him.

Jim twisted instinctively to avoid whatever it was under the water, but soon razor-sharp teeth clamped onto his left buttock. Screaming, he pulled tightly on his bound hands and swung his legs up, but there was not enough room for his body to fully clear the water. His red Superman cape shook violently as red-bellied piranhas thrashed and ripped at the flesh of his buttocks, and in agony his legs dropped back into the bloodied, frenzied, turbulent water. His body twisted and contorted with excruciating pain as his tensor fasciae ligament was eaten through and his left adductor devoured.

Lost in a Roman wilderness of pain
and all the children are insane.

Jim's screams rose above the music.

All the children are insane,
waiting for the summer rain, yeah.

And then the tugging, ripping and tearing teeth turned to his testicles, leaving a gaping hole in his pelvis and a cloud of blood in which the soft extremity loosely attached there was devoured bit by bit. The last thing he would see was his captors grinning in approval at the manner of his death, eaten alive, convulsing, with The Doors resounding in his ears.

Bound tightly and hanging from the spit, all Rich could do was listen to the screams of pain that were so extreme they became the sound of Death itself. He could only move his head from side to side, either towards the river or the forest, and he had no idea if he was still being guarded. Rich shut his eyes and muttered to himself, 'Lord help me and release me from this danger if it be your will. Guide me past the valley of death and into safety. Lord, take me from this danger.' But then a hand gently stroked his thick black hair and another threw a pile of dark, gnarled sticks beneath him.

About the same time, his cousin clambered on top of five blue barrels on a boat in Rurrenabaque and two Israelis were each handed an Uzi.

CHAPTER SEVENTEEN

They had three pozo pits to supply and the boat was loaded with barrels of sulphuric acid, sacks of soda crystals, gasoline and propane canisters. Martín was right: there was no room for Max. He was perched precariously on the barrels, holding on tightly and hoping that they were as watertight as they looked. Moshe was at the back of the boat with Martín. Esther was at the front, clutching an Uzi with the wind rushing through her hair. Behind them, the wake fanned out and hit the riverbank in a wave that crept along, until a sharp bend deflected it back into the river. This was the point at which Martín opened the throttle and spun the boat around the bend at speed, nearly catapulting Max into the river, which had been his intention all along. But Max clung on, swearing, and when he looked up, he saw a mist swirling in the distance. Within the mist a rowing boat appeared, and within that boat was a man, pulling at the oars, wearing a blue tunic with silver buttons that sparkled in the late-morning sun.

And then the mist vanished, leaving Max perplexed. The others seemed not to have noticed, and he could only conclude that he must have imagined it. He sat on those barrels, confused and bewildered. A rowing boat that disappeared was simply not real, but then neither were ghosts nor angels, and he could not say with confidence that the stories from Toocanagh were make-believe. Looking down, he spotted for the first time that the barrel he was sitting on had a black-and-white 'Corrosive' label plastered across it, and his mind was snapped back to the present just as Martín once again swung the boat aggressively in an attempt to dislodge him.

The final supplies had arrived first thing that morning, a couple of days early, and Martín had told them that he needed to leave straight away as one of the laboratories had run out of supplies. What he did not tell them was that he would deliver some propane and soda crystals to the nearest one, spend the night there and continue to the furthest laboratory, where four of the sulphuric acid barrels, most of the gasoline and a large part of the soda crystals and propane would be delivered.

The last delivery would be to a pozo pit that the Colombians and the cartel had been recently fighting over. Despite its proximity to a landing strip, it had not been used for a while because of the dispute. Now that an agreement had been reached, it was coming back on stream and Martín's instructions were to check it was secure and then drop off a small supply of precursors. It would be a quick and easy job to finish off with before returning to Rurrenabaque.

Powering down the Rio Beni, Martín was pleased he had armed guards. The business with the Colombians was unsettling. One of his friends had been killed at the airstrip laboratory, and even though the conflict was over, Pablo Escobar's cousin was now apparently in the Beni, and he had a reputation as a psychopath with unpredictable tendencies.

They reached the first pozo pit within a few hours and were greeted by men waving from the riverbank. Martín had proudly told the three of them that he was known as the 'Beni Beer Man'. His deliveries always came with river-cooled bottled beer stored in cylinders attached to the side of his boat, and for that reason alone, he was a popular visitor. The ten-minute walk into the forest was accompanied with relaxed chatter and laughter whilst the propane and sacks of soda crystals were pushed along in large wheelbarrows with single huge rubber tyres. Martín carried the cylinder of beer on his shoulder rather than add it to the wheelbarrows, as he liked to arrive in the camp bearing gifts.

Moshe laughed and pointed at Martín.

'You know, he isn't delivering scientific supplies,' he said to Max. 'Any idea what those barrels contain?'

'Well, I know it's acid. I saw the "Corrosive" labels, but I can't read Cyrillic.'

'Yeah, well, I can. You've been sitting on barrels of sulphuric acid. Since when was sulphuric acid needed to record rainfall and monitor wildlife and fauna?'

Esther looked at Moshe.

'You knew this the whole time?' she asked, gripping her Uzi. 'And you let us get on the boat?'

'Yeah, but don't worry, Estie. We're on an adventure, and the best of it is we've got the greatest gun of all time in our hands.' He laughed, patting his Uzi. 'I don't know who this guy really is, but we're armed and he isn't.'

Max watched Esther shake her head, and they walked on, past a deep hole half full of rubbish and towards a clearing with a large tarpaulin tent in the middle. Martín strode into the clearing with his cylinder of beer and strutted around the camp to rapturous applause, leaving a small trail of water behind him as he waved one arm over his head. Max just looked on and chuckled to himself; Martín was most definitely a showman, and they were most certainly in for an adventure.

The Cessna landed on the spit, turned around and left its engines running. In its hold, a huge wooden crate was tied to the floor. Weighing in at almost 250 kg, it was a special delivery for Don Escobar. That was all the pilot knew. He had a bad feeling about the cargo and would be pleased to be shot of it.

A team of men arrived with ropes and logs and got the crate out of the side of the plane and down to their boats, where it was fixed securely to a wooden platform. Taking it back up the tributary, they passed the limp form of Superman hanging in cloudy red water with the remains of a yellow belt around his waist. Other than one man making a sign of the cross, none of them took any notice of the caped superhero.

The crate would have been impossible to haul up into the camp had it not been for a large ratchet strap fixed to a tree at the top of the bank. The bony man directed the operation, pushing and pulling on a lever that pulled the cargo up the creaking logs that had been laid down as a temporary ramp. Rich had been turned around, and he now faced the camp. Managing to lift his head, he watched the arrival of the crate with horror. He imagined that it could only contain a cauldron in which he would be boiled alive after first being grilled over the fire. One of the men approached the crate, poured a barrel of water over its top and watched it disappear inside, which meant it had holes in it. Rich's fear grew worse. *It has to contain something living.*

A bottle of *pisco* then appeared from somewhere, and a toast was made to their brothers in Peru who had delivered the cargo. It had been difficult to secure, and it was a special gift from the Huallaga Valley cartel to the Medellín cartel, such was the influence of the monstrous man in the ridiculous sombrero. But they all knew that *El Patrón* would be leaving prison shortly to resume direct control of the business, and everyone wanted to create a favourable impression with his cousin.

The men raised their glasses, and the bony man began to hum and encouraged his men to join in. Rich listened to a tune he sort of recognised but could not place. Some of the men began squeaking at the end of one section before collapsing in fits of laughter. Was he hallucinating? Was he going to wake up in Beacon Hill and wander down to Faneuil Hall for breakfast? He lowered his head as he felt the last glimmers of hope fade away. One of the men approached him with a glass of *pisco* and gently lifted his head to one side.

'Drink, *güevón*, this will give you strength for tomorrow.'

CHAPTER EIGHTEEN

Martín was quiet when they set off. There was no back-slapping or chatter like before.

'What's going on, Mosh?' Max asked.

'I don't know. He turned quiet after speaking to the guy in the red shorts. You know, the one with the bright yellow shirt who tipped him out of his hammock first thing?'

They had all noticed the change in atmosphere. It was obvious that the camp was not being used for a scientific purpose, but none of them had been able to work out what they really did there. Sitting at the front of the boat gripping her Uzi, Esther scanned the river carefully for any danger, her senses alert.

After a few minutes, Martín motioned to Moshe to come and hold the throttle. He bent down and unlocked a small box that was fixed to the hull and took out a large, sheathed Bowie knife. Waving it at Max, he gestured for him to take it and then removed a Glock pistol before shutting the box. Checking its safety catch, he tucked it into his shorts and took the throttle back from Moshe, as if nothing had happened. Max looked at Moshe, who was looking a little troubled, and then down at the oversized, sinister-looking blade of the knife he had just unsheathed.

Martín's worst fears had been confirmed last night. The *hijo de puta* cousin of Escobar was just an hour further downriver, and they would have to pass his entourage on their journey. Apparently, there had been a meeting two days earlier with Ernesto and Mauricio, the two highest-ranking members of the Beni cartel who were not in prison. Nobody knew the purpose of the meeting or what was said, but it was well known that Ernesto was opposed to the agreement reached with the Colombians. Maybe he was trying to renegotiate it? Or maybe the peace was broken?

All they saw when they passed the hall was its tin roof. The building was too far back from the riverbank for them to appreciate Ernesto's potted plants. Martín slowed down. He did not want to attract unnecessary attention, but it would have been disrespectful not to have stopped and paid his respects had he been spotted. Crawling past, the compound appeared empty, with only a solitary aluminium boat tied to the bank.

Martín breathed a sigh of relief and his shoulders visibly relaxed. Bending down, he picked up some sweets from a bag next to him.

'Hey, Israeli soldiers, have one of these,' he said, and threw a packet at Esther, and then a couple at Moshe and Max.

A big smile spread over Martín's face as he opened up the throttle and shouted, '*Vámonos, güevones!*'

Fifteen minutes later they swung round a tight bend in the river, beyond which a large spit of land stretched out with a deckchair close to the water's edge. It was one of those old 1960s aluminium-framed models, with wooden armrests and a psychedelic fabric of swirling flowers. Martín slowed down instinctively. It would be a good addition to the laboratory nearby. *Maybe pick it up and quickly drop it off with the precursors and propane?* he thought. But then he shook his head, as it had clearly been placed there deliberately. *Maybe it was where Don Escobar sat when waiting for his plane to arrive?*

He decided that it was best avoided, so without a further thought, he guided the boat back into the middle of the river, opened up the throttle and raced past the deckchair. He was determined to reach the next laboratory before nightfall.

Behind them, Don Escobar sat at the same table used in the tribunal, except it was now up on a platform facing the camp and was covered in a brilliant white tablecloth. A feast was laid out on it, and a shade had been rigged up to shelter his enormous frame, but it did nothing to prevent the sweat from running down his hairline and dripping onto the starched edge of the tablecloth. In front of him, men in US Army fatigues scurried around, and to one side, Rich was shaking his head at a man trying to give him water.

When Rich looked up, he saw three others walk up to the crate and lever its side off with a small crowbar. He strained to see what was inside, but it faced the river, and all he could see was the shock on the men's faces as they jumped back and brandished some viciously pronged bamboo poles that they were holding.

In panic he tried to bounce and shake free. Whatever was in there was destined for him, and he needed to get away, fast! Yet despite his violent struggle, the spit did not sag in the slightest, and he gave up, exhausted, with sweat dripping from his red, sunburnt neck. Meanwhile, a group of men were now lining up in front of Don Escobar, marching on the spot with bamboo poles held as rifles. One of them started whistling. Don Escobar gave a wave and the bony man delivered the first chorus of a US Army marching song.

M-I-C, K-E-Y, M-O-U-S-E
We play fair and we work hard
And we're in harmony.

To which half the men replied: *M-I-C, K-E-Y, M-O-U-S-E*
Before shouting: *MICKEY MOUSE!*
The other half squeaked: *Mickey Mouse!*
The whole troop then came together for the next section of the marching song.

Forever let us hold our banner high, HIGH! HIGH! HIGH!
Boys and girls from far and near you're welcome as can be
M-I-C, K-E-Y, M-O-U-S-E
Who's the leader of the club that's made for you and me?
M-I-C, K-E-Y, M-O-U-S-E
(shout!) *MICKEY MOUSE!*
(squeak!) *Mickey Mouse!*
(shout!) *MICKEY MOUSE!*
(squeak!) *Mickey Mouse!*

The bizarre pageant in front of Don Escobar continued whilst the men by the crate guided a glistening, pointed head and sharp eyes out of the crate and into the centre of the camp. A forked tongue flicked as the green anaconda uncoiled its massive body and stretched out of the crate that had held her captive. It was the dry season, when food was harder to come by, and several weeks had passed since her last full meal. She could smell prey and was hungry. Rich strained his neck and looked in horror at the beast that faced him. He knew that it was impossible to break the bamboo, yet he bounced and shook in vain once more.

Don Escobar slowly lifted himself up and waved at the marching men to stop. From his dais he smiled, and then addressed Rich in an almost friendly manner.

'Young man, before you is the apex predator of the Amazon: the green anaconda.' He paused for a moment to mop his brow, then pointed down at the reptile. '*Eunectes murinus* is non-venomous, but she will squeeze the life out of you and then swallow you whole. This is the ultimate predator. She will dislocate her jaws and you will disappear whilst I eat my lunch, but first I have breakfast to finish.'

He slowly lowered his frame back down and glanced at Rich as if surprised by his silence. But he was too terrified to speak. The eyes of the anaconda had locked onto him, and it was now slowly creeping across the camp. Don Escobar took a sip of his coffee and watched the creature manoeuvre its enormous girth across the dirt, marvelling at the terror it instilled in the face of the young DEA agent.

He nodded in approval and added, 'Yes, I hear that you feed mice to snakes in the greatest nation. Here we feed them men dressed as mice.' He laughed loudly.

The bony man then made sure that Don Escobar had a clear view of the two-hundred-kilogram, five-metre-long, brown-and-black-spotted reptile that had now reached its prey and was about to coil around the legs of the petrified DEA agent in yellow Mickey Mouse boxers and matching Minnie Mouse vest.

CHAPTER NINETEEN

The rowing boat nudged alongside the spit of land, a spectral figure climbed out and a light mist floated past, caught in a gentle breeze that blew it towards a boat that was fast disappearing around a corner with three Westerners in it. With a nod of approval, the man watched the mist swirl into the distance before he turned around and walked up the spit, shimmering slightly.

On his chest a row of silver buttons reflected the sun across a blue tunic that was almost translucent. In one hand he held a pocket watch, and with the other he was turning a small winding crown on its top. When he reached a psychedelic deckchair, he paused, ran a hand over one of its smooth wooden armrests and eased himself into it, crossing his legs and opening the front of the watch.

Looking up briefly, he smiled as he thought about the last time he had used the pocket watch, just a few weeks ago on the Rio Mapiri – but this would be its final rewind of time. It had done its job, and he knew that his great-nephew was now on the right path. Turning back to the watch, he placed his little finger on the minute hand, moved it gently anticlockwise and looked up once more to see the rainforest blur, the river change direction and the light mist reappear with the Westerners frozen, mid-action, on their boat. Once they had passed back upriver, he returned to his own boat, climbed in and simply rowed off. It was not long before the words 'Police Boat' and 'West India Dock' could barely be seen on its hull. And then, quite suddenly, it just vanished.

Further upriver, a big smile spread over Martín's face as he opened up the throttle and shouted, '*Vámonos güevones!*'

Fifteen minutes later, they swung round a tight bend in the river beyond which a large spit of land stretched out with a deckchair close to the water's edge. It was one of those old 1960s aluminium-framed models, with wooden armrests and a psychedelic fabric of swirling flowers. Martín slowed down instinctively. It would be a good addition to the laboratory nearby. *Maybe pick it up and quickly drop it off with the precursors and propane?* he thought. But then he shook his head, as it had clearly been placed there deliberately. *Maybe it was where Don Escobar sat when waiting for his plane to arrive?*

Nah, rumours were that he was so fat he couldn't sit in an armchair, never mind squeeze into a deckchair!

Martín let the boat drift onto the spit, grabbed the deckchair and then jumped back in.

'Slight change of plan, we're going to do a small delivery to an old research station and drop off the deckchair,' he said, swinging the boat around and back up a small tributary.

Passing beneath a large, overhanging tree, they soon reached the bamboo cage and looked in horror at the body strung up there, slumped in a bizarre costume with its head bowed. It looked like a Westerner, but they could not be sure. All that remained below the waterline was a chalky skeleton hanging in the muddy river. Martín squeezed the throttle and carried on. There was nothing to be said. The *hijos de puta* Colombianos were to blame, of that he was sure, although it did not look like the body had been in the water for more than a day or so.

They continued in silence with a sense of danger around them. Moshe and Esther gripped their Uzis, alert and watchful. Max clutched his Bowie knife, but it no longer felt like the guarantee of safety that it once had. Before long, the sound of a booming voice could be heard echoing through the forest, and it was obvious that they were not alone. Martín stopped the boat, pulled into the river-bank and reached for his radio. He was clearly worried and spoke quickly and almost frantically into the transceiver, but whatever was discussed was not good news, for he now released the safety on his Glock, gripped it tightly and guided the boat slowly along with his other hand.

They hugged the riverbank for several seconds and then turned a corner where a clearing appeared with men in fatigues standing over someone, or something, on the ground. They did not notice the boat, nor did they see Max stand up to get a better look, before Martín furiously pulled him down. Everyone then crouched low, and Martín used a pole to push the boat closer to the camp, where he looked in disbelief at a group of soldiers with American flags on their sleeves and bamboo poles in their hands. They were Hispanic American soldiers about to destroy the very same pozo pit that he had been tasked with getting up and running. Martín just crouched there, staring at the men.

Max looked across at him and watched his body tense as if he were struggling with a decision, but before he had more time to think, Martín had swung the boat back into the middle of the river, jumped up, aimed his Glock and squeezed the trigger. A bullet ripped through the leg of one of the men in the camp, who collapsed, screaming in pain. His comrades scattered and then everything simply unravelled.

A bony man in a white vest was the first to reach his weapon, and he quickly returned fire, just missing Martín but puncturing the gasoline barrel next to him. Moshe jumped up, clutching his Uzi, and sent a spray of bullets into the camp, dropping three of the startled men as the others scrambled to swap their bamboo poles for AK-47s.

Martín sped the boat towards the riverbank and Esther jumped into the shallow water. From there, she waded to the edge of the bank with her Uzi held high and sprinted up the incline, only to find two men running towards her. Instinctively, she gripped her Uzi and pumped bullets into their bodies. Checking her flank, she registered the sight of a huge anaconda winding itself around a man who had been tied to a spit, but at that very moment someone appeared from behind a tree and shot at her, and she dropped to the ground and rolled for cover.

Max was now face down in the mud, watching Martín and Moshe clamber up the bank. For a couple of seconds everything became quiet, and then gunfire resumed further in the forest. He scrambled along the bank, gripping his Bowie knife, which offered no protection in the unfolding gun battle, reached some cover and lay as still as he could, listening intently. Once he was sure that the battle was unfolding in the forest, he climbed up the bank and peered into the camp. But what he saw made his blood freeze. He was met by the stare of a man in such abject terror that had he been Death itself he could not have caused such a reaction. A giant reptile was coiling slowly and methodically around the man, savouring the body that it was about to crush and devour. Max was stunned, immobile and indecisive. But then something odd gripped him.

He felt an irresistible urge to save that man. His eyes darted around the camp, and he found himself sprinting from the bank straight for the hideous reptile, but the sun glinted off the blade of his knife and the anaconda turned to face him. Lashing out with her head, she just missed his arm before the sharp point of the knife ripped through her thick skin and plunged into the vertebrae behind her skull. The horrendous brown and black scales of the monstrous reptile shook violently as she uncoiled herself and fell to the ground, writhing in agony, pulling her tail up to her head and back in a frenzied effort to dislodge the knife. But Max did not let go and pushed it further into bone, sending spasms of pain through her shaking frame until gradually she thrashed less and less, her body became still and finally her head twisted to one side, lifeless.

Max had killed the anaconda that had brought the man in front of him to the very brink of death. He had rescued him from slow torture, from the ignominy of disappearing without a trace inside a reptile's stomach, from the certainty that not even the smallest fragment of his body would remain. But somehow, and almost miraculously, he was still alive. Unconscious, with broken ankles, his feet dangling to one side and his head drooped, hanging towards the ground.

It was several minutes before Max truly grasped the enormity of what he had done, and yet despite his amazing exploit, he would never realise that the limp frame in front of him was none other than that of his distant American cousin.

EPILOGUE

One week and a day later, on 14th July 1992, DEA agent Brian Donaldson shot a civilian in a bar in Santa Cruz, Bolivia. Despite the best efforts of the local police, he avoided capture and escaped without his passport on a US commercial flight the following day. His colleague Rich McDonnell had arrived back in the US for medical treatment five days earlier.

In Lima, on Thursday 16th July 1992, shortly after nine o'clock in the evening, two lorries carrying one-tonne ammonium nitrate bombs exploded in Avenida Larco, Miraflores, killing twenty-five people and wounding 155. The Sendero Luminoso gave no warning of the attack.

On 22nd July 1992, Pablo Escobar escaped from La Catédral, the prison overlooking Medellín that he had constructed for his own incarceration. As the head of the cartel that had murdered a DEA agent and tortured another, he was a marked man. He spent sixteen months on the run before being captured and shot on 2nd December 1993.

On 1st August 1992, the US administration officially denied all knowledge of the AMR pathogen canisters that the media had claimed were evidence of a secret plan to destroy the Beni region. The Bolivian government subsequently issued a statement confirming they had been planted by the cartel, with help from the Cubans. It had been no more than a crude attempt to create a backlash against the DEA and the War on Drugs.

On 14th September 1992, Abimael Guzmán, the leader of the Sendero Luminoso, was captured in Surco, a district of Lima. He was tracked down by a discarded prescription for an asthma condition from which he was known to suffer. The movement he founded subsequently collapsed.

Frank Zappa died of prostate cancer on 4th December 1993. His family are still in dispute over his estate.

The exact date isn't clear, but at some point in 1997, Colin Dale hosted his last ever Thursday evening show on Kiss FM.

In Colombia, between 2000 and 2003, an area three times the size of New York City was aerially sprayed with Roundup, a glyphosate. In March 2015, the World Health Organization's International Agency for Research on Cancer classified glyphosate as 'probably carcinogenic in humans'. In May 2019, a US federal jury ruled that Roundup is carcinogenic and awarded two billion dollars in damages to a US couple, Alva and Alberta Pilliod, who had contracted Hodgkin's disease from exposure to the glyphosate.

In 2000, the Congress of the United States approved the use of *Fusarium oxysporum*, a soil-based fungus, as a biological control agent to destroy coca crops in Colombia. President Clinton cancelled plans to introduce it into the country for fear of being accused of deploying chemical weapons.

In November 2000, President Alberto Fujimori fled Peru to avoid charges of corruption. He took refuge in Japan, where their citizens are safe from extradition. The international warrant for his arrest caught up with him when he flew from Mexico to Chile five years later. His private jet passed through Peruvian airspace, but the head of Interpol in Lima ordered staff to switch off their twenty-four-hour Interpol warning system on the evening of his over-flight, so he evaded immediate capture. He was eventually extradited from Chile on 23rd September 2007. On 7th April 2009, he was sentenced to twenty-five years in prison for human rights abuses; his pardon was granted on 24th December 2017 on health grounds.

On 11th September 2001, the War on Terror began. Rich McDonnell spent the next four years travelling extensively throughout North Africa, Eastern Europe and Southeast Asia, where he worked as a 'rendition operative'. His experience in South America gave him a unique insight into fear, which he used to his advantage when interrogating the most hardened enemies delivered to him from the Axis of Evil.

On 22nd January 2006, Evo Morales completed his journey from 'cocalero' leader to President of the Republic of Bolivia. On his inauguration, Bolivia had the highest illiteracy rate in South America; three years later, UNESCO declared Bolivia free from illiteracy. Coca production increased under his government, US aid to the country drastically fell, and the DEA were expelled from Bolivia in October 2008. In 2013, he passed a law to combat domestic violence against women. In 2014, he became the oldest professional football player in the world, signing a contract with Sport Boys Warnes for two hundred dollars a month.

On 11th November 2019, Evo Morales fled to Mexico amid allegations of election fraud.

On 26th July 2011, Joe Arroyo died in Barranquilla. The Colombian salsa singer did indeed remain in the town he loved so much, which he sang about endlessly on the Ormeño bus down to Arequipa.

On 1st July 2017, twenty-five years after the last recorded activity of the Paraguayan bank account of Señor Boca Raton, it was closed. The funds were automatically transferred to the Central Bank of Paraguay, where five hundred thousand dollars had accrued to 13,807,179,524.08 guaraní, or $2,261,618.27, before charges. Twelve months later, the Paraguayan government confiscated the money.

It's not known what happened to Esther and Moshe; it is also unclear where Max Hansell ended up. It would be nice to think he hooked up with Sol again, and perhaps he did. The man he saved in a remote corner of Bolivia passed out after being rescued, and Max never did get to share more than a few words with him before he returned to the US.

Great-Uncle Tom still keeps an eye on his psychedelic deckchair. It has a nice spot on a sunny veranda overlooking a garden of glorious red and pink giant hydrangeas, somewhere in the town of Rurrenabaque, which now has its own airport and lots of tourists.

Martín's mother still sits on it and watches the insects coming and going from the large blooms. She reminds Tom of his retirement when he used to sit watching the men gathering hay in the fields of Toocanagh, where the stacks once stretched as far as the eye could see, and then way beyond that.

Acknowledgements

A big thank you to Christian Hayes (editing), Toby Selwyn (proof-reading), Pulp Studio (cover design) and Hewer Text (typesetting) – all of whom were an absolute pleasure to work with.

Lastly, and most importantly, a heartfelt thank you to my wife, Wendy without whom this book would not have been possible.

Afterword

Paul grew up in 1970s High Wycombe when TVs
were as wooden as the sitcoms, sherbet flying saucers
cost 2½p a hundred weight and platform shoes were
both cool *and* great for toe-punting footballs.

He lays no claim to having books published in multiple languages.

He's taught karate in Tibet and Bolivia, half built swimming
pools in Sydney and recently worked as a surveyor in Soho.

He lives in the Chilterns with his wife and ancient cat.

—

A big thank you for reading *The Man on the Rubber
Balloon or Optimism* – I hope you enjoyed it.

If so, and you have a spare moment – please review the
novel at the store where you bought it. Even better,
subscribe to my mailing list on *www.paulkellyauthor.com*
and receive updates on the sequel (out 2023) plus a link to
a free download of *Plata o Plomo (A Bullet or a Bribe)*.

Finally, a reminder that 100% of the profit from sales of *The Man on the Rubber Balloon or Optimism* goes to Young Minds, the UK's leading mental health charity for young people.

All donations are facilitated via Work for Good. Estimated profit per Amazon sale – £2.25 for an e-book (£3.99 list price) and £1.60 for a paperback (£8.99 list price, less print costs and Amazon commission).

Printed in Great Britain
by Amazon

40095164R00148